HOME TO THE WILD

FRANCESCA McMAHON

Cover Illustration by Arthur Bowling III
Cover Typography by MiblArt
Interior Design by AB Book Services
Editing by Carly Catt

ISBN: 978-1-7398853-1-1 (Ebook edition)
ISBN: 978-1-7398853-2-8 (Paperback edition)

DEDICATION

For my very own Larka. You prepared me for the world and
supported me throughout it.
I love you, Mum.

WOLF-TO-HUMAN LANGUAGE

Den – Home

False Forest – A Town

False Sun – A light

False wolves - dogs

Many suns/moons – Many days

Moon cycle – One month

Mother Wolf – "God"/Mother Nature/Spirit

Night lights - Stars

Savage Blood – Rabies

Season – One year

Shadows pass – Hours

Smoking sticks – Guns

Span's distance – A Mile

Sun pass – One day

Sun's fever – Fire

Sun's time – Summer

The cold season – Winter months

White Coat - Doctor

PART I

WHEN YOU FIND A HOME

1

LARKA

There was something in the air that night. A scent that poisoned the surrounding forest with its pungent aroma of fear and remorse. Larka was on edge, her ears pricked, her body tensed, ready to propel her into action. And yet, the Forest was still. Silence surrounded her and her family. Even the wind had fallen quiet. It was as if the land itself was holding its breath.

Larka barked an order to the group to fall into a single line; on guard and ready to engage if necessary. The wind began anew. A harsh breeze brushed against them, picking up the freshly fallen snow from the ground and creating a beautiful image in the sky. For a moment, Larka watched as the snowflakes danced in the wind. Then, a nudge from her mate, Echo, forced her into moving.

She was the best choice to lead the hunt, her white coat making her nearly invisible in the snow. Though Echo was the greater hunter, his dark fur stood out too much in comparison. Instead, he followed behind her, ready to engage when needed. Once they began the chase, he wouldn't hold back.

A rustle stopped Larka in her tracks – her eyes searching for movement in the darkness. When the sound didn't occur again, she thought she may have mistaken the noise for trees shuddering in the wind.

She went to usher the pack forward when she heard the sound again – but this time, it was different. Turning to Echo for confirmation, she saw that his ears were pricked in the same direction as hers. He turned to her, a simple answer present in his anxious huff.

The noise continued; a wail carried among the gales. Her pack was panicked, their fur standing up on edge in their unease. Larka could feel their growing need to flee, but she couldn't allow that. No wolf runs from the unknown. With a huff and a snort, she scraped her claws against the snow in warning to the wolves.

Await my signal, go nowhere else but here, she growled, and she knew they would listen. They always did.

As they stood to attention, she slipped away and approached the source of the noise with caution, hoping to gain a better look at what they were up against before attacking.

Sensing Echo at her tail, Larka felt more at ease. They weren't far from the source now, the noise growing louder and more painful to their ears, even though it seemed to be buried among the bushes. That stench of fear and remorse engulfed their senses once more, but this wasn't the time to feel overwhelmed.

They attempted to see the creature from their hiding spot, and while they could see an outline of a figure, it was near impossible to make out from the enclave of vegetation that surrounded them. Against her better judgement, Larka took a risk.

She pounced.

Larka fell towards the bush, teeth bared, and claws extended.

As she ploughed through the snow-covered branches, she snarled. Without hesitation, as the figure came into sight, she went to strike – until the creature mewled.

Larka's head tilted in confusion at the abnormal, yet somewhat familiar, sound. Blinking her eyes, she took in the little creature before her. It was small, furless, defenceless, and wrapped in a strange cocoon within an oddly shaped bush. The hairless beast stared up at her, observing her just as she did it. Grunting, the little one wiggled about, pathetic, soft whimpers escaping its lips.

What a peculiar thing, she thought as she pawed gently at the little one, snorting in surprise at the sharp delighted noise that escaped its snout.

The scent from before lingered in the air around the little one, but it didn't come from them. Instead, this furless pup held an aroma of joy. And urine. Lifting her nose into the air, Larka attempted to detect the owner of the earlier scent, and see whether they were still nearby. She found nothing.

Something grabbed Larka's fur- she turned to bite the offender but found the little one, escaped from its prison, face-first in the snow. It wasn't particularly bright, it seemed, or even that mobile. A strange garble of noises came from its snout as it grabbed and stroked Larka's fur, fascination in its eyes.

There seems to be something familiar about this creature, she said, her words soft and curious.

A deep sigh sounded behind her, and she turned to find Echo watching the two of them. His eyes focused on the little one, a sense of recognition on his face as he watched the creature hold tightly to Larka.

I thought I had long lost the memory of their smell, but I suppose it is one you can never truly forget. He turned to Larka, a sadness in his eyes. **A human. A female, if my senses are correct.**

Larka stepped back from the human sharply, trying to ignore the cry of misery it released as she did. She refused to let the noise affect her, no matter how much it sounded like her own pups. This was a human. She knew what these beasts were like all too well.

Echo approached Larka, his eyes fixed on the human who, clumsily, pulled a strange item from its mobile shelter and covered itself with it as its body shook from the cold.

It has been left to die, he said, seemingly unfeeling, and yet Larka sensed a saddened tone in his words. Echo sighed. **I had seen the cruelty of these people before; I just never expected to see it inflicted on their own kind.**

She watched the strange creature as it unsteadily held itself up on its back legs, falling onto all four intermittently, its strange cover collecting snow in patches each time. A small cry of complaint followed as its paws touched the cold ground, and its perplexed expression showed exactly how it felt about it. Larka held back a snort of amusement.

Nature will take its course soon enough, Echo continued, his tone disconnected from the words. **We should leave, so it may continue.**

Larka turned from Little One in shock. She had never known for her mate to be so uncaring in the matter of the young. Human or not, younglings and their loss was always a sombre experience. Only moments ago, he had shown sympathy for the beast, and yet now he was prepared to leave her to die? She'd never seen Echo be so cold-hearted before.

Her eyes turned to the young one who watched her and Echo in fascination. While the pup moved closer to them, she seemed to sense the tension building in the air and kept her distance enough to keep herself safe. Maybe she was not as dim as Larka had assumed. Not that Larka could ever hurt her, even the thought of it made her shudder. Harming a pup is an unthinkable act.

Echo turned to leave, drawing Larka's attention away from Little One. Disgusted by his actions, if only briefly, she rounded on him, teeth bared.

You would leave this Little One defenceless and at the mercy of the forest? Just because she is human? She snarled, only slightly aware that, from the gusting wind, her words would have been carried to the ears of her pack nearby. Not that she cared much at this moment. This was the right decision, the right action. She would be damned if she did not fight for it. **Little One is just a pup we—**

Little One? Echo asked, a tilt to his head.

Taken aback at the question, she paused. She realised that in just a short time, she already felt attached to this useless little thing. Larka watched as Little One toddled about, the shiver more prominent in her body, but the joyful noise never faded. She didn't know why, not yet, but she knew what she had to do next – no matter what Echo thought.

A huff drew her attention to Echo who Little One was now bothering with inquisitive touches. Just as she had with Larka, her small claws tugged at Echo's fur, and occasionally she would lean forward to bite him. When she grabbed or bit too hard, she would receive a little nip, which seemed to not bother her at all – if the strange cheerful noise that escaped her was anything to go by.

Electing to ignore Little One's attention as best he could, Echo turned to Larka, pretending a human wasn't poking his ears.

The natural world has its balance, Larka, you know this. Little One grew bored and stumbled instead towards Larka, a smile on her face.

A human in our world. He sighed. **It is unheard of. I saw how they lived, and it is a far cry from how we do. Their kind is not built like us. Her chance of survival...** He didn't finish his train of thought, but his focus on the shivering young girl said it all.

Her furless exterior was not sustainable in this environment. On instinct, Larka stepped closer to Little One, a momentary hope that her own warmth could delay the seemingly inevitable end.

Larka had had no direct experience with humans before. That was Echo's area of expertise. She didn't understand them or their limits, but this young one seemed resilient. The scent of the creature who abandoned her was faint when they first arrived, showing it had been some time since Little One was left to die. Yet, even in her furless state, she had survived.

Just as I saved you from the humans, I will save her, Larka stated. **She is strong, Echo. She can make it; I am sure of it.**

Little One clutched at Larka's fur with her claws, digging them into its warmth. For a seemingly useless creature, she was intelligent enough to understand how to keep herself safe in this climate.

A sigh drew her attention away from Little One and back to Echo. His expression was a mixture of many: dismay, humour, and adoration. He stepped forward, bumping his head softly against hers.

You are incorrigible, my soul, he said, a teasing tone to his words.

Larka pulled back, insulted all the same. **Incorrigible? How dare you! I—**

A grunt stopped her in the beginning of her tirade as Little One fell with a thump into the snow once more. Instantly, she turned her attention away from Echo and onto the pup. Crouching down, she softened the maw of her jaw onto the soft muscle of Little One's foreleg and pulled her up and close to her, making sure the strange material stayed wrapped around her pale skin.

From the corner of her eye, she saw Echo step towards them. A tenseness built in her shoulders and her hackles raised instinctively, an action she had only done when protecting her pups at the Den.

Echo slowed his pace, sensing this change, and lowered his head submissively before he spoke. **Her strange nest will be best for her to be kept in right now, away from the cold and wet ground.** He stepped slowly closer, his eyes never leaving Larka's. With a tilt of his head, he asked for permission to take Little One.

Realising her irrational attitude, Larka stepped back.

Without a word, Echo turned from her and towards the pup. Using his teeth carefully, he soft-mouthed his jaw onto her forearm and dragged her towards her nest. After placing her inside, Larka watched as her smitten mate carefully laid the soft material atop her to keep Little One warm before he lapped his tongue against her cheek and pulled away.

I understand what has drawn you to her, but I am afraid our pack will not... Echo said, trailing off, his eyes still on the child before he finally turned away. Stepping towards Larka, he nuzzled the side of her neck. **But I will support you when we return home with the human pup.**

He drew back from her, his eyes holding hers. His actions left Larka in a state of shock. Loyalty was a quality she had always treasured in her mate; nevertheless, it surprised her each time. Larka watched him, love in her eyes, as he bowed his head and told her he would speak to the pack to prepare them. Then, Echo set off into the woods.

Watching him leave, a sense of warmth filled her. It was only the attention-seeking whimper that finally drew her away. As she headed over to Little One, who thankfully was entangled still in her strange contraption, she looked at her fully for the first time. The young pup stared at her, eyes wide with wonder and what seemed to be love. Larka wasn't sure why she had been left to die in the forest, but she knew she would not let that happen.

Come, Little One, she purred. **It is time we went home.**

2

LARKA

Carrying Little One's shelter back to the Den was a lot more complicated, and tiring, than Larka expected. She dragged, pushed, and carried it as best she could, but with the distance they had travelled for their hunt, she wasn't making much progress in getting closer to home.

If her family hadn't been nearby, she would have been concerned about her vulnerability. She listened once more to the delicate padding of paws on the crunching snow around her, the sound of their presence calming her. Empowered by her pack, she tried again. Latching her teeth and locking her jaw on the arch of the nest, she lifted.

Slowly but surely, she made progress. And as the forest grew denser, she knew they were getting close. Larka relaxed. Soon she'd have Little One fed and warm alongside her pups.

Then she heard it.

Larka stopped sharply in place, her ears pricking to a new set of pattering paws. They stepped slowly and deliberately, as if trying to hide their arrival.

Putting Little One's nest down, she positioned herself into a protective stance above her. With teeth bared, she searched, trying to pinpoint the direction of the prowler.

It didn't take long before the predator revealed themselves, their scent too easy to identify. For a moment, Larka relished in the idea of finally putting this creature where it belonged. That was until she realised her pack was not close enough to fight with her.

My, my, what a treat we have here.

A low growl built in her chest. Larka's amber eyes locked with the golden pair of a bark-coloured cougar. Its feline features caught the reflection of the moon in the snow, giving the creature a sinister look as it bared its own fangs in a wicked smile of mirth. The cocky attitude was unmistakable.

Hye, Larka snarled, unchecked rage dripping in her words, like the saliva that trickled down her maw. **What a displeasure to see you again. And in the pack's territory of all places.**

With a stretch, exposing his sharp claws, Hye yawned. **I was just on a short night hunt, preparing for a restful night on a filled stomach.** He smiled. **I must have been distracted is all.**

A likely story, cat, Larka snapped. **You know the rules.**

Not looking in her direction, and at a comfortable distance for them both, Hye strolled in a wide arc around them, paying her no mind.

I assure you, Larka, it was a simple mistake. He smiled. **No laws have been broken here. Something I am sure** – Hye turned his golden eyes on her pup with a smile – **you know all about.**

A sense of trepidation built within Larka. Humans hadn't been seen in the Forest in many generations, and with good reason. Though, from what she knew, there was nothing in their laws about keeping a human pup. But even Larka knew that not all creatures from their world would be as open as her pack appeared to be. Could there be consequences she hadn't considered?

Keeping her attention on the predator, Larka lowered herself closer to the nest, shielding Little One from view as best she could. Hye had never attacked the pack before, but things were different now; she couldn't let her guard down for a second. She could only hope that this would not turn into a confrontation. She did not know how she could fight while saving herself and Little One.

Fascinating, Hye purred as he settled into the snow, his eyes studying Larka with a benign interest. She didn't relax, however; cougars were well known for hiding their predatory instincts.

Silence fell between them with the Forest following suit. Curiosity marked his gaze as he watched them, his head tilting to the side, his ears flickering at the sound of Little One's fussing.

Then, all too suddenly, Hye was up and moving, walking away with his back turned away from the two. Larka tensed in place, preparing for a sneak attack that never came. As he disappeared into the trees, he left Larka with his final words.

A human is an interesting pet to keep, my dear. I look forward to watching this play out.

As his tail disappeared into the nearest vegetation, Larka stood still, watching, waiting. Hye was one for dramatics and trickery but had never been one to enact brute force. Sadly, with a human, this was a different game for all. She searched for any sign that he had returned. One could never be too careful. Especially with cats.

Larka?

Turning away reluctantly from where Hye had left, Larka faced Skai - a junior member of their pack, who's grey and brown patchy fur stood out from the mature members of the hunt. She was a nervous one, and she held her head low as she approached, her river-coloured eyes dotting back and forth between Larka and Little One.

They sent me to check on your well-being; Echo sensed you had fallen behind. Skai's nose twitched, and she turned toward where the cougar had headed, a growl building in her chest. **Shall I call for the others?**

With the presence of another pack member, her unease had faded. **No**, Larka responded, **Hye is of no problem to us.** Stepping back from Little One's nest, she checked to make sure she was fine and found her still sleeping. **We will be fine carrying on with the others nearby.**

Skai bowed her head but didn't leave. Huffing at the apparent order Echo had given the young wolf, Larka focused on Little One. Gripping the nest's roof once again with her teeth, she began her journey anew - her security following suit.

She had hoped that, after a break, carrying the nest would be less burdensome and painful. She was wrong of course, but she tried to ignore the pain it caused her as much as possible. When a particularly sharp part of the nest caught her foreleg, she held back a whimper as the scent of fresh blood filled her senses. As she awkwardly continued her walking, Larka questioned whether she had made the right decision.

Maybe this is a sign, she thought as her clumsy walk continued.

As she carried her, a niggling of doubt built in her mind. And as they came closer to the Den, her worries grew all the louder in her mind: *Could she have broken some unwritten law of the Forest? Was she risking the safety of her pack over some human pup? What if her own pups reject the human? What if she made—*

Mother!

Her thoughts vanished at the sound of the delighted yips and barks of her pups. She could hear their awkwardly placed paws as they stumbled around the snow outside the Den, just over the hill.

Only a few days ago, they had been allowed to explore the outside, and each new day was an adventure for them all.

In her excitement to return to her puppies, Larka stepped just a little too quickly, briefly forgetting the precious cargo she was carrying.

The nest caught her injured leg and, with a yelp, she dropped it. The pain wasn't unbearable, but the shock stunned her briefly. It was the cry, however, that caught her off guard.

From the overturned nest, Little One's cries echoed across the snow-covered ground. Rushing to her side, Larka buried her head into the pup, offering comfort in her presence and warmth. Pulling the nest up from the ground and away from the cold, her senses went on alert, searching for any sign of harm.

Skai came up alongside her, but Larka paid her no mind. It was only when the young wolf snorted in disdain that her ears twitched in her direction, a distrust rising within her.

There is not a scratch or injury on the hairless creature. Such a fuss over nothing. What utter—

Larka snapped, her teeth biting the air just before Skai's forelegs. The youngling jumped back in fright, her head bowing low when she reached a safe distance.

I am sorry, Larka, I did not mean to speak poorly of the human.

Rising from her position by the nest where the pup had since fallen silent, Larka stared down at the young wolf who dropped into the snow beneath her. Gazing into her stricken eyes, a huff slipped past Larka's lips.

Turning away and back to Little One, Larka checked on her one last time before she began dragging the nest the final length of the journey up the hill, forcing herself to ignore the pain from the injury to her leg in her desperation to see her pups and get Little One acquainted.

Just over the ridge, her pups awaited her. Their eagerness and excitement at her return led to her being overrun by the littluns as they vied for her attention and play. Nips at her tail, jumping up at her mouth for food, or playing fighting with one another to show off. It had only been a short period of time since they left for the hunt, but seeing her pups again warmed her heart, and she felt herself release a breath of relief. She hated being away from her young.

Your food smells strange, Mother, an inquisitive voice said, drawing Larka's attention away from the pups and back to Little One's nest. With paws holding on to its edge, Rae, the smallest of her litter, bent her head over the side of the nest, her tail wagging in interest as she gazed inside intently.

A momentary panic built up within Larka as she made a dash for Rae, intending to pull her away quickly. It was only when she caught sight of them, she stopped in place. There was a playful curiosity between the two pups.

The two sniffed, licked, and pawed at one another. After a nip from Rae out of interest, she watched as Little One tilted her head, just as Rae had, and returned the bite playfully. Leaning over the side of her nest, Little One tumbled out into the snow. A noise of delight escaped from her as she stumbled about in the snow playing with Rae.

Unlike Rae, she was very unstable on her paws, awkwardly wobbling on her two back legs, her forelegs waving madly in the air – not that Rae seemed to mind. She was finally the fast one for once.

As Larka watched the two clumsily playing together, she laid herself down to rest, allowing her pups to feed. Her milk was all they would get today, though surprisingly, her pack hadn't returned yet, and even Skai had skittered away since. *Maybe they have gone in search of something more?* she wondered but decided not to think about it further. Instead, as her pups drank, she found herself amused by the sight of the two oddballs before her, lost in their little games.

It seems the signs were wrong, she thought, smiling.

Little One thankfully had stopped her incessant shivering

now, and while here, at the Den, she hopefully wouldn't feel the cold as deeply as she would elsewhere.

The Den was a sanctuary for pup rearing. Atop the hilly surface, they could keep an eye out for predators and use the natural wilds around them to protect their young from view. Even more so, the trees surrounding them kept her pups safe from the heavy snow and chill.

As the runt of her own litter as a pup, this Den had been her saviour. The safety of its slight warmth was the difference between her life and death. Briefly, the worry that had faded reappeared as she wondered if humans were different.

Could I just be prolonging the inevitable?

At that moment, a heavy weight fell against her back. Lifting her head and turning slightly, she met the wide-eyed and open-mouthed sight of Little One who was taking this moment to dig her paws and snout into Larka's fur. It was a strange sensation, being huddled into in such a way.

Her feeding pups were not pleased at their mother's distract-edness. Little One's continued fidgeting interrupted the litter's peaceful meal. Irritated, the pups trotted away from Larka and went to play instead, their hunger sated for now.

Here, Little One clambered onto her back and lay there, wiggling every so often, trying to get comfortable, until Rae pulled her off the other side. With an *oof*, Little One fell atop her sister, and the two awkwardly wrestled – awkward on Little One's part at least.

Enough! Larka barked. Rae, understanding her mother, stopped instantly, but Little One was still new to this world and continued to play.

Directing a low growl and a snapping motion of her jaw Little One's way, Larka, unwilling to fail, repeated: **Enough.**

This time, the words seemed to break through, as Little One dropped to the ground beside Rae, sitting still.

Turning to look at her other pups who, to her relief, were distracted by the arrival of Skai, Larka rolled to her side once again. Rae slowly crawled to her mother, her eyes darting towards her siblings nervously, before she slowly leant forward to drink.

Unfortunately, Little One wasn't a simple case. She stayed where she was, watching, her features scrunched up in confusion. It seemed she would need a little bit more convincing. Thankfully for Larka, she was not alone in her teaching this time.

Echo appeared over the hill, the rest of the pack following close behind, and he headed straight towards Larka, their pups jumping up at him, desperate to play. For now, he passed them by, a gentle baring of his teeth to warn them to behave as he met with Larka. Locking eyes, he bowed his head to her and stepped forward, lapping his tongue gently against the broken skin of her leg, soothing the ache as best he could. Larka brushed her head against his in thanks before he stepped towards Little One.

Knocking her ever so slightly to put her off balance, Echo sent her tumbling into Larka's stomach. Little One turned her young and clueless eyes on Rae, taking in everything she was doing. It was when Echo came back into focus, stepping close beside her, that she refocused on him. He was her guide now.

Leaning forward, he brushed his nose near Larka's teats, and then repeated the action at Little One's maw. Larka released a content sigh at the scene, Echo often claimed that she was the one with the soft heart, and yet here he was. Smitten.

Finally, after continued encouragement, Little One drank.

Echo huffed happily; his job complete. With a nuzzle to Larka, he went to step away, until the grip of the young pup caught him. While he could easily pull himself away, her strength not as strong as she may think, Larka watched as Echo almost instantly lowered himself to the ground and placed his head beside Little One.

Later that night, when the elders and the pups retired to the

Den, Larka watched as Little One and Rae curled up beside Echo - Little One, in particular, squeezing in close. Echo studied her with fascination before leaning forward and licking hers and Rae's heads before going to rest his own.

Larka came and snuggled up near them, their pups curled around them. With her nose touching her mate's, she waited for the signs that their younglings had fallen asleep to speak.

It appears I am not the only one drawn to the human pup, she said, a smugness in her words.

Echo sighed in response and pretended to have fallen asleep. For a moment, Larka believed he had drifted off and intended to do the same herself. As she closed her eyes to rest, she fell asleep with a warmth in her heart at his last words:

She is a survivor, my soul.

3

―――――――

LARKA

*L*arka hadn't realised how difficult it would be. She had raised four litters of puppies now and believed that in doing so she had understood how to be a mother. Even though she knew there would be problems in taking in the human pup, anticipated it even, she never thought that the bond between her two youngest would turn out to be the biggest challenge.

Little One, though not born a wolf, learnt faster than Larka expected. While she didn't speak the language, her understanding of the wolf's way grew every day. Unfortunately, it wasn't always Larka's or Echo's teachings that she was learning from.

Rae had always been rather passive, and while Larka couldn't blame her, her actions now put another at risk. Little One couldn't afford to follow the same path as her sister, but she idolised her far too much that even Larka struggled to undo the damage.

As the other pups ate and drank first, Rae and Little One would hang back and wait - occasionally crawling forward hoping to receive permission from their siblings to join them.

They never did.

It was because of this passivity that Larka stayed home from the pack's hunts to focus on the two of them by providing extra meals and teaching them how to assert themselves. She had never seen reason to do so with Rae in the past. Somehow, she had survived with ease and found success in her methods.

Her methods, however, would not last now there was another mouth to feed. Especially for one as … delicate as Little One's.

Only a few moons had passed since Larka had brought her home and, to her dismay, she was deteriorating before her eyes. Echo's words from the day they found her about nature taking its course came to mind every time she saw her frail body. Even now as she watched Rae and Little One play, all she could focus on were the scratches and bite marks that covered Little One's skin. They weren't deep, but as her rib cage stuck out against her furless body, Larka's anxiety for her grew.

She needed more time, and more aggression, from the both of them. Their softness would get them killed – whether it be at the hand of an enemy or by the failing of their own inept natures. Larka refused to let that happen.

Sadly, she knew what needed to be done to help them survive.

This will not be pretty, she thought as she headed over to her other pups to set her plan in motion, Rae and Little One none the wiser.

The pups instantly focused on their mother, vying for her attention, only stopping when she snapped her jaw at them in warning. Lying down, she faced them all. **We're going to play a game.**

SHE FLINCHED as the first pup pounced on Little One, latching their teeth onto her fragile skin. The yelp of pain echoed in her ears as the others ganged up on her, tugging at her for attention and play but far rougher than Rae had ever done.

Little One wasn't prepared for this.

It felt crueller to sit and watch, so Larka paced back and forth, waiting for any sign or moment that it had gone too far. Only then would she step in.

Little One, for all her worth, did not let the play phase her. She fought back with her own nips, but they were harmless against the thick fur of the wolves. It didn't deter her from trying her best. It was only with a particularly painful bite to her side that drew blood that Little One went wild. She threw her paws widely, trying to scare her siblings backwards, even grabbing the ears of those closest and yanking with all her might. But it didn't help, her actions weren't strong enough against full-blood wolves.

She just wasn't wolf enough to overcome the onslaught.

The anxiety built up in Larka as she jittered in place, bouncing back and forth considering how to react. She knew she couldn't rush this, Little One had to be tougher if she was going to survive. But it didn't mean she had to enjoy this.

Mother!

Larka froze. The voice was one she had not heard before. It was … unnatural in its usage, the pitch high and strange, its owner clearly unfamiliar with the tongue.

Help, Mother, Little One cried out, her innocent eyes seeking Larka's.

That was the final straw.

Charging from her spot, Larka called to her pups to stop. But before she even had the chance, whines and whimpers sounded one after another as the pups rushed away from Little One.

Rae doesn't play fair, Mother! one of them yelped.

Ahead, only a few of the pups remained, going on the offensive, no longer play fighting. Larka watched as Rae – small, submissive, and nonconfrontational Rae – charged her siblings. Her teeth were not as sharp as theirs, but she dug them into the nearest pup's leg throwing them aside and then used her smaller claws to smack another away. She attacked each one of the siblings left who stood too close to Little One.

As she snapped at the last of the pups, leading to them rushing away, Rae backed up towards Little One, who stood with minor cuts on her body, and growled something fierce for one so young.

Hurt her again and see what happens, Rae snarled, her striking blue eyes going cold, just for a moment, as she stared down her siblings. Her tufts of grey and white fur standing up on end in warning.

Larka had watched the entire scene, and she found herself awestruck. She watched as Rae stood protectively in front of her sister, eyeing her other siblings in distrust. It was only then that Larka knew what she needed to do.

Children, stay here and behave, she said, her eyes not leaving the two pups. **I must speak with Rae and Little One. Alone.**

She didn't wait for an answer as she walked away, heading to the hill's edge. She didn't need to tell them to follow, though a moment's hesitation from Rae concerned her until she heard the patter of paws following closely behind.

Reaching the bottom of the hill, Larka continued walking. While they couldn't travel too far, they needed a semblance of privacy for their conversation. When they arrived at the trees' sides, she turned to face them, taking in briefly the protective stance Rae took in front of Little One. Pride swelled in her chest. But now was not the time for that.

You must protect each other, she began, staring them down individually, her tone holding no room for arguments. Taking a step forward towards Little One, Rae's small body lurched slightly, as if to attack, but stopped when her eyes locked with Larka's. As they held one another's gaze, Larka continued.

But you must also learn to protect yourself.

Turning away from Rae, she looked at Little One, whose body was covered in tiny cuts. Small trickles of blood were splattered across her fragile skin, but she looked relatively unfazed.

A pack is a family. Yet, we are all fighting to survive. Leaning forward, she began to soothe the wounds on Little One's body with her tongue, a hiccup of a whine reaching her ears as she hit a sore spot.

As she soothed Little One's cuts with her tongue, Rae began to relax, though her eyes never left her sister.

If you are not strong, you will not live. She looked at the two younglings, who had today experienced first-hand the reality of the world and stared it down.

Weakness cannot be an option. Larka turned to Little One. **You must fight or nature will come for you, and it will not be as kind as your siblings.**

Larka's ears pricked, and she turned away from them and looked into the distant wilderness as pounding paws caught her attention. The excited heartbeats and breathless pants could only mean one thing: their hunting party had returned.

She turned back to them, a warmth in her heart as she watched Rae continue to ease the cuts of her sister.

I tell you these things not to shame your nature but to show you the truth. The strength of the wolf is that of its pack. Be strong and work together and you will survive. She locked eyes with Rae and found a mistrust within them. For one so young, the image was painful, but as a runt, it was needed. **The hunting party is back. It is time to eat.**

Pushing Little One with her muzzle in the hill's direction, Larka watched as she clumsily stumbled ahead, calling out to the pack as they emerged from the trees. Larka was amazed at her resilience and went to follow until a small voice caught her attention.

You told them to fight her, Rae asked, not moving from her spot. **Didn't you?**

Larka didn't turn to her, instead she moved forward and towards the hill. When Rae finally followed, Larka slowed, waiting for the sight of the small grey furred tail to pass beside her before she responded.

To survive, we must endure.

She was met with a heart-wrenching silence. She watched her daughter walk up and over the hill, away from her without a word. It was only when Larka herself reached the top, the Den and her family in front of her, that she knew she had made the right decision.

The passing of meat to the pups progressed as it normally did, but instead of waiting on the sideline, Little One demanded the attention of one of the hunters. Pushing aside one of her siblings, she held control and was one of the first of the pups to eat.

Echo came to Larka's side, carrying a chunk of meat, and placed it at her feet and turned to face the others, allowing her to eat in privacy. For once, Larka found herself able to relax during their mealtime, no longer finding herself worried over the survival of her youngest.

While she ate, the tension in her body melted away, and she began to feel the ache within her bones. She knew she had been growing old; she'd just not had the chance to feel it till then. A heavy sigh left her.

Laying down her head, she watched her pups feed, only to find her eyes drifting to the two who had since finished their meals. Little One and Rae were practicing play fighting – Rae teaching her sister how best to defend and attack. Larka smiled and thought with pride, *Nature will not claim my children. I will make sure of it.*

_4_

RAE

Two Seasons Later

Her new grey-white coat had fully come through the last moon cycle. With the warm sun's time soon to end, it was a relief to have her winter coat return. She had feared that during the first few weeks she may have been at the mercy of the winds as they scoured further out into their territory to hunt, following the herd as best they could without encroaching on another's land.

As she led the pack, her senses heightened, her legs powered through the snow, and her heart pounded with the intensity of the moment as she tracked their prey's scent. The trail led them down to the river. It was here she paused, the pack following suit, as she focused on the surrounding sounds, searching for any sign.

It didn't take long.

Caribou to the east of the river, she said. **Unsure of the amount but moving slowly.** She turned to Echo, expecting him to give the direction for what to do. He stayed silent, waiting for her. A simple movement of his head told her this was her move.

While she had been their best tracker since she had joined the hunt, she'd never been given the opportunity to lead the stalking and herding of their prey. She didn't hesitate in taking the chance.

Fall into a line of threes and follow me, we will corner them near the mountain's edge, she ordered, smiling internally at the instant obeying of the wolves.

Turning away, she led the charge. They would eat well that day.

WELL, that was disappointing, Skai muttered as they travelled back to the Den. The wolves' stomachs were barely sated from hunger, while Echo and Kali each carried chunks of meat for Larka and Little One to eat. **I wonder why the herd has been retreating.**

Shadow, a dark-furred elder who was closer to Rae's father, huffed. **I believe Hye may be our answer to that. His hunting has been erratic and careless as of late.**

Damn cat, Akala grit out, **how are we meant to survive if we cannot-**

Enough! Rae snapped, irritated. **We have eaten; that is enough. I will hear no more complaints.**

Thankfully, and surprisingly, the wolves fell quiet after that. When she turned to them, she found their heads bowed in respect, though Skai somewhat begrudgingly. Rae smiled before turning back to the hill and running up it to her waiting sister.

Before she could even step a full paw onto the hilltop, a body was crashing into her, knocking her into the snow with an "oof".

Rae! Rae! What did you get? Little One whined playfully, pushing at Rae's stomach and sides to irritate her. **Did you chase the deer? Oh! Did you feed well?** She lent in close and grinned. **Will you feed me well?**

Huffing at her sister's antics, Rae pushed her over and pawed at her in return, careful not to use her full strength. **You will not eat at all if you keep this up sister. I am stronger than you, remember?**

Little One smiled and rolled away from Rae's paws and jumped up, positioning herself in a fighting move.

Children, please. Larka sighed as she rose slowly from her position on the ground, hiding as best she could the wince that followed. **Rae, will you put your sister out of her misery?**

Rae bowed her head before gesturing to Kali to bring forward the deer's leg he had been carrying for Little One.

With a bow of her head to Kali, Little One dove in, devouring her meal. Rae watched as her father brought her mother's meat to her and turned away at the loving touch the two shared, offering them privacy. Instead, she refocused on her sister, feeling the warmth of her love for her rise in her chest as Little One finished her meal and began playing with their other siblings.

Since Little One arrived two seasons ago, she had grown from a sickly human runt to a strong and brave wolf. Now, after many teachings from herself and, later, her mother, Little One spoke and played easily with the rest of the family. She was a wolf, and the pack was just as proud and accepting of her as Rae and their mother were.

When this last season passed, Rae watched Little One branch out and away from her protection, now able to hold her own. It was when this began to happen that Larka took over Rae's role as her guide and bestowed the honour of leading the hunt onto Rae.

Rae knew it was not just a reward for her protection and teaching of Little One – she had seen how much her mother had been struggling in keeping up with and guiding her grown pups. Now, when the pack hunted, Larka would spend her days with Little One, whose curiosity of the world allowed Larka to keep up her athleticism and skill without having to travel the distances needed for hunts.

Rae was concerned about her, not that she would ever show it. Her mother was far too proud, and if anyone saw the slightest hint, she'd push herself too far to prove a point.

For now, Rae kept her thoughts to herself and instead felt grateful for the focus Little One had gained from their mother. While she was the height of her elder siblings, she was still closer to a pup than a grown wolf – which wasn't helped by the fact that, unlike the pack, she needed sustenance more often than them. They'd coped well enough during her first two winters with them, but as they headed into their third, with the caribou numbers fading and them travelling further out of their territory, they weren't sure they would be as successful this time. Rae knew Little One had grown stronger in mind and body, so she wasn't too nervous, but she still had her moments.

Just that morning, Little One had run snout-first into a low-hanging branch as she chased one of the local hares. She had herself a good little whine, but as she has been taught, she calmed down not long after Mother took a look at her and dealt with any injuries.

Not that there ever were any. As the family had learnt, compared to themselves, Little One was very dramatic. Minor inconveniences would become big ordeals. Though it didn't take long for Rae to realise that, in making a commotion, it gave her more time with Mother.

Rae had laughed at the realisation. *Such a mother's pup,* she thought, with a rush of love for her trickster of a sister.

Of course, because Rae took so much after her worrisome father, she found herself concerned by the level of attachment and reliance Little One was building with their mother. She had thought that she'd outgrown this need by now with her, but it seemed she was falling back into old habits, and to Rae's surprise, Larka was indulging her.

As a leader whose primary focus had always been training and teaching Little One to adapt and understand wolf life, Larka seemed to be faltering on her own lessons. *What happened to "you must strive for your own survival", Mother?* Rae wondered bitterly, watching her hard work fade away in front of her.

Rae shook her head gently as Little One rushed ahead and around the hilltop, stopping only briefly to come and nuzzle Rae, before dropping to the ground and rolling down the hill, squealing as she did.

She began playing in the slowly growing snow. While she was still susceptible to the cold, she had shown her resilience in not allowing it to phase her, though she would occasionally use the strange material that she was found with to cover herself if necessary.

Little One had always been a curious one, but more than that, she was stubborn beyond belief. *Like Mother like daughter*, she thought with a rueful huff. Rae could only hope that that would continue to keep her strong.

5

RAE

It didn't take long before something went wrong with the pack's happy picture. Rae should have expected something – the natural world was prone to irony – but didn't expect it to happen so soon.

The last few suns that the pack had hunted, they had found no caribou in their territory. While they weren't without prey, with winter incoming, they needed bigger animals to sate their hunger for longer, and deer and rabbits wouldn't help with that.

That day, Rae cancelled the hunt and, instead, she sent out her wolves in threes to go in search of the herd. Echo, Akira and Shadow made one group; Chase, Rune and Swift another; and finally, Kali, Una and Lobo. She hoped that by sending them out in multiple directions, they would find where the herd had travelled to without scaring them off with their numbers.

It wasn't helped that there'd been more reports of Hye hunting erratically in the recent moon cycle, Rae feared that without any large meals soon, they'd not have the strength to fend off a possible attack from Hye or any other rival pack. She was sure that by now she would have driven herself mad with worry, but Little One was always ready to help. And today was no different.

A few shadows had passed since she had sent out the searching party of wolves for the herd and they hadn't returned since, which led to a build of anxiety within her. Before she could spiral, she found herself being held by Little One who patted her back and spoke strange nothings to her.

She'd never experienced this as a wolf, nor was it particularly wolf-like, but it was very Little One.

The two of them stood there, Little One's forelegs around Rae's chest and back, and her head tucked in and nuzzling hers. It didn't take long for Rae's anxieties to fade away. Little One always knew how to make her feel better.

With her work done, Little One licked Rae's face lovingly before tumbling down the hill towards a rather disgruntled looking Skai. It was time for Little One's training lessons, and for once, Rae intended to watch. She wouldn't admit it out loud to anyone but her sister, but she needed Little One. There was something about her sister that helped her fell less hopeless. Whether it was her kind heart or her belief in Rae, she wasn't sure. She just knew she needed her. So, for now, she would rest and enjoy the sight of her sister having fun – much to Skai's annoyance.

Skai had been tasked recently with teaching Little One about hunting, though Rae couldn't understand why. The grey-furred wolf wasn't exactly known for her patience, especially with Little One.

She watched as her sister practiced her pouncing, and from Skai's snapping, she was prepared to intervene when her mother appeared at her side.

As Larka laid down next to her, she too turned towards Little One's class. A deep sigh left her as she watched, drawing Rae's attention away from her sister and to her. Reaching forward, she nuzzled and licked at her mother's face briefly, before pulling back. Larka had closed her eyes, taking it in, before sighing again.

The snowstorms have been quiet this time, she said, a tenseness to her voice. **You know what this means.**

Rae nodded – the signs of the weather drilled into her since she was a pup. The fewer the storms and the sooner the bears hide away in their caves, the harsher the colder days.

Larka opened her eyes, and she turned towards the fading sun in the distance. She looked older than Rae had ever seen her. And so very tired. **Little One will need looking after more**, she said.

Watching her mother, Rae felt conflicted. She had noticed the weariness in her eyes and the ache in her gait for some time now. A wolf is never to mention weakness, both out of respect but also for protection. Once it's brought into the open, it becomes only a matter of time before the pack, and later predators, notice it.

That can be its own death sentence.

But she desperately wanted to ask if she was okay. She had given her so much. She had trusted her with Little One, confided in her about her worries, and even allowed her to lead the hunt. Even now Rae didn't understand why. So, while she couldn't ask what she needed, she asked what she wanted.

Why me, Mother?

Larka turned to her, and for a moment, the exhaustion in her eyes became wistful and loving. Her posture changed as she sat herself up and, once again, shone as the prominent leader and mother of the family, the symbol of strength and power. She looked at Rae with pride, huffing happily towards her.

You ask me why, yet the answer is clear as our light and dark. Larka gestured to the land below, where Little One had begun a game of play with Skai in the freshly fallen snow. **You have given our pack something I never could. A chance to enjoy life and live it fully, as a family.**

I have spoken for too long about survival over all else, and in it, while we have thrived, we have not lived. Larka nuzzled her softly, continuing, **But you, you gave us that once again. You gave me that.**

It was then Larka turned back to Little One who now, shivering, was playing with a disgruntled but amused Skai. Thankfully for them, they knew not to play too rough with the fragile one. Rae lowered herself to lie down as she watched them, waiting for her mother to continue.

Then there is the biggest reason of them all.

The two of them stayed silent, watching and listening to the joy of the youngest and kindest of them all.

Rae felt a warmth in her chest as she looked over at her sister. While the two hadn't spent as much time together recently as they had when they were younger, the love they had was still as strong. Rae continued to teach her, and unexpectedly, Little One had taught her as well.

There was always something about her. Even when I found her, something drew me to her and gave me a sense of...

There were too many ways that her mother's feelings could have been described, but it was in that moment that a high-pitched howl echoed around them.

6

RAE

In an instant, Rae was on her feet and charging in the cry's direction, her heart pounding so hard she could feel it in her paws; she barely acknowledged the presence of her mother and Skai following quickly behind her.

She could smell blood in the air; it was fresh and came from a span's distance from the Den. Whoever had been hurt, it had happened in their territory. *Was this an act of war?* Rae thought fearfully. *Have the packs sensed weakness in us somehow?*

Rae didn't dwell on that for long as she, Larka, and Skai bounded through the prickly bushes and onto the scene. Snarling faces turned on them instinctively until Akira and Shadow realised it was them. A sigh of relief left them as they took up their protective positions once more in front and behind the injured Echo. Echo lay on the ground, his blood staining the crystal snow. His back leg oozed; the scratches were deep but nonthreatening. Quiet whimpers escaped him, a sign that, even though it was nonfatal, it was serious. Echo never complained about injuries.

Larka moved to him instantly, tending to his wound by

licking it clean. **My soul, what happened?** she cried, turning to him for answers.

Before he could respond, from the bushes, three of Rae's siblings appeared, their breathing harsh from their pursuit. Without a thought, they turned to Rae and told her what happened.

It was Hye, Rae, Rune said, anxiety in his voice as he stared at their father. **We were returning to the Den when we heard, but we … we arrived too late to stop him.** For a moment, Rune paused as he noticed their mother tending to Echo, he looked conflicted as to whether he should be speaking to Rae or her.

Swift took over from him, her white fur like their mother's stood on end in rage. **We do not know what he wanted, but he fled as quickly as he arrived,** she said, her tone sharp. **The coward refused to turn back and fight.**

Frowning, Rae turned away from the wolves and sniffed the air. She could definitely smell Hye, but there was something strange about his scent. Stepping closer to the area where the scent was strongest, she drank it in deep. While there was a sense of anxiousness that Rae could smell, there was also something else that frightened her.

Excitement.

That's not right, Rae thought, taking in the scent again. *Why would he—*

Her head flew up, eyes darting around every aspect of the Forest in front of her, her ears twitched at every sound as she searched for answers, bracing her legs, ready to pounce into action when she found it. And then she did. The heartbeat of Little One, waiting for her pack to return, and then—

Another heartbeat. Slow, deliberate, patient. The soft breaths of a hunter preparing to pounce.

Rae turned to her pack. The recognition and fear in her eyes passed to them, and then she turned to her mother.

Larka was the first to spring into action, taking the lead in the most reckless way Rae has ever seen her do: charging right towards the danger with no stealth or plan in place to attack.

IT TOOK Rae and the others too long to react after her mother had charged away. But when they did, Rae instantly took lead. **We need a coordinated attack,** she barked, pausing only briefly when the other trio from the search arrived. *Thankfully, we have the advantage of numbers*, Rae thought as she issued the rest of her orders. A group of four to the left, another four to the right, with Rae herself following Larka's path straight ahead.

Skai, stay with Echo and make sure no other predator seeks him out, Rae finished, a soft growl in her throat when Skai attempted to protest. **Everyone, go, now.**

Then, Rae turned tail and ran. While she was fast, she was deliberate in her movements, following the exact trail that Larka had left behind to soften the sound of her approaching steps. While Hye would have heard and sensed her mother's presence, with her actions now, it'd be less likely for him to notice her.

It was only when the snarling and hissing started that she quickened her pace, loping into the action over the hill as safely as possible. Once she emerged into the open, she was met with a standoff between Hye and Larka. Hye stood low to the ground, his claws extended and mouth open, exposing his long, sharp teeth as he focused in on Larka standing tall with her legs braced and ready to pounce. She stood in front of Little One protecting her from view. Though to Rae's surprise, Little One wasn't cowering like she thought she would be. She was growling at the cat just like their mother.

Rae closed in, a snarl building in her own throat, as she stepped closer to her sister, adding another protective body in front of her. Making sure to not lose sight of Hye, she checked on Little One out of the corner of her eye. She appeared unharmed but dazed as she watched Larka paw at the ground in front of them.

Yet, even with her show of defiance and the growing aroma of pure hatred rolling off her, Hye was not backing down. There was something in his eyes: a thirst, a need to do this. As he and Larka sized one another up, prowling back and forth in front of another, Rae took him in.

There was an anticipation in his movements, but he looked different from the last time she'd seen him – a tiredness about him – and she was sure she could see his bones showing through his thinned-out fur. He may have had the jump on Echo, his blood coating his outstretched claws, but that action alone had exhausted him.

His breathing was heavy as he paced, eyes never leaving Larka, even with Rae and the others in view surrounding him. There was something personal about Hye's attack that Larka seemed to understand as she commanded to the group:

This is our fight. None shall interfere.

The family was silent. They had not expected a command for them to stay away, and so they moved closer. It was only when Larka snapped her jaws in their direction, her intentions clear, that they stopped and stepped back. You never interfere with a mother wolf.

Only Rae refused, keeping as close to her mother and Little One as she could, and if her closeness meant she could jump in to help, if necessary, well that was just a coincidence. Though if Larka's stance told her anything, it was that if she interfered, she would face worse than whatever she would inflict on the cat. With that, she nudged Little One further back towards the hill. And with a quiet bark to the nearest wolf, Rune, she issued the order for them to retreat with Little One to the Den.

She followed them briefly, giving extra protection to Little

One as Rune escorted her up the hill, and watched her mother engage with the cat.

Larka had always been an incredible fighter – Rae herself had witnessed this first-hand when they hunted – but this was different. She was in a frenzy, her teeth and claws lashing out at Hye to keep him back from the Den's hill. Hye always made the first move, desperate and aggressive, but with no skill or precision, making it easy for Larka to push him back with a swipe of her paw.

Turning away from the fight, Rae checked on her sister, only to find herself surprised at what she saw in her eyes. Anger. And then their locked eyes.

Help her, Little One said, her voice more controlled and firmer than it had ever been before.

Rae smiled and nodded her head before turning back and rushing down the hill to her mother's side.

That was the wrong decision.

Her reappearance and movement caused Larka to lose focus, her eyes dropping away from her target and towards Rae, giving Hye the opportunity to strike. He leapt forward, teeth bared and claws outstretched, ripping them across Larka's side. A high-pitched whimper of shock tore from her throat as she was knocked sideways from the blow.

Barely standing, blood dripping from her side and down her maw, Larka shook herself slightly from the shock. Rae was ready to issue the order to the rest of the pack before Larka released a howling snarl and pounded forward into action.

7

RAE

The viciousness of the fight took Rae aback. It was like nothing she had ever seen before. She watched her mother spring back and forth, side to side, lashing out with a snap of her teeth towards the cat. Rae could understand why her mother had held onto her power for so long.

Larka was a strong and calculated fighter, which gave her the advantage as she weakened her opponent as a wolf does their prey. With Little One no longer in sight, and even with Rae standing guard at the Den's entrance, Larka was able to push Hye harder.

She got in close and personal, taunting him to swipe at her only to jump out of the way in time and send him off balance with a snap of her jaws at his swinging paw. After each attack of hers, she put space between them quickly so he wouldn't have the chance to retaliate. His teeth were deadly. One precise bite could end it all.

Around her, Rae could sense the pack's unease and frustration about not being able to fight. They knew that together, Hye would be dealt with quickly and easily. Their family was not one for spectating; it wasn't in their nature.

But this wasn't a normal fight. Rae knew that the cat had been seen around the pack acting strange for many moon cycles now, but he and her mother had never had reason to quarrel. As she studied Hye more, she took in his wild state. Around his maw frothing saliva dribbled down and onto the ground, his fur was matted and parts of it had been torn off showing sore skin beneath. Hye was not acting like a normal animal. He had become an unhinged one.

It was by focusing on Hye that she saw it.

The mistake.

Larka darted forward, jaw wide to target the cat's neck with her teeth. A killing strike. But Hye was ready for her. He threw his head to the side, blocking Larka's target, and leapt forward with his own mouth wide.

The sharp whimper echoed around them as her mother fell with a thump to the ground, her blood spattering across the last of the sun's time grass and tainted the fallen snow, the flesh at her neck torn by the cat's teeth. Rae howled and charged towards her mother's side, ready to protect her. Her cry spurred on the pack, and they charged towards the enemy, ready to destroy him.

As wolf after wolf lunged, snapped, bit, and scratched, Hye grew more reckless. His movements were weak. Every swipe he made gave the pack the opportunity to strike him in return. But even as more of his blood stained the ground, the feral glint in his eyes didn't fade.

Rae was sure that she had seen something like this before, or had heard tales of it at least. Of beasts who turned on their own or grew a thirst for blood from a hunger that could not be sated. As she watched the wild cat grow weaker, but never stop trying to kill, she realised it must be true.

Larka had told the stories, she was sure of it. Savage Blood, she had called it. Rae turned to her injured mother, who lay beneath Rae's protective stance. Larka's breathing was shallow, but her eyes were open and alert, staring at Rae. She knew that she had figured it out.

Rae needed to keep her pack safe, but she wasn't sure how to signal the danger Hye posed without letting him know. As it turned out, she wouldn't have the time to do so anyway.

The wolves were becoming just as sloppy, their anger making them reckless and less focused, and soon Rae and Larka were left in the open, a perfect line of attack. And Hye noticed this before Rae could bark an order out.

Even as claws ripped at his side, Hye barely reacted as he charged towards Rae, and she stepped away from her mother, closer towards him, ready to fight till the end. With wolves at his heels and bloodlust in his eyes, he lunged. Rae braced herself, teeth bared to attack, when a snowy white figure flew past her, colliding with the cat.

Silence surrounded them. The heavy thud of a single body and the pants of another were the only sounds that could be heard.

Shocked and in awe, Rae stared at the image of her mother standing tall. She was hurt and bleeding from her wounded neck, her maw and fangs coated in fresh blood that was not her own. She stood above the lifeless body of Hye, whose eyes laid wide open, his mouth frothing with blood-coated saliva.

The pack stayed silent, their breathing the only noise left in their once peaceful sanctuary. It was only when Kali, one of her siblings, broke that stillness by cautiously stepping towards Hye, that a growl echoed across the snow, stopping her in her steps.

Cold eyes turned to the young wolf, their voice leaving no room for argument. **Respect is to be given to our fallen comrade. His actions and mind were not his own,** Larka snapped as she limped towards the cougar, her movements tight and sore. **He deserves to be returned to his home. So be careful in doing so** – she turned to the pack – **as we will take him there.**

The family was slow in their reactions to her orders. The separation from their ways, the foolish fight, and now her injury had all brought her skill and leadership into question. Loyalty, however, was a powerful thing among the wolves. It was only after a secondary nod by Rae, given behind her mother, that the pack moved into action. Their steps cautious so as not to sour her temper.

Kali, Shadow, go collect Echo and Skai and bring them back to the Den. The rest of you... She looked at her mother out of the corner of her eye. **Do as you have been ordered.**

As they set to work, careful not to dig their teeth in too sharply, or come close to the frothed saliva, Larka stepped back. She turned away from their work, and before realising Rae could see her, allowed the pain that clearly was overwhelming her to show.

Her legs shook as she stepped away, and her jaw wobbled as if she were trying to hold back a whimper. It was only when she noticed Rae that she stood tall again, controlling her breathing as best she could to mask the pain.

Keep an eye on the others. I must check on Little One and make sure she is unharmed, she said, not meeting Rae's eyes. **Have Echo brought to my side when he returns.**

Rae was unsatisfied with this. **Mother, we must care for you first. You are bleeding! You cannot just—**

I will not be spoken down to, pup! Larka snarled, snapping her head in Rae's direction, her teeth bared and visible to the root. **Remember your place. You may have the freedom and the authority over the others, but I can take it away as easily as I gave it.**

Without another word, Larka walked off. There was an obvious need to limp in her stance, but her mother was prideful. No matter the pain, she refused to show even the smallest sign of it as she headed up the hill towards the anxious cries of Little One. It was as her figure disappeared over the top that Rae allowed herself to breathe. She'd never been afraid of her mother before, let alone been afraid *for* her. She took in the sight of the drops of blood that stained the newly fallen snow.

After a pause, waiting to see if her mother would return, and maybe apologise for her actions, Rae turned to the pack and trotted towards them, taking hold of a limb herself to help with the pulling of the body. Hye had been a large creature, and in death, his weight doubled. His territory was far, and it would take time to return him.

The sun was still high in the sky and so, with the respect for the wild that was ingrained in all its creatures, the pack began their journey.

8

LARKA

The ache shattered her. Not that she could show it, at least not until she was alone. Ferocity was her weapon for now. It was the only way to dissuade the enemies that would come once they knew of her weakness. A sick sensation built within her at the fear and betrayal in her daughter's eyes caused by her actions. That sight alone was far more painful than anything she was feeling.

As she climbed over the hill, she was met by the whining cries of her pup. The pain, while still unbearable, fell to the wayside as she rushed to her side. Nuzzling her face, she breathed in her scent as her eyes took in every inch of her to make sure she was unharmed. It was only after a thorough cleaning of the minor cuts on her body that she felt satisfied with her pup's well-being.

You are hurt, the small voice said. Placing a hand next to the injury on Larka's neck, Little One whimpered. **They hurt you, Mother.**

Just as Larka would her own pups, and as is the way of the wolf, Little One leant forward and licked her wound. While she gagged initially at the unexpected taste, she continued with little to no complaint, cleaning Larka's wound as best her small tongue could.

Eventually, Larka nudged her to stop. The ache hadn't lessened, not really, but in her mind it had dulled. Little One stepped back, her mouth and nose covered in Larka's blood. It was a jarring sight.

She cleaned the blood from the youngling's face, relishing in the squeal it elicited. After finishing and determining her pup to be clean and no longer upset by the sight of her injuries, she turned to the wolves arriving behind her.

Echo, limping himself but not severely, came as quickly as he could to her side, with Skai, Kali and Shadow following slowly behind, head bowed. They stood in silence, awaiting her reaction and command.

Larka stood tall as she held their gaze, her tone and words holding no room for arguing: **Hye is being returned to his territory. Join the pack and help them complete the journey.**

The wolves stayed still, a few sharing a look between themselves; however, after a brief pause, they bowed their heads and quickly trotted past Larka before disappearing over the hill to join the others.

Only Echo didn't move. His injury was shallow but had caught a vein, making the pain and blood flow more freely than normal. Even though it was clear that Echo didn't have the capacity to help the pack in removing Hye, his disobeying of her orders affected Larka more than she expected.

She jumped at him, her body low, her teeth pulled back, the warning simple: *disobey and suffer.* Echo, however, was not one for such acts of violence or attempted dominance. They were equals, as they should be. He always, and would always, see her in that way. Instead of pushing back and responding, he released a soft and calming whimper.

The growl dissipated, and she loosened her position, knowing it was ridiculous to have tried. Slowly, after hearing how far their pack had travelled from the Den, she surrendered. Sliding to the ground and rolling onto her side, she released a heavy breath. Then another, and another.

Finally, she allowed the pain to take hold. While she was quiet to not alert any predators nearby, the agony she felt nearly tore her to pieces. Every ache, every tear, and every scratch came at her all at once, and she could feel herself almost losing consciousness again because of it. Echo and Little One, the two beings who seemed to know her better than she knew herself, came closer. Little One curled up by her belly, her paws petting her softly in comfort. Echo walked to her side, and with a gentle nuzzle to her head, he sat down and began surveying the land. From his position, he would see whatever might come their way. His language was clear: He would protect her so she could be weak.

A heavy sigh left her. With Little One at her side and Echo as her guardian, Larka allowed herself to rest.

As a leader, Larka was used to holding the image of strength. She held her head high, her tail taut in the air. The obedience that her presence demanded was enough to make it clear who held control. The cold days had passed since her attack, and from the intensity of the storms making life even more difficult, she had grown used to the pretence of wellness.

Her fur had grown back over the bite marks, but if sought out within her fur, the healed scar wasn't hard to see. Other than the war wounds, something most wolves gained at one point or another, Larka appeared to be the picture of health. She had returned to leading the hunts on occasion, with Rae resuming her duties to Little One's teachings in those times.

She ran her normal speeds, killed with no struggle or strain, and provided for her pack as she had for many seasons. It was only as her family slept that she would slink away in the night to release the painful tension in isolation.

Each day was different. Sometimes it involved rolling her wound in the cold snow, dampening the painful heat it omitted. Other days she caused smaller injuries to other areas of her body to distract her, if only briefly, from the pain. A small puncture from a branch, irritating a porcupine, or running so fast that the ache in her limbs would dull it.

Only Echo knew what she did in the night. Her exhaustion was never easy to hide from him. With him knowing he was able to cover for any weakness she showed. In doing so, it left her pack, and those who could seek them harm, none the wiser.

However, as the new moon drew nearer, the ache in her jaw grew stronger. Eventually her bones became weaker, to the point where it felt like they could give out at any moment. She grew more confused and irritable as each day passed. She knew that soon she would be too dangerous to be near her family but losing them would be far more painful.

That evening, as she took her leave to relinquish her pain, that thought troubled her again. She plotted in her mind how long she could have to stay with her family before … well, she didn't want to think of that part.

She attempted to trace the changes in Hye in the lead-up to his attack. He had appeared to be erratic for a moon's time before the assault. His fascination with the wolves had grown, she had assumed, because of their growing numbers. However, when he had finally struck, he appeared smart enough to choose a single target, Little One.

Is it the human scent that drives Savage Blood to the extreme? she thought as she made her journey around their territory's edge. To any enemies, it would seem like she was patrolling, a warning sign to any who wished to encroach. In reality, the further and longer she could travel, the more her aches faded and migrated elsewhere.

Thankfully, she didn't have to worry about her pack questioning her absence; her beloved had been keeping guard for her ever since she had started this. Though she hadn't told him directly, she was sure he knew what was happening. She could think of no other reason as to why he would leave her be like this.

As she travelled, keeping her focus on the surrounding area, the mysteries of Savage Blood continued to plague her. She had never learnt or understood the complexities. No being had. All she knew was that it drove the creatures to a bloodthirsty madness. They wouldn't be of sound enough mind to target and stalk their prey, their actions too brutish and desperate for that. Often, they would die before they could even cause harm.

Yet, Hye hadn't. Instead, he had come for Little One. Would that happen again? Would this sickness that was spreading through her lead her to attack her own child? Was there something about Little One that led the Savage Blood to seeking out beings like her as prey?

Could it be possible that Little One's mere presence put the pack at risk?

The thought made her pause. That her pup could be the reason for what is happening to her now brought a strange heat to her chest. It was anger. Not at the thought that Little One was responsible, but that she, her mother, could even consider laying blame. Shame washed over her.

It was as she began her return to the Den that she resigned herself to what she had to do. Plotting Hye's own journey, his interactions with the land, and how he reacted did her no good. Nature was a fickle creature, and as her own mother used to say, a tree never fell in the same place twice.

Her journey with this would not be the same; she just had to hope her spirit could hold out a little longer so she could say goodbye in her own way.

To her surprise, when approaching the Den, at the bottom of

the hill sat Little One, waiting and watching. Larka turned to look for one of her other children but couldn't see or hear any movement from them in the Den above. She approached the youngling and softly bumped her head against hers. Little One sighed. Her careful paws raised up to hold on to Larka's muzzle.

Mother, she began, stern and forceful, before the power in her voice left her, **you are still hurt, aren't you?** She whispered. So quiet that Larka was briefly unsure she had spoken at all. Upon realising, she pulled back slightly to look at the pup. There was innocence in her eyes, but also a wisdom too powerful for one so young.

It seemed Larka was not as subtle as she had thought. Of course, she couldn't keep much from this pup of hers. She sat down at her side, a wince the only sign of her continued pain, and sighed.

You are right, Little One. I am sorry I hid it from you, she said, her words genuine. While she knew protection of the pack was of the utmost importance in their world, keeping this secret and her pain from her family was unbearable. **It was for our safety, if you can understand.**

Little One crawled to her, sitting herself between Larka's front legs, allowing for Larka's head to rest upon hers. Paws once again held her, and her body relaxed, the pain subsiding for that moment.

She could feel the confusion in her voice as Little One spoke. **You taught me that ... when you are hurt, you are to tell. That is the only way we can make it better.** Her small weight rested against Larka's chest as she continued. **The strength of the wolf is that of its pack.**

A snort escaped Larka in her amusement, surprising Little One. She didn't mean to find it funny, but after only three seasons with her darling pup, she had already outgrown her. Little One was strong at heart, even if she didn't know it now.

You are correct, my pup. But I am not strong. She pulled back from Little One, making sure she didn't fall. She waited for the pup to turn and face her. **The pack is strong, and its strength lies in the bonds of family. Yet life does not last forever, and neither does family. Nature does not make life easy that way.**

Larka's ears pricked, a familiar noise gaining her attention. She was no longer just speaking to Little One.

You must be the life. You must be the family. When we are together, our lives and family are one, holding and powering our strength to survive and withstand. We have our leader, we have our young, but above all, we have life and love. It is why we say that the strength of the wolf is that of its pack.

Little One was enraptured by her words, but it was those last few that caught her attention. Larka listened in as Little One repeated them quietly to herself, imprinting it to memory.

Life does not last forever. Soon I will be gone from this world. Little One let out a whimpering cry, but Larka ignored it as best she could. **It will only be the love of this family, of my children, and my children's children, that my life will continue on.**

Behind them, a slender figure emerged from the darkness, but Larka stayed focused on Little One. She could feel Rae's attention focused solely on her, and for once, she felt confident in her weakness.

You are life and love, Little One, and that is the soul of a pack. Do you understand?

For a moment, her pup stayed silent. Her expression seemed confused, and Larka feared that, for now, something so metaphorical was not within Little One's capability at such an age. Then, suddenly, Little One leant forward and laid her paw on Larka's beating heart.

I am loved by the pack, and they are loved by me.

Larka was taken aback by her youngest's wisdom once more but did not have time to respond before she was met with a wide and loud yawn. The pup clambered to her feet, and with a loving nuzzle to Larka's side, she scaled the hill, ready for sleep.

She sat silently for a long time, almost forgetting that her other daughter was waiting at her side until she spoke.

Sometimes we forget how bright she is, Rae said, her eyes on the hill. **You have raised a fine wolf, Mother.**

Stunned, Larka turned to speak to her, only to find that she had disappeared. She could only hear the pounding of paws as Rae fled into the night to patrol.

A sense of relief and sadness filled her at realising that her daughter had fled her presence. Larka stood still for that moment until the pain returned. She stretched out hoping to ease it before walking a small circuit around the hillside once more. Subconsciously, she knew she was stalling, hoping to put off what was to follow as long as she could.

Her ears pricked once again, the soft paws on fresh snow letting her know that Rae was still within earshot. Somehow, knowing this resolved Larka to her choice. This was the right decision, even if it was one of the hardest.

With a heavy exhale, one that shook her to her core, she lifted her eyes to the moonlit sky. Where she was going, she knew that her family would be with her, even if it was only in spirit.

She ran out into the wilderness, the sound of a mournful howl from her beloved Echo following her as she disappeared into the darkness.

9

LITTLE ONE

The Den had felt smaller these last few suns. Even though her father and, on the odd occasion, her sister Rae were resting with her there, she couldn't shake this feeling that something was missing.

She had found herself waking up that day, shivering, and struggling to breathe. Only rushing out from the Den into the open air and gulping it in could she calm down and lose the tightness in her heart.

There was something missing within her. There was someone that should have taken up the empty space beside her at night, and she didn't understand why they weren't. So, on the fourth sun's day, she finally broke.

Where is Mother? Little One snapped, baring her teeth just like Mother would.

Rae, however, was not amused. She growled back fiercely, making Little One stumble and fall in surprise. Rae stood over her, staring her down, her lips pulled back over her teeth as she stood in silence. They may be the same height now but Little One still instinctively backed down and away from her.

Do you think your disobedience in her absence will

please her? Rae barked; eyes narrowed. **I have told you many times, sister, when I have an answer for you, I will share it.**

Little One went to speak once more, ready to moan about how unfair this was, until she noticed how exhausted her sister looked. Her usually beautiful and bright blue eyes were dulled and sullen, her grey-white coat was matted from the great distances she had been taking the pack in search of the herd and their mother. Even her usual tenderness with Little One had faded, replaced with a consistent tiredness that left no room for play.

Rae had been leading the pack in hunts for a season now, but since their mother's disappearance four suns ago, she'd found herself with the sole responsibility of the pack on her shoulders. What kind of a sister would Little One be if she kept pushing her?

Instead, as she always did when she sensed her sister's turmoil, she laid her head against hers and offered what little comfort she could. *I can always ask Father*, she thought as she felt the tight muscles in Rae's jaw relax, even if only briefly.

When Rae pulled back, she looked calmer than before, a little light returned in her eyes as she affectionately nudged Little One with her nose before pushing her over with her paw.

Little One barked a laugh as she tumbled in the snow. Bouncing to her paws, she faced her sister, ready to play fight, when a voice drew their attention away from their games.

Rae, they are waiting for you, Skai said, words clipped with barely hidden irritation. **I have been ordered to watch** – the grey wolf paused, as if she were considering saying something else before she continued. – **Little One while you search.**

With a nod of recognition, Rae came to Little One's side and nuzzled her, ignoring Skai's huff as she sulked towards the farthest corner of the hilltop away from the two of them.

Little One snorted at the older wolf's behaviour. *She acts more like a pup than I do.*

Behave for Skai, sister. We should not be gone long, Rae said, a smile in her words as if she had heard Little One's thoughts.

Why can I not come? she asked, trying not to whine. **I want to find Mother too.**

Rae sighed and stepped back, preparing to leave. She, and most of the pack, did this whenever Little One asked to join them in anything outside of the Den's quarters. Whether it be a hunt, patrolling, or anything else her siblings had been able to do for so long now, the answer was always the same.

Not this time, dear sister, you are not strong enough yet, Rae said, turning away before Little One could push for a better answer. **Be good. We will be back soon.**

Then like that, Rae ran down the hillside towards the pack that stood waiting for her. When she reached their father, who stood at the front, she barked her orders, and they loped into action and out of sight.

Little One tried to listen into their pounding paws as they went, hoping to stay with them as long as she could, but her hearing wasn't as strong as the other wolves, and eventually she gave up trying.

Sighing, she shuffled to her own side of the hilltop, staying as far away from the grumpy wolf on the other. Skai didn't like her, and for that reason alone, Little One didn't like her in return. Staying out of each other's way was the simplest way to keep the peace.

She wondered how she would keep herself occupied while the pack was away. Their searches and hunts could last up to five shadow passes, and with Skai, Little One was limited in entertainment.

I wish I could be out there with them, Little One thought, her chest tight with emotion. *I wouldn't slow them down ... I think.*

Another sigh escaped her, which received a frustrated growl from Skai in return. Trying not to anger the wolf, Little One kept quiet, leaning against the solid bark of the tree Den and keeping herself out of sight.

She knew she was different from the others. She knew why they wouldn't let her join them in their search. She wasn't fast like them, cunning like them, strong like them, even her fur wasn't like theirs. Everything about her was different. She'd always known it, but only recently had she felt it.

After Hye had hurt Echo and Larka, she could feel the resentment towards her from her siblings build. Before, they would have played with her, shared their meal with her, and even gone on walks with her near the Den. Now they could barely stand being in her presence, though they tried to hide their distrust of her by bearing it when necessary.

It was the one thing she respected Skai for. At least she was upfront in how she disliked Little One.

That was why she wanted to help search for their mother and bring her home. When Larka was here, she didn't feel so alone. Even Rae had new responsibilities now. While she did take time to be with her, Rae was often distracted. With each day Larka was gone, the more of a burden Little One felt.

In the back of her mind, in a place she wouldn't go, she thought of how her mother's leaving was her fault. Hye had only attacked because of her, and now, even though that had been two moon cycles ago, her mother hadn't been the same since.

Even now, the words her mother told her the night before she disappeared played in her mind. Something felt final about them. As if she knew she wouldn't be with her again.

Little One shook her head of those thoughts. They helped no one, especially not her mother.

She needed to do something, she couldn't just sit there and wait, proving to her pack just what they thought: that she was the weak link. Whether or not her pack acted like it, she deserved to help find her mother too. She was just as much a member of this pack as the rest of them. She was a wolf. Wolves support the pack. Wolves are a family.

Then she heard a yawn from the other side of the hill. Turning, she watched as Skai stretched, the signs of weariness clear in her movements. It was then that Little One hatched her plan.

10

LITTLE ONE

*P*atience wasn't her strong suit. Sitting, watching, waiting for Skai to fall asleep was exhausting. She just had to hope that she'd rest soon before the pack came back. The only issue with that was relying on a hungry wolf to fall asleep without a full belly.

Little One herself, unlike her family, slept far less than they did. She'd always been grateful for that fact, even though it was one more thing that set her apart from the rest. The only reason she enjoyed it was that, when her pack rested, she could explore.

Often, she would take her cover with her, wrapping it around herself, as she strayed further than the boundaries she was given. Once she'd even befriended a local raven, a creature who was the friend to the wolves, and the two had chased each other until she had grown tired.

Recently, however, with the lack of successful hunts, the hungry pack struggled to sleep, which meant no adventures for Little One. And an empty stomach.

It was while she was lost in this memory that the tell-tale signs of a sleeping wolf met her ears. Turning, she saw the deep inhales of the grey-furred wolf who had laid onto her side to sleep. Little One smiled in relief.

Standing from her spot, warm cover in hand, she took a step towards the edge of the hill. A soft groan froze her to her spot. Looking over her shoulder, Little One checked to make sure Skai hadn't woken. Thankfully, all that happened was Skai curling herself into a ball, continuing to doze.

Slowly, and as quietly as she possibly could, Little One left the Den, following the paw prints of the since-departed pack to silence her steps.

It had been far too long since she had been outside the inner land of their territory. Her mother used to take her great distances as the pack hunted. Showing her their land, teaching her the history behind it. Now, without her, she had barely made it past the great oak less than half a shadow's pass from the Den.

As Little One walked, her paws sinking into the fresh snow, her cover wrapped around her shoulders, she became aware of the safety her mother's presence and knowledge had provided her. The trees looked taller without her – bunched and curled together, creating frightening shadows on the ground, one of which looked like a pair of teeth trying to swallow her whole. Everything melded together making it hard to follow the path she took with Larka. Too many times she took the wrong turn and had to find her way back to where she came from.

The only positive that came from almost getting lost was that, with every wrong path she took, she discovered something new about her home.

Once, when she took a left at the collapsed tree instead of climbing over it as she was meant to, she stumbled across a small stream that was frequented by the smaller animals of the Forest. She took a moment to have a drink and politely greet the birds, bunnies, and hedgehogs before she headed back the correct way.

Even if I do not find my mother, she thought as she bounced down the snowy path, *at least I can show that I am capable for the hunt.*

Little One would prove herself to the pack no matter the outcome. She knew what she was doing, where she was going. She would be the one to find Mother. She had to be. The only thing she had to do was find the river.

The river marked the end of their territory and bridged the space between their pack and others. Mother had taken her there a few times whenever the pack was travelling far for their hunts. Each time they went, the more the river became somewhere that was just hers and her mother's place.

One time when they had been there, they had walked the line of the river and seen a rival wolf across the bank. A calm and silent standoff occurred, confusing Little One. Then, the rival turned and left, their tail low to the ground, and it was over.

Mother had sat down after that, a sigh escaping her, as she turned to Little One. **Nature is not kind to those who do not stand up to it, my pup. To be in balance with this hostile world, one must find a way to fight with and against it.**

Her mother often spouted wisdom like this, and Little One never really understood them. But she knew they were important, so she held onto the words in her mind for when she was older. Mother told her that she would understand it then.

A wolf is always learning, never stopping, and forever building. Even I still have much left to learn, she'd said on their last visit to the river. She had turned to Little One, who had taken to splashing in the shallow of the water to cool down in the warmer time, and nudged her. **Maybe even you will teach me something I have not learnt before.**

The two had then played together in the water, chasing one another across the banks until it was time to head back. Thinking of these memories pushed Little One to keep going, following the path she remembered to the river. She was sure this was where she must have gone. Her mother had always seemed at peace when they were there. It felt right that she would go there to rest from her injury.

The only fault with this plan was that the journey to the river was a half-sun's walk there and back. She could only hope that her pack would be out hunting longer than usual for her to make it undetected.

Still, her mother was out there somewhere, and she would bring her home where she belonged, no matter what. So, she continued her walk, her steps high to keep them out of the deep snow, sometimes even jumping when it got too much to stop her from getting stuck. To distract herself from the cold that seeped into her bones, she focused on the Forest around her.

It was abuzz with tentative excitement, and she wondered if maybe she was the reason. A lone pup was a rare sight after all. Small prey wandered near, curious about Little One, though nervous of her connection to the wolves. She snapped her small teeth at any who came too close, a warning at just how well she'd been trained. While she had yet to hunt properly, she had enough experience with her play fighting to feel some confidence in her ability to protect herself.

There was also the underlying fear that with so much prey nearby, any predators that may be on their hunt may find her. Mother had said there was an unspoken law of the Forest among the predators, a "we don't hurt you, you don't hurt us" courtesy. But Little One had never been sure if that included her.

She shook her head. **Pay attention, Little One**, she chastised herself.

Trudging on, she took in her surroundings, stopping every so often at certain trees, checking the markings left behind by her mother. She had used these as a teaching method for Little One when they used to travel to the river.

Mother had told her that, with her lack of scent and memory tracking, plotting a path was important for her to do. It would help her find her way back home to safety and her family. Little One smiled at the memory as she followed the scratched-out path. Some had faded over time, but most were still visible. As she continued, Little One's memory of the journey grew stronger.

The giant weeping tree that fell across the sky, blocking out the sun's light, meant she was at the halfway point. With the moss-covered rocky faces and the smaller pine trees that followed, Little One's confidence grew. She knew what she was doing.

Her only difficulty now was dealing with the cold. Her paws felt numb and uncomfortable, and her attempts at high-step-ping out of the snow tired her more than she expected.

Somehow it had been easier with her mother. With her, she had always managed it just fine, even in the height of the cold. A sadness washed over Little One then. It had been too long since she and her mother had adventured together. So much had happened in such a brief space of time, and somehow it also felt as if nothing had changed.

Lost in thought, she tripped over a snow-covered rock. Tumbling down an incline, her small body bounced atop the snow, the cold biting into her skin as she went, making her yelp in pain.

She landed face-first into the ground at the bottom with a thud. Spitting out the snow and brushing her face clean of the flakes, Little One clambered up from the ground. Her skin was soaked, as if she had just been bathed, and she could feel the flakes melting into her fur.

Her body tremored; the intense cold covered her from head to toe. She'd been cold before, but not like this. Her teeth hurt, an incessant chattering hurting her jaw. She pulled her warm covered tighter around herself but it made no difference. It was as if the chill were biting into her very bones. All her toes curled in on themselves, forcing her to stumble awkwardly on her numbing limbs.

Little One could feel panic building in her chest, making her breathe harder and heavier, but she couldn't afford that right now. Not out in the open.

But her sister's voice suddenly spoke in her mind. *Panic and defeat will do you no favours,* she had told her once after one of their siblings had played too roughly. *You can never show weakness, or it will be the death of you.*

Rae had always been there for her. Even though she was different now, and so far away, she was still protecting her. Then she pictured her mother and her sister together once more, Rae no longer burdened by the stress of leadership, her mother happy and with her once more, and Little One felt herself relax.

Taking a steadying breath, she forced herself to walk on, ignoring the sharp pains she felt shoot up her back legs.

Little One's throat was tight and sore, and in desperate need of water. Shakily, she scooped snow into her mouth, hoping that would sate the worst of it until she reached the river.

It was when the shadows grew thicker around Little One and the Forest around her that she realised her mistake. From her slow pace, it had taken her longer than usual to travel to the river. At this point, by the time she reached it, it would be dark. Too dark to make it back to the Den safely, or without her being noticed by the pack.

Little One considered turning back. She could always try again tomorrow.

Then she heard it.

Rushing water. As fast as she could in her state, she charged ahead. The sounds grew louder the closer she came. She could hear the crashing of the water against the banks and even splashes of the jumping fish that swam within its waters. She stumbled on her numb limbs through an opening in the trees and fell at the edges of the slowly icing waters. It was just like she remembered.

The river spanned a tree trunk's distance between the pack's territory and their rivals. It was colder now, so the colourful plants had withered, but the snow here was thinner, showing the grass beneath her paws. Every so often she would see the fish leap out of the water before they disappeared underneath it once more.

Even as her teeth chattered and her toes numbed, her heart warmed just from being there. As she crawled close to the bankside, she dunked her face into the icy waters and drank. With her thirst finally quenched, she celebrated her victory. She'd made it. And done so all on her own.

Bouncing up and down, she let out a yip of glee. Though she could still feel the cold, her cover around her body doing nothing now to warm her, Little One could hardly care. Until of course her stomach growled and spasmed, causing her pain.

She needed food. Soon.

As she looked around, she saw there was nothing of substance in the area for her. No forgotten carcasses that she could feast on to fill her stomach, and she had never been successful at catching fish, so she took to nibbling on the grass at her feet. It'd help in the meantime at least.

Now to search for Mother, she thought, taking in her surroundings.

Ripping out a chunk of grass to chew on, she began her trek. Her initial plan had been to call out to her mother as she went, but with darkness coming, she didn't want to alert any nearby predators of her presence. Instead, she stayed low to the ground, using her paws to seek out any signs of her mother while her eyes stayed watching around her, examining every movement of a tree branch or rustle of a bush.

She checked the thicket near the riverbank, under fallen

trees, and even at the water's edge - though Little One made sure to hold onto a nearby rocky patch to keep her balance so as to not fall in.

As she searched the length of the riverbank, her smile faded alongside the dwindling light of the day. There was no sign of her mother, and she still had a lot of river to check.

They will have found out I am gone by now, she thought, her heart racing with anxiety. *And I will never be able to get to the Den safely in the dark.*

She'd never been away from the safety of the pack for this long before, or alone for so long. Now she was experiencing both at once. She felt just as she had that morning, waking up without her mother again. Her heart felt hollow, as if it was no longer there. Her skin was feverish, though she was still cold. She found herself struggling to catch her breath. Little One tried to ignore it as best she could, continuing with her search, but as the first of the night lights arrived, she began to wonder.

Would she die out here? How would her pack even find her this far away from the Den? Would they even want to look for her?

Tears trickled down her cheeks, blurring her eyes. Brushing her face, she pushed those thoughts away. All Little One knew was that she needed her mother; she'd fix everything. She'd tell her the truth and love and care for her no matter what. Mother would—

Up ahead, hidden beneath fallen snow and shielded with reefs and flowers by the riverbed, was the distinct sight of pure white fur. Little One froze.

Are my eyes playing tricks? she thought.

Well, she didn't care if they were. Running towards the mound of fur and snow, her cold paws making the action clumsy and awkward, she couldn't stop herself from calling out to her mother.

Coming around the riverbed, she fell into the soft fur coat of her mother and openly wept in relief, the tightness in her chest finally releasing as she let go of all the pain she had felt in missing her. She nuzzled, cuddled, and cried into her fur, grateful to be back with her. It hadn't been that long since she had disappeared, but it felt like a lifetime as the joy at seeing her warmed her.

Oh Mother, I missed you! she whined, still nuzzling her side, soaking up the warmth she always provided. Her nose twitched slightly this time as she picked up a potent scent from her mother's fur - one that made her gag. **You smell strange, Mother, what were you doing?**

For the first time, she turned to her mother's face. The cold that had riddled her body even now with tremors suddenly felt like nothing. She could feel nothing.

Larka's eyes were wide open and shiny, frozen trickles of blood speckled around them as if some animal had tried to feast on her too soon. Her muzzle was wide open. Her tongue was dry and had flopped onto the grass bed beneath her, the edges of it missing, likely having been eaten by a nearby pest. Her once-pure white fur was caked in mud and blood, with her claws broken at the tip. The warmth that she always provided was no longer the same, it was a warming stench of death.

Her mother was dead.

Little One sat in horrified silence. Her eyes never left her mother's. Around her, the Forest seemed to take a palpable breath, its own heart breaking for the loss of one of its own. What neither Little One, the Forest, nor its inhabitants expected was the wailing howl of a heartbroken cub.

11

RAE

$\mathcal{S}$he had never considered killing a fellow wolf before, but for Skai, she was willing to make an exception. Echo and Shadow were the only ones keeping her from pouncing, their muscled and larger bodies blocking her path to the grey wolf.

How could you! Rae snarled, her teeth bared and hackles raised. Even if she had to leap over her elders to get to the beast, she'd do it. She was ready to show Skai exactly what traitors got.

But then she heard the howl.

Every member of the pack fell silent, their heads rearing up, ears standing to a point. Around them, the wail echoed, the sound drifting on the wind and swirling around the territory. The howl swallowed the air with its pain and anguish. Rae turned to her father, who gave her the same look.

Little One.

Without a word, Rae turned and loped into action, knowing her family would follow without question. Her paws pounded against the solid snow, barely leaving a print from how fast she ran. The wail, though now silent, continued to play over and over in her mind.

As she ran, her senses were on high, searching for any scent or sight that could help guide her. It didn't take long for her to latch onto her sister's familiar smell, a mix of pine, wolf, and lavender, though it was muted by an intense smell of fresh water.

The river, Rae thought and changed course for that direction, following the path her father had taken her on when they explored the territory during her first hunt.

Echo appeared at her side; his gait as desperate as hers. Even in his old age, he soon surpassed her in speed and spurred ahead.

Pushing herself faster, trying to catch up with Echo, Rae's mind ran away from her with worry. If Little One was by the river's side and seen with or without Mother, an all-out fight for dominance could break out with the riverside wolf pack. So Rae ran faster, the trees blurring around her till all she saw was the path she must follow.

The smell of fresh water and the sound of its rushing stream grew louder as wolf after wolf pounded the ground in their race to the river's edge. Then, the Forest opened up to the boundary line, and the pack stopped in their places.

Ahead of them, Echo stood still and silent beside the banks, his head low, ears flat against his back, tail tucked between his legs. A soft mournful whine reached Rae's and the pack's ears, and they all fell quiet. It was then that Rae smelled it.

Death.

Taking a breath to keep herself calm at the intensity of the scent, she slowly, head low, approached Echo. He did not turn to look at her, instead he stepped closer to whatever he was looking at, falling to the ground in grief.

Then the image of a heartbroken Little One came into view. Her skin was covered in mud and blood, her tears tracking lines through the muck. The sight alone was enough to break Rae's heart, but when she stepped towards her sister, she finally saw her mother.

She stopped. Her instinct to comfort her sister was ripped from her as she fought back the growing sickness in her stomach as she took in the sight of her broken mother. Rae stepped backwards, the need to flee rising within her, but she stumbled, her legs feeling numb beneath her.

This... this can't be, Rae whispered, barely able to take her eyes off Larka's empty golden ones.

Little One let out a cry, one she'd clearly been trying to hold back as she slapped a paw against her mouth in anger.

Bowing her head, Rae continued to her sister's side. She pressed herself against her cold body, noticing that her cover had been placed atop Larka, as if Little One was trying to keep her warm. Rae closed her eyes, her own tears threatening to spill at the sight.

Instead, she leant down to softly nuzzle her mother's body. This would be the last time she would see her mother, and while she knew this would mar the memory of the unbreakable strength she had, she would honour and respect her as any wolf would.

May Mother Wolf guide you, she said, her tongue brushing Larka's jaw.

At that, Echo broke, his once mournful whimpers rose to a devastated cry as he pawed at Larka's side, desperate for her to wake up. Rae had to turn away, as did most of the pack. When a wolf found their mate, their very souls tied together. To lose their other half is to lose themselves. While Rae, and most of the others, had not found their mate, they could understand the pain. He would not manage well without her.

Watching his grief take hold, Rae knew she had to step up. So she turned to address the pack.

Larka, provider and protector of the family, leader and

survivor – her eyes met with every wolf – **is lost. We will honour her as she becomes anew.**

One by one, the pack lowered their heads, and their tails flattened against their bodies. Any creature who saw them now would understand its sign and feel the change in the air. They were a pack in mourning, united in grief. Their bond would grow stronger as they supported one another. However, it was within their grief that they also became weak to other predators.

Rae kept a watchful eye on the outer banks of the river. They were exposed here, their grief visible to any that walked past, and that put them at risk for attack. She hoped to delay the other pack's knowledge of their loss as long as possible, and that meant getting out of sight.

We shall say our goodbyes and return—

This is the runt's fault! Skai snarled. She stepped out from the grieving pack who, in their surprise, raised their heads and tails to attention. As Skai approached Little One, she cautiously lowered her body, ready to pounce, and bared her teeth. **If she hadn't come, Larka would have still been here!**

Watch your tongue, Skai, Rae snapped. **My sister is not responsible for the actions and consequences of my mother just as you were not responsible for losing Arnou to the caribou.**

Skai growled a fierce growl, her eyes burning with rage. **Do not compare me to such filth.** Skai came closer, eyes flickering between Rae and Little One, who sat solemnly, her eyes never leaving Larka. **The human was a curse from the start.**

The she-wolf turned to the others, daring them to disagree with her. **Who among us can think of a single moment when this beast provided help or support to our family?** The wolves moved uneasily. **Yet, I guarantee that you can think of a moment of strife that it has caused for us.**

Skai turned from the others, and her eyes settled on Little

One alone. The hunger and hate that reeked from her pores was palpable to every member of the pack. It disturbed even Echo from his private grieving.

For a moment, just a moment, Rae looked at the stance of her family, and took in the look in their eyes. They were hanging on every word Skai spouted. Whether it be grief, anger, or frustration guiding them, they seemed ready to take up action if asked.

It was the small voice from behind her that cemented her decision.

My fault.

The wolves' ears pricked towards Little One, who no longer sat frozen in her sorrow. Now she stood facing them all, her head held high, a deliberate disgrace of tradition to appear confident in her action.

Her small body trembled as she stood, the blood of their mother covering her skin. Rae knew she was still young and learning, but as she turned to face the wrath of the pack, her features guarded yet determined, Little One appeared as strong as Larka herself.

It is my fault. I deserve this. Little One locked eyes with Rae before facing Skai who was satisfied with this announcement. **A life for a life.**

Then she dropped to the ground, her eyes to the snow, as she stretched out her neck - exposing her throat. The pack was stunned into silence, unmoving. Life for a life was an archaic tradition, brought in generations ago when their ancestors had been reckless in their hunts and had been practically outlawed soon after. How Little One knew of it was beyond Rae.

She saw the pack falter, their indecision palpable. They no longer seemed sure on what to do. Only Skai was. She didn't care what Little One's actions meant. All she saw was an opportunity.

Little One's eyes were closed tightly when Skai tensed her

muscles. A snarl built in the she-wolf's throat as she bared her teeth to strike. Then she pounced, her figure high in the air and her target locked. What she didn't expect was teeth at her own throat.

With a yelp of pain, Skai was thrown to the ground, her body thudding heavily. While she bled, the wound was superficial, enough of a warning sign of what would come if she tried again. Skai turned to her, eyes wide with fear and betrayal. Rae stared her down, a snarl of her own leaving her body as she stepped close. She took pride in Skai's flinch.

By the laws of this pack, you will not harm your own, Rae growled, bearing down on Skai who lay defenceless at her feet. **You have deliberately caused discourse among our family amid the loss of another.**

Rae considered showering her mercy, understanding that these were emotional times. However, when Skai continued to show her teeth in defiance, even from her position on the ground, Rae knew that the wolf would not be easily pacified. Even now, her eyes darted to the sides of Rae in search of an escape. Whether to go for Little One again or to gain the advantage, she wasn't sure, but she refused to give her the chance.

When Rae stepped towards Skai, the other members of her pack stepped backwards, their heads bowing in respect. Rae ignored them, for now, as she focused on the still-fighting wolf. When Skai snapped her teeth towards her, Rae retaliated, hard, letting her teeth sink into Skai's ear, only yielding when Skai whimpered and pulled back. Stepping forward, teeth on open display, a growl grew in Rae's throat. A small satisfaction rose within her as the grey wolf fell back, her position subservient.

You have disrespected the pack, Skai. Her voice boomed, making sure the others held onto her every word. She had seen the weakness in their eyes, and she would make sure they learnt never to cross their sister again. **As our mother passes, you**

seek to blame an innocent as the reason for her loss, just because she is different.

Skai's eyes fell away, and she slowly lowered her head to the ground, the surrender clear in her actions. With her submission, Rae stepped atop her, holding her in that position.

Mother Larka raised Little One with us as one. Yes, she may be different, but this should not drive a pack apart. Rae met each wolf head on, staring them down. **I will deal with any who seek to oust her. If you do not yield** – she turned to Skai – **you will be exiled.**

At that, Echo stood up from Larka's side, his attention fully on Rae now. Rae was laying out the law to the pack and, from the look in her father's eyes, he was both proud and grateful.

Skai laid completely still beneath her, fear in her eyes. Rae knew that her words were having the effect they needed, though she doubted that Skai would ever understand Little One's value.

To turn on our own is to disobey the great laws of our kind. She held her head high as she spoke. **The strength of the wolf is that of its pack.**

Rae stepped backwards and away from Skai. She never took her eyes off her family as she came to stand by the one she knew she would always protect. **Mother once told me, whether or not I understood it at the time, that love and life sustain us all.**

Little One's paws came to Rae's side and curled within her fur. The reassurance and love that Rae felt from that single connection sustained her through what she needed to say. **Our sister taught Mother this lesson, because she is love and life, just as we are. She is a wolf, and she is part of our pack.**

Silence fell across the banks as the wolves took in her words.

Then, Echo stepped forward and licked her muzzle – a sign of respect and submission. Turning to Little One, Echo brushed away her tears with his tongue and laid his head against hers.

After that, and without a word, he turned away, his head low and tail tucked, and he headed into the Forest. Whether he was to return home or wander until he too passed to be with his soul, Rae was unsure, but she was grateful all the same for his acceptance.

One by one, the wolves followed suit, various signs of acceptance to this fresh change in leadership. A few stopped to pay their respects to their fallen Mother and even offered a small amount of comfort to Little One with a lick to her face or nuzzle to her soft head.

They then took their leave and set off to return to the Den. A time of grief and recuperation was needed, and this would last as long as they all needed. Only Rae and Little One remained, their mother's body beside them.

The two embraced, wrapping tightly around one another. They stayed in this position for a time, Rae's heat restoring warmth to Little One, and Little One giving her a moment to be weak as the two sought comfort from their grief. She was unsure how much time had passed as they stood there, but with the moon high in the sky, it was far later than Little One had ever been out.

As Rae licked her sister's head to calm her whimpers, a flicker of movement across the water caught her attention. Just through the hedgerow, Rae spotted a rival wolf. His grey-brown fur blended in with the surrounding trees, and from how well-hidden he had been, she could only assume he had been there for quite some time. Watching.

The two locked eyes and held one another's gaze. Normally, such a stare-off would be dripping with dominance, but this wolf seemed different as he tilted his head curiously at Rae. Then, in a flash, he turned and vanished into the shadows of the trees.

She was unsure what that meant. Were their rivals now aware that there had been a change in leadership? Would they be planning an attack to steal their territory? It could mean many things, and it was the unknown that she feared the most.

For now, though, it was time for her and her sister to leave. As if sensing her thoughts, Little One turned to face her sister.

Home? she asked.

Home.

12

LITTLE ONE

Rae hadn't been sleeping much these days. She was often still awake when Little One was, which – though not concerning – was strange to say the least. As Little One watched her issue orders to the pack, she tried to remember the last time she'd seen her sister sleep.

It had been a moon cycle since Rae had become the new leader of the pack, and Little One thought she was doing a great job. But it was clear that, from the lack of sleep, the tenseness in her muscles and the exhaustion in her eyes, it was taking its toll. Though she had been in the role of leader for some time because of Larka's illness, acting as leader and being one are two very different things.

Little One tried to help her relax, just like she had once before. With a gentle hold, a loving nuzzle or even gaining the attention of the pack with play fighting to give Rae a chance to breathe, but nothing seemed to help her now.

What was worse, at least to Little One, was that beneath the pressure she felt as leader, there was something Rae was hiding. She seemed distracted, distant, as if she were waiting for something. Whatever it was, it was buried under Rae's thick exterior, and she had not confided in her about it.

Little One hated secrets. Especially when it was Rae keeping them from her. But she didn't feel able to ask her for answers. So instead, she watched her.

It was in doing so that, in the dark of night, she saw Rae disappear into the shadows. Little One was never able to stay awake long enough to see her return, but every time she awoke, she would find Rae nearby. Whatever she was doing, she always made sure to make it back to her sister before morning.

Even Father Echo seemed unaware, and he was the most observant of the pack. Or maybe he was, and he just let it go. He didn't seem to care about much anymore, Little One had noticed. The ache of losing her mother weighed on her heart, but she could hardly imagine what Echo must be feeling. Though if his loss of appetite and never-ending cries as he slept were a sign, he was struggling more than he showed.

Rae had warned her that, in losing his soul mate, it wouldn't be long before they lost him too. But Little One didn't want to hear it.

She tried her best to comfort him. She laid with him as he slept, her head curled in close to him, her paws atop his, just like he had done for her as a pup. Little One stuck by him during the day, trying to entertain him, as well as the other members of the pack, with the fun tricks the ravens had taught her to bring some joy back to their home.

Her mother and Rae had spoken of the importance of life and love, and so Little One was determined to make sure it returned to her family.

The fun trick the raven had taught her was to snap a stick from a tree and chase it around. She herself didn't fully understand the appeal of the throwing and fetching, but at the few barks of laughter that followed, mainly after she slipped on the snow, she knew she was on the right path.

As the next few suns passed, Little One continued to play her games until eventually a few others began to join her. While the grief of losing one of their own never left, at least it was beginning to feel less painful.

It was on one of those days while she and another sibling were engaging in a play fight that a strange scent filled the air, forcing the wolves to stop and stand to attention.

A trespasser, Shadow growled, his hackles raised as both he and the other wolves eyed their surroundings, ears flicking in every direction in search of the enemy.

While Little One's senses would be of no help, she stood near Elder Una, a white-and-grey patched wolf who stepped closer to her, shielding her from any possible threat that could arrive.

Then Little One realised they were missing someone.

Rae, Little One hissed out in panic, **where's Rae?**

As if summoned, Rae appeared in the clearing ahead, looking relaxed for the first time in a long while, which surprised Little One.

Why was she so calm? she thought, confused.

Rae, taking in the fighting stance of her pack, frowned before crouching herself into position.

What happened? she demanded, her eyes searching them and their surroundings for a sign.

A rival wolf, Elder Una responded, stepping forward towards Rae, with Little One following automatically. **Shadow picked up its scent just now. Did you see anything on your return, Rae?**

Little One saw it then.

A slight pause before her answer, one so small that only she could see it. **No ... No, I saw nothing, only a loathsome fox.** Rae responded quickly, stammering at the start. **Possibly the fox ... the fox may have carried a scent from a nearby territory.**

While the other wolves seemed happy to accept their leader's words, Little One knew Rae better than them. Rae never stuttered her words, unless she was lying. And Rae never lied to the pack.

As Rae came closer to the Den, Little One saw her chance. Under the guise of seeking comfort, she walked over and nuzzled into her sister's side. While her nose was not as strong as that of her families, she took in a deep breath, searching for what she was sure she'd find. And she did.

Alongside her sister's scent came another. It wasn't strong, the scent having been washed away as much as it could be with mud and snow, but it was there, and different from any of those of their pack.

We will hunt soon, my sister. Our bellies will be full and then we can rest easily, Rae said to her, aiming to comfort her. **Do not fear.**

A rest will be good, Little One said, pleased with herself. Then, a plan formed in her mind. **Will you come rest with me now?**

Rae smiled at her and licked her face to clean the few scratches she had gained from her play fights. **As you wish, dear sister.**

The two of them rested atop the hill together, enjoying one another's presence as they watched the pack go about their day. As they sat together, Little One worked through her plan. Tonight, as her sister snuck out into the night, she would follow. When Rae sighed lovingly and nuzzled her side before relaxing once more, her curiosity at her sister's secret wolf faded, exchanged quickly with guilt.

She had promised her sister after what happened with her mother that not only would she never leave the Den alone again but she would not seek out answers to something she doesn't need to know.

Little One just couldn't do it though. Her sister was keeping secrets from her again, and she refused to be kept in the dark this time.

LITTLE ONE HEARD her sister leave that night, just as she always did. This time she followed. She wasn't fast like Rae, so stealth wasn't an option here, but she did the best she could. The Forest was always livelier at night, making following her sister all the more difficult.

Unlike usual though, Little One found herself keeping up with her sister. Normally even Rae's walking pace was hard to keep up with, but as Little One caught sight of her through the trees, Rae slowed down, almost stopping in place as if she were searching for something.

Frowning, Little One stepped closer to the tree-line, trying to catch sight of her sister's expression. But when Rae stopped moving and sat down, waiting, Little One froze in place. Had she been caught? When nothing followed, Little One relaxed slightly and continued to watch as her sister scanned the tree-line in front of her.

What could be so important to search for in the dead of night? Little One wondered.

Rae sat silently and patiently, her tail twitching nervously while her ears pricked in the direction she watched, waiting.

It didn't take long for Little One to grow bored. She considered returning to the Den, exhaustion overwhelming her the longer she waited. Just as she was about to make her decision though, something else made it for her.

Hot breath rolled against the back of her neck, making her thin fur stand on end, as a low grumble of a growl followed. Before she could even react, she found herself being yanked away.

Teeth held tightly onto her arm, pulling her along. Thankfully the grip was gentle and didn't dig in like her siblings. To her side, an enormous wolf with grey-brown fur was pulling her out of her hiding place and towards her sister. When Rae turned towards them, her muzzle pulled back, exposing her teeth towards the stranger.

Release her now, Kiba! she snapped, legs bent, prepared to strike.

In an instant, the wolf let her go. Little One rubbed her sore arm and turned to the strange wolf. Though it would have been the safest option, she didn't move far from their side. Her Mother would have called it a wolf curiosity; her sister, however, would call it a twig in her paw. Still, she stayed close to this Kiba, and could not keep her thoughts to herself:

Who are you? And why do you know my sister?

Kiba barked a laugh in response, surprising both her and Rae, who stepped back in shock. Lying down at her feet, Kiba kept his eyes on Little One and huffed his amusement once more.

I have heard much about you, young one. Your inquisitive nature is refreshing. Little One smiled at that.

Kiba... Rae warned, the anxiety in her voice as clear to Little One as it was to him. Only when he turned towards her, a warm smile on his face and a bow of his head, did Rae sigh and nod her agreement.

The wolf turned back to Little One.

To your first question, my name is Kiba. I was once a member of the pack across the river but broke out on my own a few moons ago. He kept his focus on Little One, his eyes locked on hers, engaging with her fully. No other wolf beside her parents and Rae had ever done this. **As to your second, it is not my place to speak on your sister's behalf. If she wishes to tell you, that is her choice, not my own.**

It was refreshing to have an older wolf, and one not even of her pack, to be so easily engaged with her. Few wolves spoke to her the way he did – with a kindred respect. She smiled widely, forgetting all about her sister, though she had drawn closer to the pair of them, and asked directly about him.

Why did you leave your pack?

For the reasons many do, to strike out and find a new home, and sometimes – his eyes flickered briefly to Rae – **to go in search of their soul. Mine, I suppose, was a little more adventurous as I left to find both.**

How do you know if someone's your soul?

Kiba exhaled and closed his eyes, and Little One's smile fell instantly. She knew those sighs too well - she had overstepped in her questions or asked too much.

How does the moon rise and fall? Little One was startled at his words. **Why does the deer sense danger so quickly? There is never a correct answer to such things. Often, most senses just fall into place.**

Little One turned to her sister, asking for confirmation.

He is right, Rae said, her eyes on Kiba, a strange softness within them as she stared. **When you meet your soul, you will feel it in your very bones.**

Turning back to Kiba, she found he too was watching Rae, before he looked back to her and smiled.

As wolves, we decide to follow what the Forest tells us, or change fate to our wishing. Kiba leant forward and nudged his head into Little One's body. **You are evidence of that, young wolf.**

Little One was stunned into silence. The kindness of this strange wolf was unexpected and deeply needed. Ever since Skai's outburst by the river, though she had left the pack soon after, her words had stayed with her. Especially the word "human". She didn't know what it meant and had been too afraid to ask. What she did know, however, was that it meant she wasn't a wolf.

To be named wolf by a stranger outside the pack, and to be

seen as an equal by a fellow wolf, made an unexpected difference. She had never realised how desperately she needed
another being to see her how she saw herself.

Whether this was a trick or not, Little One didn't care.
Dropping to all fours, she leant forward, staring into Kiba's
eyes, and pressed her snout to his. He watched her in return,
only breaking it when his tongue licked the side of her maw in
play. Little One smiled and turned to her sister.

Can we keep him? She smiled. **I want to keep him.**

Kiba released a quiet huffed laugh, clearly hoping that Rae
wouldn't hear him. From the look in her eyes, she had, and she
was unamused. Walking towards them, a gleam in her eyes, she
stood tall in an attempt to show her strength over the two
fiends. Kiba was the first to submit, rolling playfully to his side.

Little One, on the other hand, wasn't one to give in – especially not to her sister. She darted away, deliberately pouncing
on her sister's side, before charging ahead. Normally her sister
would have chased her and a game of keep-away would have
followed.

This time, when Little One turned, she caught sight of Rae
and Kiba together, lost in their own world. Kiba laid on his side,
his legs curled up to his stomach, head lifted towards Rae. Rae
pawed at him gently before she bounced back and forth as he
attempted to get closer to her from his position on the ground.

Confused, she watched for a moment longer as this game
continued. She'd never seen a wolf act this way before, let
alone Rae.

Then she noticed it.

It was a small action, invisible to any who wasn't paying
attention. As Kiba rose, Rae dropped to the ground, a position
no leader would put themselves in – except with their equal.
Here, Kiba stood at her side, his forelegs stretched over her
body, towering over her. Normally, Little One would have been
nervous to see her sister so vulnerable to a rival wolf, until she

saw Kiba turn away from Rae and look to the Forest around them. Slowly, ears alert, eyes focused, he surveyed the area.

Little One had only seen this action once before but knew what it meant. With a smile, and a sly quickness that was worthy of the name "wolf", she slipped away from the clearing and returned to the Den.

Once she had, she curled up at her father's side, the excitement of the day and the night catching up to her. Before she fell asleep though, she thought back to what she had witnessed and smiled.

Her sister had found her soul mate, and her soul was a kind and loving one. She wondered why Rae had not brought Kiba to them, until she heard her father's sleeping cries for Larka.

Rae must now understand the ache of their father and didn't wish to hurt him by bringing her love to the pack yet. Little One nuzzled in closer to her father, resting her paw against his heart, until his cries faded away into silence.

As she held Echo who dreamed of his soul, she thought of her sister being with hers, and found herself smiling wider. Rae deserved such devotion without question. With a new warmth in her heart, and visions of her sister's happiness, Little One finally rested.

13

RAE

After her secret was uncovered by Little One, it wasn't long after that Rae made the decision to introduce Kiba. While the pack itself was open to his arrival – the usual animosity a newly joined member faced was non-existent due to his connection to their leader – Rae still felt anxious. Especially towards Echo.

Echo had acknowledged her soul's presence when he arrived, but since then he hadn't engaged with either of them, returning to his never-ending slumber. Rae understood now the level of grief he was feeling at the loss of his own soul, but as a daughter, she had hoped he would have been happier for her.

Thankfully, Little One's open love and joy with Kiba joining them was enough to cover that aching loss of her father's acceptance.

Rae watched as Kiba and Little One played with one another atop the Den; their barks of laughter brought a smile to her stoic image. She knew she had found the one when she met Kiba at the riverbanks, even if she had tried to kill him for trespassing then. But seeing him that night with her sister, giving her the respect and care she deserved without question or prompting just proved to her that he was her soul.

Kiba had not only charmed Rae though; he had found his way among the pack with ease. He knew how to work with each wolf depending on their strengths and wants.

Una, she enjoyed a direct approach with orders and conversations. Kali, a lighter touch. Then with Shadow and Akira, they enjoyed being involved with the discussion together. Each wolf had their own personality and tastes, and Kiba found them all within the first four suns of his arrival.

He went on to impress Rae, and the pack, even more after that. He may be her soul but his ease with leadership surprised even Rae. On their first hunt as a pair, with the others at their heels, they fell into perfect harmony. With each turn, twist, and stalk of prey, the two moved as one. It was because of this that in only a half-moon's cycle, Kiba had proven himself worthy to the pack, and to Rae herself.

Now, in the growing height of the migration season, their need to hunt was becoming more potent. The caribou were their largest provider, but recently, their numbers had been small. Most appeared to have moved further in-land to the treacherous rock-filled meadows. The pack could follow well enough, but it would mean a two suns' journey.

Thankfully, there were still plenty of prey that stayed closer to their territory during the warmer moons, though they were far more complex to hunt. The rabbits could sustain a pack, but with their large numbers, even if they caught one each, it would not fill them all.

Usually by now, several wolves would leave the pack in search of their own pack or for a soul - just as Kiba had done. Only Skai had left, her refusal to respect Rae's leadership or Little One as a wolf led her to be forced out not long after the confrontation at the river. However, from the packs' shared grief over Larka during the cold season, and the now-growing anxiety towards Echo's fading form, none of them wished to leave during this migration season.

With their numbers larger than ever, and their food supply running low, Rae feared how they would survive. They still had some time before the cold season arrived, which gave them time to seek out the herd, or for a few wolves to head out on their own. But as the suns passed and nothing changed, Rae considered her last resort.

If a pack ate well, they would not have to hunt as often, their stomachs holding the sustenance of the meal for longer. It wasn't a practice her wolves were used to, but if they needed to do it, they would.

The only problem was Little One.

Little One didn't have the stomach of a wolf. She was still, for all intents and purposes, a young pup and needed more food than the rest of them. Without a nursing wolf among them, this wasn't a possibility. Because she didn't hunt with them, Little One had only ever received the scraps of a meal. She'd never been able to have her fill, leading to her always being on the smaller side.

One night, as her sister slept fitfully on an empty stomach, Rae made a decision. It was dangerous and unwise, but right now it seemed to be the only option to ensure her sister's survival.

It was time for Little One's first hunt.

Kiba thought the idea was madness. His fear and concern for Little One's safety in such an environment was tangible from the frustration in his words. He was smarter than to speak harshly of her idea, but he did express his worries.

You know the hunt is a vulnerable position to put her in, Kiba said, his tail flickering nervously as he paced back and forth across the hilltop. **While our own will not turn on her amid their stalk, we cannot control what other creatures may do.**

I am aware, Kiba, Rae huffed, lying down on the melted snow to watch her pacing soul. **But if she is to survive this already questionable cold passing, then she must come with us.**

Pawing the ground slightly, Kiba responded without looking at Rae. **I know you wish to prove your worth to the pack with this impending fear of what may come, but we both know that Little One is not strong enough to withstand such an outing. What if she gets hurt?**

Rae ruminated on his last point; she couldn't bear the idea of her sister getting hurt. But then she remembered how he had started his argument. Rae would not admit it to herself, but she knew that this was a genuine fear of hers. Not being good enough. Failing in her duties as a leader. And just like her sister, she wasn't exactly reasonable when afraid.

Then my heart would break. Rae stood and stepped forward, pushing her head against his. **But what will break my heart more is knowing that if she does not survive, it was my fault for not trying everything in my power to save her.** She pulled back and looked him in the eyes. **I know you would not want to see Little One suffer in that way.**

She felt a slight guilt, knowing that would be enough to pull Kiba to her side. He was as devoted to Little One as she was. The two desperately wanted her to be with them for all time. But to Rae, this hunt was the only way to guarantee that.

With this, their decision was made, albeit reluctantly. Little One would hunt with them. A small hunt of easy prey, with only a few wolves to keep them safe from any predators who may come their way.

When they went to speak with Little One, they found her play fighting with Kali in the fresh grass by the tree-line, her laughter and excitable nature contagious with their fellow wolves who had also taken time to play and relax with one another in the warm sun.

Without being asked, Little One ran to Rae and Kiba's side, attempting to start a game of keep-away with the two of them, her smiles enough to calm the anxiety in Rae's mind – if only for a moment.

Come play, come play with us, she yipped loudly as she bounced in place, tugging at Kiba's ear.

Rae got to the point.

Wolves! Rae barked, gaining the pack's attention and bringing them in close. **A new wolf is to be initiated into the hunt today.** There was an excited jitter that followed, the pack's energy boosting Rae's confidence in her decision. She looked to her sister.

Little One, daughter of Larka and Echo, will you accept this initiation to the hunt?

The reaction was instant.

A small howl was released into the air, followed by a chorus of them from the rest of the pack who cheered on the newest member of the hunt. As the family celebrated with their sister, she found herself taking a step back to breathe, anxiety gripping tight on her heart.

She could only hope that not only would this hunt ensure her sister's survival but prove to her that she was a worthy member of the pack. As much as she, Kiba, and the pack could treat her like she was, Little One needed to prove it to herself. She was a wolf. She just needed to believe it.

A FEW SHADOWS after Little One's celebration event, the hunting party set off. The team was composed of Rae, Kiba, Shadow, Akira, Una, and Kali. All of Little One's favourite members had volunteered themselves to join.

Walking at a languid pace, with Little One excitedly trotting at their sides in the middle of the group, the wolves headed to the closest thicket. The plan was to catch a rabbit or small deer, something that could provide a quick and simple meal. Little One herself would not be the one catching the animal - instead simply watching and waiting until they called her to eat.

Rae was not leading the hunt today, Kiba having volunteered for the task. Instead, she walked alongside Little One in comfortable silence.

A nervous energy passed between the two, and they knew that the anxiety was for different reasons. Rae was nervous for her sister's safety, even second-guessing her decision, but she shook it off as best she could. It was Little One's nerves that concerned her.

She could sense the anxiety beneath her excitement. This was her moment to prove her bravery and wolfness, and she was ready to take it. The wolves around them sensed her buzz of energy, increasing their apprehension.

She would have to monitor Little One throughout the hunt. She was always inquisitive and impulsive, but in this environment, such qualities could be a death sentence. Her misadventure when searching for their mother was proof enough of that.

As they progressed, the snow began to reach their knees, and the wind picked up. Rae stepped closer to Little One to ensure she didn't get too cold. For a moment, she wished she had thought of this plan when the weather was kinder and not working against them. Then, from the thicket, a startled deer broke into the open.

The hunt was on.

The pack fell into formation, charging after the creature, corralling it from either side and snapping at its hind legs with their teeth. Due to its small size, the deer struggled against the snow. It attempted to jump out and make away in leaps, but strength and speed weren't in its favour.

Rae leapt at the small beast from the side, knocking its legs out from under them. Once it was down, the wolves pounced.

There was nowhere for it to run now. Slashing at the back legs to immobilise it, Rae stepped forward. Standing over the body, Rae struck the final blow and sunk her teeth into the deer's soft neck and held tight as it thrashed, twitched, and then finally stopped.

Elation filled the group with their success. They hadn't been out long, and yet, the Forest had provided. The members of the hunt went to seize the body, hunger taking over them, but a swift snap of Rae's teeth put them back in order.

Little One, you may feast now. Turning to look behind the pack in search of her sister, Rae rose from her position in fright.

Sister? She looked around the expanse of the killing area, searching for any trace of the pup. Facing Kiba, who was sniffing the air to seek Little One, a horrifying realisation came to her.

In the excitement of the chase, the pack had given in to their instincts and charged, leaving the slowest of them all behind. The deer had given quite the chase, and they had no idea how far back they had lost Little One.

Split up, find Little One, and bring her to safety, Rae barked, taking off in one direction with Kiba following and the other wolves heading in opposite directions. The hunters had become the seekers, searching for any sign of the lost pup.

Rae was beside herself. As she ran, the revulsion at her recklessness grew. How could she have been so idiotic? Their territory was filled with predators of all sizes. Cougars, foxes, bears, even a rival wolf could see a young pup and consider them dinner. In trying to save her sister, and raise her own status among the ranks, she may have just signed her death sentence for her.

With Kiba at her side, Rae searched across the vast ground, seeking her sister's scent – a task which turned out to be much harder than she thought. Many herds had passed through this land recently, and their scent stuck to the ground and air around them, masking any chance of latching onto Little One's.

Then, in the distance, she heard pounding hooves. Their movements jerky, disjointed, and fleeing. Her wolves were nowhere near them. Something else had to have frightened them.

Please, Mother Wolf, let this be her.

Rae darted off in the herd's direction, nose pointing to the air as she ran and Kiba followed. It was he who was the first to find Little One's scent and guide them towards a large thicket of oak trees.

But it was Rae who smelt the blood.

In a fit of terror, she sped ahead of Kiba, tracking the stench of blood to its source. Its rancid scent poisoned the air around her, its intensity so strong it brought tears to her eyes, until it was the only thing she could smell. Drops of it left a trail, a stain against the pure snow. It was, while following these drops, that Rae heard noises nearby.

Rounding a corner of oak trees, Little One came into view and Rae let out a relieved sigh. Looking her over, she searched for wounds. While there were many cuts, blood trickling from each one, it was not as severe as the scent had made it appear. The surprising part was, while Little One was injured and appeared startled if not a little confused, she was smiling widely.

Rae immediately felt on edge, the appearance of Kiba and the other wolves doing nothing to soothe her nerves – especially when Little One revealed the source of her glee.

I found it! she said, pride in her voice.

In the bushes behind her was an unfamiliar carcass of a creature not native to the Forest. Its fur was a collection of tight curls and, while matted with blood and mud, the whiteness of the fur stood out among the bush, blending in with the snow.

Its face was dark, contrasting with its fur, and while marred with savage slashes, it was clear the animal had been well cared for previously. If the torn stomach was anything to go by, then the creature had never feared for a lack of food. It was not as large as a wolf, but it was bigger than a fox which would make it a prime target for any hungry predator. Yet, Rae had never seen anything like it before.

But Kiba had.

As her soul came to her side, she could feel the terror rolling off him in waves. The other wolves could feel it, and a tension fell over them as they anxiously watched the area around them.

Young one, he asked calmly, his eyes on Little One, **have you fed from this creature?**

Little One shook her head no. **I wanted to show everyone what I found, but I didn't know where you were, so I waited.**

And the cuts? Rae asked her.

Something scared the deer. They caught me with their hooves, and I fell. I walked around, trying to find you, but then I found the food.

Rae could see that her sister was picking up the unease around her and, confused and curious as ever, she went to speak. But Rae couldn't risk the chance of her asking questions.

To counter, she nuzzled her sister's side. **You did well, dear sister, but sadly the animal is not well, and I do not wish for you to become sick from it. We will try again another time.** Rae turned to Kali, who seemed to sense what she was planning. **Kali will take you to the Den while we return to the deer we caught for you.**

Never one to question her sister, or pass up time with her favourite playmate, Little One nodded. With Kali at her side, and her paws curled into her fur, the two of them left.

With them out of sight, Rae snapped into action.

Kiba, what is it? she demanded.

But he didn't answer her. Instead, he turned to the fastest wolf of the group.

Akira, quick, reach the Den first and send Father Echo my way. Go, now!

The grey wolf charged into the woods without question, far from where Kali and Little One had gone so as to not draw the pup's suspicion.

With Rae, Kiba, and the other wolves left behind waiting for Echo, an unsettling energy weighed upon their shoulders. Though none but Kiba knew the significance of it. They were all too afraid to ask.

All except Rae that is.

Kiba, she stepped forward towards her soul, whose heart she could hear racing wildly in his chest. **What does this mean? Why have you called for my father?**

Closing his eyes, Kiba sighed heavily, his body tenser than Rae had ever seen him. Then he opened his eyes and turned towards her.

Your father and I are the only ones who know the tales of this beast's masters, he said, his voice hollow. **We have both lived with the scars from meeting the monsters.**

Turning to the fallen creature beside them, Kiba swallowed hard.

Rae couldn't stand to see her soul in pain, but she had to push him. If they were to face this together, she had to know what they were up against.

What does this mean? she asked, her eyes seeking his.

Kiba turned away from the beast and towards her. She didn't have to hear his words to see the terror in his eyes. Then he turned to their pack and stood tall – a picture of leadership for a time when it would be needed most – and said the words no wolf wishes to hear.

That we are no longer safe.

14

RAE

A rival pack has entered our lands, Rae declared, the sound of her packs' growls echoing around her.

After finding the animal in the woods, the wolves waited for Echo to arrive. When he did, he took one look at the beast before confirming what Kiba had feared, and what the pack thought they may never have to face.

A human's animal.

It was with that that Rae's worst nightmare as leader of the pack was realised. She wanted to run away and her family as far away as possible. But she couldn't. She had to be strong, even if her pounding heart was giving her away.

They had the beast quickly removed from their territory and disposed of elsewhere before they returned to the Den to inform the rest of the pack. They would have no part of what this rival pack was delving into; the pack would not tolerate the dangers they brought on their land.

What have they come here for? Shadow asked, his voice filled with hate for these trespassers.

Rae could feel Kiba's eyes on her then. His presence kept her calm when she felt she couldn't be.

To cause trouble for us all, Rae announced, standing tall and looking each of her wolves in the eye. It was as her eyes fell on Little One who, now without her warm cover, stood curled into Kali's side watching Rae as she spoke, that she felt her confidence wane.

She couldn't keep something like this from her pack. They needed to prepare themselves for what may come, but she feared what would happen to Little One once they knew what danger lurked nearby.

No, Little One is strong. She can survive this, Rae thought, and continued her speech.

They have stolen animals from the human's land and brought them into ours.

A ripple of shock spread throughout the pack. None here, except for Kiba and father Echo, had even seen or interacted with humans before. Or at least, none that they saw as human.

It was then that eyes began to drift to Little One.

We have left these humans in peace for this pack's lifetime, and they in turn have left us alone. But our enemies now seek to change that. The wolves turned away from Little One and back to Rae; she released a silent breath of relief. **In these times, as food becomes scarce, we can become desperate. This rival pack has become just that and now threatens our very existence by breaking this most sacred law.**

They all knew this law, its words passed down to them within their very DNA from their ancestors.

Never steal from a human if you wish to live.

We must work together to save our pack and stop these rivals from bringing this danger into our lives.

The wolves stood in relative silence after she had finished. Her ears twitched nervously, seeking out their heartbeats, and her eyes watched them all, waiting for a sign of weakness. Would this be the moment they turned away from her and sought stronger leadership? Maybe an elder pair could provide for them more.

When Akira, one such elder, stepped forward, a sense of unease grew within her. But, as he lowered his head in respect, the fear passed. He asked: **How shall we proceed, Rae?**

A sense of gratitude filled her. Akira had always been a responsible member, following the laws of the pack without question. With his guidance, the other wolves fell into place. Their ears pricked to listen, eyes trained solely on her, and their heartbeats lining up in a calming rhythm showing their synchronization.

For now, we must be wary of leaving the Den. We do not know if this pack is still in our territory nor how long this has been going on for. Rae stared them all down. She knew they would not disobey, but that didn't stop her from worrying. She refused to lose anyone else. **Everyone is to be on high alert, and stay in groups if you must leave the safety of the Den.**

Kiba stepped close to her side, a show of support in her decision. **We will arrange territory tracking to show our presence across our grounds to dissuade these trespassers and any who may follow their lead.**

From the corner of her eye, Rae watched as Little One slinked away from the group, stepping just out of view. As Kiba issued out orders, the other wolves giving him their undivided attention, Rae took the opportunity to check on her sister.

She found her sitting outside the Den's entrance, her back legs curled up to her chest, her warm material around her shoulders and under her maw. Her eyes were closed and as Rae came closer, she could feel the frustration rolling off Little One's skin. It smelled bitter.

What is wrong, sister? Rae asked, lying down at her feet. Little One didn't meet her eyes. **Are you afraid?** Rae pressed, her paws reaching out to push against Little One's forelegs. **It is natural for you to feel as such. **Fear is just as much a part of the natural order as—**

I am not afraid! Little One snapped, her paws knocking away Rae's in anger.

Rae shuffled back, surprised at her sister's rage – especially towards her. She'd never seen her this way before. Little One couldn't even look at her as she curled tighter into her hiding place, trying to cover the emotions on her face.

I want to help, but I cannot. She sniffed bitterly before she finally turned to look at Rae. **Because I am human.**

Stunned into silence, Rae watched as Little One stared her down, almost begging her to deny what she had just said. Though, from the wobbling of her throat as she attempted to hold back her tears, she knew Rae wouldn't lie.

But she wouldn't let this change her sister.

And that makes you less of a wolf, does it?

Little One went to speak, as if she were about to argue back, but Rae wouldn't let her. Instead, she jumped to her feet and stepped into her sister's space, her nose touching hers.

You are as much a wolf as any of us. Yes, you may not be able to help us protect and patrol our territory, but that does not make you lesser.

I—

Rae didn't let her finish. **In fact, if it had not been for you, we may have been in a more perilous situation. You may have saved us from an attack we would not have been prepared for.**

Little One's protests died in her throat as she stared back into Rae's eyes, seeking out signs for a lie. When a small smile slipped across her lips, it was clear she didn't find one.

I helped? she asked quietly, still somewhat disbelieving.

Lying back down to appear less aggressive, Rae leant forward and nuzzled her softly. **You are always a help, dear sister. Even when you do not realise it.** Little One looked confused at that, and so Rae explained. **Yes, you are different from us in many ways. But you have never allowed those differences to define you or stop you from being just as important as the rest of us. Mother knew this. Kiba knows this. The rest of the pack knows this. You have shown us all that, truly, the strength of the wolf is that of its pack. And you** – Rae nudged her with her nose – **you are that centre.**

Little One was silent for some time to the point that Rae began to feel nervous, until suddenly Little One crawled forward and, in a strange move, wrapped her forelegs around Rae's neck and held her close. The instinct to snap at her nearly took over, to be so close to a vulnerable spot would put any on edge. But the softness of her sister's action gave her pause. It was not the wolf's way, nor was it wolf-like at all.

No, she thought, turning away from her instincts and relaxing into the position as her sister held on, *but it is the Little One way.*

Eventually, Little One stepped back and let go of her before curling in tightly over Rae's paws to rest. She was too big for this now, just coming up past four seasons, but the familiarity was enough for her not to care. Resting her head atop Little One's body, Rae released a content sigh. It had been too long since she had been able to find a quiet moment like this with her sister, and with the pack nowhere in sight, she found herself able to rest easily without the weight of responsibility on her shoulders.

They didn't realise they'd fallen into a deep sleep until Kiba came and woke them many shadows later. Little One was delivered a piece of deer carcass that they had caught. It was strange to think, as she watched Little One devour her meal, that earlier that day they had taken her for her first hunt. Now, everything was different.

Rae went to stand, preparing to meet with the wolves to

issue orders on what would happen next, but Kiba stepped in front of her, blocking her path.

Stay and eat, my soul, Kiba said, his tail flicking nervously. **I have already sent the wolves out to begin their search.** Before Rae could even argue back, he continued, his tone leaving no room for argument. **You were in a deep rest, which is something you have not had in a moon cycle. I am the leader of this pack also. Allow me to take some of this burden from you.** He leant in close, his amber eyes soft and loving. **Please.**

Like most she-wolves, she couldn't resist eyes like his, and relented quicker than she'd like to admit. Though Little One's barely hidden laugh made it clear it wasn't hidden well enough. Trying to save her ego, Rae ordered Kiba to report on his plan.

He smiled. **The initial plan is to check the mountain's side on the next sun's day and continue from there across the rest of the land until we reach the river.** His eyes briefly touched on Little One, still eating, before he turned back to Rae. **When at the mountainside, we will stray as close to the human's border as we can without being caught, to seek out possible further carcasses or signs that the humans have noticed. A small patrol has checked within the weeping trees borders and around to make sure we are safe here.** Kiba nodded solemnly. **We are.**

Rae released a sigh of relief; they should be safe for now. She could only hope that this was just an anomaly in the lead-up to the cold period. Even so, she knew they couldn't lower their guard until they knew for sure.

This is a good course of action. For our inner territory, we should always have a few wolves patrolling in case they are within our lands. We must all be on high alert from now on. If the cold season is to be as bad as we expect, we must be prepared for an attack.

Kiba nodded in agreement, he bowed his head and left to relay the information to the pack. When he was out of sight,

Little One tugged at Rae's side to gain her attention, then spoke up.

Are you scared?

Rae sighed before turning towards her sister, her eyes flicking to the unfinished meat in her hands. A sudden hunger pulled at Rae, and as Little One passed the food towards her, she tucked into what was left, buying herself time. It wasn't much and she was still hungry afterwards, but she wouldn't be able to ignore her sister's question forever.

Yes, Rae whispered, fear growing heavy in her stomach as she looked out to the horizon. **But then, I am always afraid.**

15

RAE

In the end, the cold period was far more ordinary than the pack had prepared for. Though all signs pointed to a difficult time – the lack of prey, the anxiety of the rival pack and human interference, and the heavier snowstorms – the pack thrived, considering the circumstances.

There had been struggles, just not the ones Rae had expected. As the temperature fell to its lowest point and the pack huddled together for warmth within the Den's burrows, Echo had left in the dead of night.

A storm raged for three moons after he disappeared. It was only after it faded that she sent Akira and Kiba out in search of him. It was them who found him at the riverside in the very spot where Larka herself had passed. Akira didn't return with Kiba after their discovery, taking that moment to leave in search of another pack. He and Echo had always been close, and Rae understood that it was hard to lose a friend.

Little One took Echo's loss the hardest. When Kiba told her, she'd fallen silent, unable to comprehend what he'd said. For many days, she refused to leave the Den, curled up in her warm cover, barely eating or speaking to those around her. Even though she was the same age as her siblings, she was still young in mind. It was hard for her to handle the loss of their father. He'd kept close to her ever since Larka was lost, and now he was gone as well. Rae knew how she felt, even if she herself could not express her grief as deeply as Little One. She had a pack to protect.

Unlike Little One, the rest of the wolves knew this day would come. He had been without his soul for too long. They knew he had only been holding out to see them through the impending danger. Now, with his passing, he would be with Larka once more. There was happiness for him, but like any loss, they grieved for him too. So, for a moon cycle, the last one of the cold periods, they mourned until they could do no more.

When the deep snow melted to its normal depth, filling the rivers to make them flow again, Rae finally felt at ease. She was sure that whatever had killed the strange creature must have died in the cold, or maybe they had fled after her pack spread across their territory in a show of dominance.

Soon the caribou would return to their area of the Forest, and they could eat fully and well once again. They had kept Little One strong enough during the cold, relying on the smaller prey like rabbits and small deer to keep her well-fed. It was during this time that Little One grew taller, now standing over Rae and the others in height. It left Rae wondering not only how much bigger she could grow but how much of a difference this could make to her eating habits. She could only hope that the bigger she got the less she would need.

While her sister's ribs did stand out against her furless body, just as it had when they were pups, and she felt the cold more these days due to the loss of fat, she had not fallen ill, which Rae took as a success. If they could catch bigger game, she could return the fullness to her sister's size soon enough.

But that was easier said than done.

On the first hunt of the new season, as she and the wolves

loped across the receded snowy grounds, relief in their tired bones at the long-distance run across simpler terrain, they hunted for their prey.

As they searched, senses on alert for the tell-tale signs of the caribou herd, or even the wild deer, they slowed their pace to not overdo themselves. They retraced the usual path that the herds would take to their grazing grounds, but there was no sign of hoof prints, no broken twigs or gnawed-at freshly grown grass to show that they had arrived. Confused but not deterred, the pack explored elsewhere.

It was as the sun faded and night was upon them that the pack retired, only finding and killing a small deer, a creature that would only just about satisfy Little One let alone a whole pack. The promise of returning the next day in search of larger prey was the only thing that kept them calm.

When the next day ended with the same result, followed by the next one and the next one and the next one, frustration grew. Fights were breaking out, tensions were heightened, and even resentment of Little One who needed to eat more regularly, which reminded the pack of their hunger, began to grow. It was when Kali, who had been close to Little One, snapped at her, breaking skin with her teeth in anger that things changed.

In the moons that followed, members of the pack slowly began to break off, leaving in search of a new pack or food of their own. First went Kali, then Swift and Lobo. Soon, as more went, their overwhelming twenty-member pack had fallen down to a reasonable eight. At least, for now.

ONE MORNING, on the day of another search for the caribou, Rae felt uneasy about leaving the Den. Even though she had only eaten lightly throughout the last two moons since the end of the cold period, she had grown. Now, as exhaustion overwhelmed her, she wished to be alone.

Any who came in or towards her hole would be chased off by an instinctive growl and baring of her teeth. Even her beloved Kiba and Little One. Her breathing was often laboured, and she found herself sleeping more than she ever had before. She didn't understand what was happening, only that she would be safer in the Den.

Every so often, regurgitated remnants of a kill would be quickly dumped at her resting place's entrance. Any who didn't move away fast enough faced the snap of her jaws before she took her meal. Yet, even as she ate, she never felt satisfied. No matter how big her pieces of meat, it wasn't enough.

Even with little food, she continued to grow, and the ache in her muscles and bones never faded. The few times she left the safety of the Den, usually in search of water, each step sent sharp twinges up her legs and across her stomach.

Then, on the eve of a new moon, pain overwhelmed her. She flopped heavily onto the solid ground of the Den, whimpering and whining as her body pushed and throbbed completely against her will. Everything around her was heightened. She could smell Kiba's wooden scent as he laid outside. She could hear a nearby rabbit's nervous heartbeat. And even the glow of the moon's light hurt her eyes. She wasn't sure, but at one point she thought she saw Little One come near her. Whether she had or not, her presence calmed Rae, her breathing evening out.

At some point she must have fallen asleep, as when she came to, the pain had gone. Instead, a small irritating sensation rubbed against her stomach, pinching at her. When she went to move, she heard a chorus of pitiful barks.

Lifting her weary head from the ground, she looked down to find six soft, tiny, blood-covered furballs curled into her, suckling awkwardly at her teats. Rae's heart swelled as she looked at them, a motherly whine of awe slipping out of her throat.

Leaning forward, her tongue lathered across their backs, cleaning the blood that had been caught in the little fur they had, before she pulled back.

They are mine, she thought wonderstruck as she looked at what she and Kiba had made.

As her pups suckled, Rae looked to the world outside her burrow and felt for the first time the fear her mother must have felt for her and her siblings. Curling tighter around her pups, she stared out into the snowy world. She had only just met her pups, but she would die to save them, no matter what.

THE PACK SEEMED to have grown accustomed to her absence, knowing to keep their distance. Only Little One struggled to keep away. As Rae fed her pups and cared for them, she often found Little One watching from the outside of the Den.

She had grown more since Rae had isolated herself. Her body had filled out, her patch of brown fur on her head now reached down her back, and her bright forest green eyes glowed in the moon's light as she stared down any that came too close to the burrow. Even though she was still not as strong as the others, she stood guard over her sister and her pups and made sure that any who attempted to approach the Den, even Kiba, would not get far.

Her growls were pitiful, and if it were to come down to a fight, it wouldn't go her way, but her protective stance was enough to warn them off, leaving Rae to rest with ease.

It wasn't just her presence and protection that she offered her. As the other wolves hunted, Little One would speak to her. Her voice kept Rae, and her newborn pups, calm and peaceful.

Caribou have been spotted, but they are a small herd, so Kiba doesn't want to hunt them yet. The pack isn't happy, but he put them in their place.

I lost some teeth to a bone but now have another one growing, so I will be okay.

We found Kali. She did not make it to another pack, Kiba said. We gave her the peace and send-off she deserved. I am sorry she did not find a new home.

Each tale kept Rae informed and her pups entertained as they grew. Soon, they were wobbling on their paws, and getting far too interested in joining Little One outside of the Den. The fact that they were branching out was a good thing, especially when Little One revealed the latest news one sunny afternoon.

The rival pack is back.

In an instant, and for the first time since the birth of her pups, Rae dashed out from the Den, startling Little One. Turning this way and that, Rae searched for Kiba, or any of the wolves, who may provide more. Often, they never informed Little One well enough to know all.

They all went out to help track and chase them out, it will be fine—

Before her sister could even finish, Rae was loping away from the Den, almost forgetting she had new responsibilities now. Knowing Little One was still there, she let her instincts take over. Her fear of what the return of these wolves meant took over her mind as she went in search of her pack.

The excess energy she had built up from her time cooped up with her pups allowed her to exert herself fast enough to find her wolves. They had come to a stop at the split mountains, the marker to the human's land, and as she arrived, the tension she felt in the air scared her.

The wolves heard her coming and, while surprised, they gave way for her to come to Kiba's side. There, she came face-to-face with her worst nightmare.

Another kill.

It was the same animal they had stumbled across before the cold season, one of the human's own prey. Its white curly fur was torn to shreds and splattered with blood; its carcass torn to the bone. While there wasn't much of the creature left, the killer having devoured all it could, there was no denying the similarity.

It is another of the human's beasts, Shadow said, a statement and not a question.

They all knew what this meant, what this was.

The peace they had experienced during the cold season was gone.

What do we do, Rae, Kiba? Una asked, stepping forward, her head bowed in respect. **We have never faced these humans before. How are we meant to protect our pack against them?**

Rae turned to Kiba who, out of them all, had the most knowledge of humans, but found him turned away from her and the pack. As he stared out into the distance, looking to the mountains, Rae could hear his heart pick up in speed. Confused, she turned to look at what he was looking at and felt her blood run cold.

Beyond the split mountains before them, past the small pasture of thinly snow-covered trees, and into an open crevice of land, was the world of the humans. And it was there that they saw it.

Smoke. Growing and rising into the sky, a deep orange glow, like sunset, below it. Human land never looked like this. Something had changed.

They will come soon, Kiba whispered, his voice the sound of a frightened pup.

Anxiety grew among the pack at that. None of them had ever seen a human, nor understood entirely what these signs meant, but every natural being knew of the stories and what humans could - and would - do. Not from their own experiences, but through the generations of lived trauma passed onto them.

Humans are always to be feared.

Our enemy has feasted on the human's land and brought it to us. In doing so, they have put us all at risk, Kiba said, gaining the pack's attention. As he pulled himself to his full height, Rae followed suit. Their pack was anxious; they needed to be strong for them. **Humans in the Forest have almost always meant death. Now these rivals have brought this threat to us.**

Love swelled in Rae's chest at his words as she turned to him, watching as he led and guided the pack with honour. There is only one human she knew who came under that "almost".

We will find this treacherous fiend and rip them limb from limb before they alert any human, he stated, his words brittle and dripping in rage. Then, in a raised voice, he said their pack's proverb.

The strength of the wolf is that of its pack.

For a moment, there was silence. Then, Shadow, the last of the original Elders from the pack stood, his darkened fur standing out amongst the others. In a gruff yet strong voice, he repeated:

The strength of the wolf is that of its pack.

One wolf after another followed suit, Rune, Una, Chase, Selena, repeating back their saying. Rae watched as their pack stood strong and proud, the want for survival stronger than any fear of what may come. Rae stood at Kiba's side, the strength the two boosted the morale of them all. Yet, inside, Rae felt as if she couldn't breathe. Trepidation grew as a single question plagued her, and no matter how much she tried to push it away, it kept coming back.

What if we are already too late?

16

LITTLE ONE

Secrets were no longer being kept from her. For the first time, she was included without question. And for the first time, she would have rather been left out. She knew the word "human" and knew it referred to her too. What if Skai was right to be wary of her? And what if this was the moment the rest of the pack realised it?

Thankfully, she didn't have time to worry about these things. Since the human's prey animal had been killed, her responsibilities at the Den had doubled. It was now her duty to monitor and protect Rae's pups while she and the others were out hunting for the traitors.

She enjoyed this newfound faith in her abilities and the fact that she was so easily trusted to care for and raise her sister's young. As she watched the playing pups bounce and tumble with one another, she smiled. It had only been five seasons ago that Rae had taken on the role to protect and guide her when they were pups, and now she was doing the same for the next generation.

It helped that, in looking after the pups, she was able to feel needed within the pack. Finally, she could show her worth to them all. Add in that, unlike the rest of the wolves, the pups didn't know of the word "human" and that she was one. They knew her only as their Elder and a fellow wolf. Not a human.

Little One could remember when Skai had called her human, almost two seasons ago now. She knew the stories of course. The monstrous humans who had once, so long ago, tried to wipe out all the wolves in the Forest. Since then, they had both avoided one another, sticking to their own lands and never crossing the boundary.

Until Little One.

She knew she wasn't truly a wolf. She had told Rae as such. With no fur, no ability in speed or strength, or even the ability to walk on all fours like them, she wondered how stupid she could be to not have realised it sooner. But here, with these pups who relied on her, knowing she was different didn't matter to her anymore. The otherness she always felt faded away whenever she was with them. She was useful, and she took her role seriously.

It didn't take her long to realise that teaching a pup was far more difficult than learning as one. Her patience was limited, as it always had been, and teaching the young was no different - but she tried hard to contain her temper.

Originally, she had hoped to follow the formula of Larka's teaching by taking the pups around and explaining what they could see and have them repeat it. However, with the pack on high alert, she didn't want to put them at any additional risk - or face Rae's wrath if she did. So she taught them within the safety of the Den's high ground. Unfortunately for her, the pups had other ideas.

Just like when she was young, all they wanted was to play or ask pointless questions.

Why do bears sleep in winter? Where do the rabbits go to sleep? How come you do not have fur like us?

Briefly she wondered if somehow, she'd imprinted her

curious nature onto them. Though it did make her smile that some quality of hers was now in them too. The idea of Rae's reaction to it, the huff of irritation and wide-eyed stare, made her laugh aloud, startling the pups nearby. Or at least, that's what she thought had startled them. Until she felt a change in the air too.

All six pups stood in silence, their ears, while still floppy from their young age, flickered wildly, searching for the sound that grabbed their attention. She knew never to disturb a wolf when they were seeking, but she needed to know what was going on if she was to protect them.

What do you hear? she whispered, casting her eyes around for any sign of danger.

It was Fenris who answered, his glowing amber eyes, just like his fathers, dancing around in the same direction as his ears. **Running paws, loud noise. Coming here.**

Then, all six of their heads snapped toward the trees nearest the hill, their eyes never leaving it.

Not even a second had passed before all havoc broke loose. Wolf after wolf burst through the thicket, and while the sight of them should have brought a sense of ease, Little One's heart jumped into her throat. Each wolf was splattered with blood; large clumps melded into their fur and covered their paws. At the head of the group was Rae, her snout and teeth dripping in blood. She barely looked at Little One and the pups before she and the pack turned to face whatever was following them, snarls growing in their throats as their hackles rose.

Instinctively, Little One herded and dragged the pups back into the Den, blocking the exit with her body. Whatever was coming, she would protect the cubs with her life.

Of course, she could have never predicted what would come. Or the pure unadulterated hatred that would boil within her when it did.

From the thicket, three creatures stepped out. Their coats

were mismatched and strange in colour, both blending with and standing out against the natural image of the Forest. In their forelegs, they carried a wooden smoking stick. It didn't appear peculiar itself until she smelt smoke that spewed from it. It burnt her throat, nearly making her gag. She took in everything about them, but it was the last part about them that terrified Little One the most.

Their faces were like hers.

Short noses, round heads, small ears, and no muzzle. She'd never seen a creature like her before. Yet, while they may have looked like her, they weren't the same. It was their eyes that told her this.

They were here to kill.

She turned to the pups who, terrified themselves, had crawled to the back of the Den. Her last look warned them not to move, and she knew they would obey. Then, quietly and quickly she stalked forwards, coming to Rae's side.

Little One could feel the human's eyes on her the moment she came down from the Den, but it was only when she stood by Rae that she looked at them, meeting their eyes head on.

Their expressions changed when she did – a curiosity lighting in their small eyes as they tilted their heads, confused. Little One could feel a growl of her own growing in her throat as she prayed that her curiosity hadn't come from the beasts.

One of them stepped forward, their smoking sticks still in their paws, but Kiba jumped forward, teeth bared, warning. The human stumbled back and raised the stick towards him.

Little One didn't know what it was, but before she could stop herself, she was jumping forward.

No! she snarled, only stopping when Una and Chase stepped in her way, keeping her safe.

It was her snap that drew the human's attention away from Kiba and back to her. From there, neither group engaged again.

The humans only observed from their position, their eyes

focused only on Little One, so much so that the pack began to feel nervous. Una slowly pushed her backwards with her head, sending her towards Rae at the edge of the Den.

As Little One was moved further away from them, the humans exchanged another look before they too slunk away, their eyes never leaving Little One and the pack as they disappeared into the thicket.

Even with them gone, the pack didn't cease their snarls and snapping of teeth until long after the sun had set. Little One could feel the tension bubbling around the Den, taste their fear in the air itself. It was almost a guarantee that no wolf would sleep well that night.

As Kiba organised a new patrol of the inner regions of their territory, Little One and Rae retreated to the cove where the pups lay whimpering and frightened. Only when their stomachs were filled did they fall asleep, their troubles fading with them. The two sisters had no such luxury.

As the pups slept, Little One watched her sister care for them before she found herself staring at the drying blood on her fur and maw. A horrifying image of her sister's body in place of her mother's played in her mind at the sight of the blood.

What happened today? she asked quietly into the night, her eyes staring into her sisters as a silent question played in the back of her mind. *And why were they looking at me?*

17

RAE

EARLIER THAT DAY

A full moon had passed since they had discovered the most recent animal killings. Since then, alongside caring for her pups, she spent much of her time patrolling their territory. Their hope? To find and kill the rival pack who had brought danger to their land before any human came for them.

In doing so, they had found another four bodies across their lands. Most congregating near the border to the humans', but thankfully they were far enough from their main territory. If any retaliation from the humans came, Rae could only pray that the bodies were far enough from the Den that her pack wouldn't be held responsible.

Still, the anger and disgust at the desperate actions grew strong among her pack with each new carcass. But there was one thing she didn't understand about these rivals.

While the numbers in the caribou weren't as vast as before, her territory was far more prosperous with them and other creatures. While feasting on their prey would be an equal insult, it would make sense. So far, however, this pack seemed to be hunting *only* the humans' creatures. Why? Rae had no idea. In fact, she was reaching the point of no longer being interested in an answer.

It was while out on another patrol that Rae and her pack found themselves nearing the gap in the mountain, the separation between the two worlds. They had avoided going closer to the mountains since they'd found the carcass, but they were running out of places to find the rival wolves. This was the last place to look within their territory.

The split mountains were unnerving as ever, the small thicket of trees that lay between the lush shrubbery with fresh leaves that stuck out from the fallen snow, giving it a disarming outward appearance. The closer the wolves walked, the more uncomfortable the terrain became. Small bumps of sharp rocks ran under their feet, making it difficult to walk with speed, and the open ground within the trees left them dangerously open to attack. The very land itself was designed to turn against the wolves.

What was worse was the silence. The further they travelled in, the more still it became, even the sound of the whistling wind disappeared. For a wolf, silence was perfect for hunting, but right now they weren't hunters.

Instead, they felt like the hunted.

Kiba came to her side, his eyes trained on every crevice of open land he could see, homing in on the shadows caused by the mountains as if they were an enemy in disguise.

I am not surprised that we have not passed this barrier before, there's something... He didn't finish his thought, his body suddenly recoiling in horror. Raising a paw, he scraped at his nose, as if trying to rip it off. Confusion sprouted across her features, but before she could ask what was wrong, her own body spasmed from disgust.

She smelled it too.

The air was rancid, the pungent odour seeping into every crevice. Her wolves gagged at the overpowering nature, some even burying their nose into the ground to dampen the intensity, and Rae joined them. But even with their noses buried deep into the mud and snow, they weren't protected from the scent. It was as if the odour was consuming them, and they couldn't escape. Even a decayed kill didn't smell as badly as this. No, this was something else. Something unnatural.

Rae knew they had to find it, no matter how painful it was.

The strength of the scent made it easy to track. The pack held back their whines and whimpers as the smell grew stronger, making their eyes water and their other senses fade away. As much as they wished to turn and run, they knew they had to see this through. They had to be prepared for what may follow. As they crossed through a close-packed area of the thicket – the rotting smell now the only thing they could sense – and stepped through a bundle of bushes, they came face-to-face with the source. And it terrified them all to the core.

It took a moment to realise what the creatures were as the tell-tale signs of their wolfen nature had been removed. Only small remnants of grey and white fur that couldn't be removed, and the shape of their skulls, indicated who and what they were.

There were five carcasses in total, though from how they had been hacked and ripped apart, it was possible there were more. Their bodies, while usually covered in fur, had been stripped and skinned, leaving them bare to the world. From their hairless appearance, it revealed the sorry state they had been in before death. They were pure skin and bones, starved almost to death before their hunter got to them to finish the job. Now, all that remained of them was a lifeless carcass.

Their blood spattered the green grass and the patches of snow, staining the land around them. More blood dribbled onto the ground as ravens pecked and ate at their exposed bodies. *They have to survive too,* Larka's words played in her mind at the sight. *It is how it must be.*

They were not even given dignity in death, Kiba whined,

unchecked anger making his voice break. He turned away, unable to bear the sight of it any longer. **They were tortured for sport.**

Unlike Kiba, Rae couldn't take her eyes off them, enraptured and horrified to learn what she looked like underneath her fur. Instead, she walked closer, ignoring the tingling in her nose as it protested at the proximity to the carcasses. She snapped her teeth at the ravens, tearing the feathers off one of them, scaring them away. It was as she swallowed away the taste of the raven's blood that a scent attached to the body closest caught her attention.

She stepped closer to it and inhaled deeply.

No, she whispered as a scent that felt so familiar and yet so wrong filled her. **Please, no.**

Panic tried to force itself into her limbs, but she refused to let it. She had a duty.

Her head shot up high, turning this way and that, ears pricking and flicking in every direction. She could feel her wolves tense, preparing themselves for what she had uncovered, and ready to react in whatever way was needed. In this case, it was a single word.

Run.

Before they even had a chance, a powerful roar pierced the surrounding air, startling the wolves into freezing. It was only when another roar ripped through the air, penetrating the ground near the dead wolves, spitting up snow and grass, that the pack moved into action.

Darting across the land, they moved rapidly back and forth across the Forest ground, their movements fluid and precise as they ran through the trees and bushes. Again and again, the roaring blast would sound, most hitting a tree or the ground. Rae had no idea what it was or what it would do if it hit them.

It was a high-pitched yelp and the heavy thump of a body falling to the ground that told her.

Rae chanced a glance behind her, her eyes falling to the still form of Shadow a distance behind them. He'd grown slower in recent times from his old age and now it had caught up with him. Her heart broke, but now was not the time to be distracted. She had hoped, more than anything, that a wolf's strength, stamina, and speed would give them the upper hand. But as she turned to look upon the monsters, she feared they could be outmatched.

The beasts that followed them rode upon an animal of pure darkness which growled fiercely as it followed. The brutes that controlled them, of which there were three, howled wildly in excitement as they chased the pack. The long smoking sticks in their hands were pointed towards them.

Rae didn't know how to lose them. They seemed able to avoid any obstacle thrown their way. Whether it be a thicket or collection of trees, they found a way around. Her only hope was drawing them to the centre of their territory where the steep hills, gnarled and sharp bushes, and small gaped trees would stop the beasts they rode. Without the beasts, they'd be vulnerable, she was sure of it.

Kiba! she barked, her eyes locking with her souls at her side. **We must get them to the Den it may be our only chance.**

He was anxious, his chest heaving in fear and exhaustion, but he trusted her. With a nod, he turned and snapped the command to their pack. They continued their scattered run, hoping to dodge any attacks. They were only a shadow's pass distance from the inner territory, close enough to the Den, but far enough away to keep the pups and Little One safe. Especially Little One.

Bursting through the thicket into the mainland, the snow kicked up into their faces as they landed roughly on the ground. Though their bodies were cut up and worn ragged from their escape, the wolves didn't pause. Fanning out around the hill's edge, they formed a line of protection making sure there was no chance of the devils breaking through to the Den.

For a moment, all was still. The only sound that could be heard were the growls of her wolves as their eyes darted around, searching for danger. Behind her, over the hill, she could hear her sister ushering her pups inside the safety of the Den's internal cover. The lights of her life were safe, and she would make sure it stayed that way.

Training her ears and eyes to their surroundings, she waited to hear the growls of the animals, or the piercing roar of their attacks. But she heard nothing.

Then, the soft crunching of snow underfoot reached her ears. Snaps of twigs and bending of branches as they were pushed aside helped her pinpoint the position. The beasts had separated from their creatures to pursue them, just as she had thought they would. From how far they were and how slowly they moved, her hope for her pack's survival grew.

Their power comes from the roaring animal. Keep yourself ready. Now we may have a fighting chance, she snapped to the pack whose raised hackles and salivating jaws had intensified in the wait for their enemy.

Kiba at her side, his snarls more ferocious than she had ever heard them, echoed her. **We do not know their strength alone. But, whatever happens, we keep them away from the young. Do not engage until they do.** He snapped his teeth. **Then we tear them to pieces.**

Behind her, Rae heard the frightened noises of her pups. Her motherly instincts told her to go to them, and she almost did, until the creatures showed themselves.

From the thicket, the strange beasts appeared. Their fur was a mismatch of skin, some parts appeared smooth, others rough. She could not distinguish them properly, this strange fur covering most of them from sight. Everything about them felt

... wrong. It was the sticks in their forearms that drew her attention, smoke billowing from one end.

She had only seen smoke like that up close once in her life, and that was amid the sun's fever that ravaged the woods across the river. While their lands had remained untouched, the air was rancid with the smell of burning for many moons.

To see such a sign atop their sticks gave her pause and concern. Their roaring enemy may have been the sticks themselves. Just as the wolves used their claws and teeth, these beasts used their smoking sticks.

From their emergence, she expected instant antagonization and attack. However, they stood very still, observing. Neither moving to attack or preparing to defend, just standing there, watching. It was as they stood that Rae finally saw their features.

Her heart dropped.

Humans, she growled quietly, enough for her pack to hear and no one else. She didn't want to push the humans to attack, nor did she want her sister to hear her. Better yet she hoped her sister wouldn't see them.

Of course, as Rae's ears flickered at the sound of approaching paws, she knew fate would not be kind with this wish.

WITH THE COAST clear for now, the pack got to work with Kiba leading the charge.

Patrols from now until... Kiba started, but didn't know how to finish. The truth was, none of them were sure how long this may need to last. **We only leave in threes. No wolf goes alone. Is this understood?**

The pack nodded in agreement, fear still holding tight onto them.

Shadow... Selena said, stepping out from the group, her grey patched fur glowing in the moon's light. **We must return for Shadow.**

As the wolves discussed arrangements to find their Elder and provide him with the final farewell, Rae and Little One slipped away and back towards the Den. Rae needed to be with her pups, the only things in her life that made sense right now. She was exhausted, but as her pups fed and fell asleep against her, she knew that her day was not done.

What happened today? Little One asked quietly, though from how she shied away from looking at Rae, Rae knew that wasn't what she truly wanted to ask. But she knew her too well to ignore it.

We were too late. Rae whispered and turned away, looking to the distance where the split mountains lay. **We found our rivals bodies by the split mountains. And then...** she sighed. **Then the humans found us. It was humans that came here to our home and we have no idea what they will do next. But to your other question** – she ignored her sister's surprise – **while I know not much of their kind, just as the wolf knows their kin by sight, so must a human recognise theirs.** She turned to her sister, who sat with a fearful and devastated look in her eyes. **That is why they looked at you.**

18

LITTLE ONE

In the dead of night, Little One found herself unable to sleep. While most of the pack rested, barring the few on patrol, she lay wide awake. Finally giving up, she silently slipped out from the Den and away from her resting family. She considered joining the patrol, but with her lack of skill, it'd be safer if she didn't. Instead, she found herself being drawn to the trees where the humans had stood.

A shiver slipped down her back, but not from the cold. She could picture them even now, their smoking sticks pointed at Kiba, their murderous eyes watching her, a fascination and intrigue in them as they followed her movements. It was so vivid that she had to shake her head to remind herself that they weren't here. The familiarity she had seen in their eyes frightened her. Rae's words played in her mind. *These monsters see me as kin. What does that make me?*

Little One walked closer to the spot, searching for something, anything, that would show that these beasts and her were the same. She knew she was human, but seeing these beasts close up and knowing they were supposedly like her, all she could feel was resentment at the possibility.

She was a wolf. Or at least, she felt like one. But there was always something that threw that out of balance. Hye's attack, losing her mother, Skai turning on her. Then Kiba arrived, and he helped heal the hole of the past. Now, once again, there was something else to remind her, and the pack, that she didn't belong.

These creatures were like her, and they brought horror and destruction. Just as she had led to her mother's death, these monsters had led to Shadow's. Who would she or her kin hurt next?

Little One had sworn long ago that she would never run off alone again. Her sister had made her promise, the fear in her eyes the only reason Little One agreed. Now, as she sat within the trees, staring at the paw print of the beasts like her, she wondered if it would be for the best.

I did not think you would be the one to succumb to our enemy so easily.

Little One didn't turn, keeping her eyes on the thicket of trees instead, hoping that the voice would turn and leave if she didn't engage. Of course, her sister was never one for giving her what she wanted.

She came to her side and laid down next to her, exhaustion clear in her movements, and the subsequent yawn proved that. The two sat quietly, staring into the shadowed abyss of the trees, finding a calm in one another's presence. Briefly, Little One believed her sister had fallen asleep. When she looked at her out of the corner of her eye, she saw Rae staring at her, her head on her paws.

Little One sighed. She had no chance of getting out of this. Rae's patience, though spotty at best, was better than hers without a doubt. She was just waiting for her to make the first move. Waiting for her to say what she needed to say. Rae always knew what she was feeling and thinking, but she let her come out with it on her own terms. It was something she always appreciated. Even if it was sometimes frustrating at how well her sister understood her.

I do not belong here, she said, quiet but earnest. **I should not be here.**

Rae was silent for a moment, her eyes watching Little One, as if she could see into her very soul.

Why do you believe that? Rae responded, lifting her head from her paws.

Because I have eyes! Little One snapped, throwing a stick from the ground beside her into the shadows. She'd hoped the action would have released some tension. Instead, it just made her want to throw more. **I have brought nothing but chaos to our family and our home, all because I am human.**

Once again, Rae stayed silent.

I am no wolf! I am the killer of them! Just as these humans killed our rivals, I too have killed. Who's to say I will not become exactly like them once I am grown? She didn't know when she began pacing, but she didn't stop. **Would what happened with mother, Hye, and the humans, have happened if I was not here?**

Her heart pounded heavily against her chest, hurting her. She had laid out every negative and angry thought she had had about herself bare before Rae who, even now, stayed silent. While Little One wished to be angry and force her to react, she didn't have the strength to try.

No.

Little One turned to her sister, surprised.

No, none of that would have happened if it were not for you.

In that moment, every one of Little One's worst nightmares came to light. Her heart felt as if it were being eaten from her very chest. The one person she feared would eventually turn on her had done so.

It would have happened in another way, eventually. Rae looked away from her, turning to the moon in the sky. **That is the way of nature. To put the blame on a single being for the fallout of all the trials we face is to forget the power of the Forest.** Rae turned to Little One, her eyes calm and loving. **Dear sister, you are not as powerful as nature itself. As much as you like to act that you are, your actions do not control fate.**

Little One stared at her sister in shock, surprised by her words. She went to speak, but Rae wasn't done yet.

You are a member of this pack, and though, yes, you are different from us, you are part of the natural order all wolves follow. You feel you do not belong? Then that is your own doing. She went to protest, but the soft growl from Rae stopped her. **You better than anyone should understand. We feed off one other. If I can tell when you feel conflicted, even from a distance, the rest of us will as well. By believing you are different, you tell them you are.**

But Skai—

Her resentment at being made to care for you was a catalyst, yes, but Skai had never felt like she had belonged. Whereas you, you fit in easily. Were accepted easily. Only you believe that you do not belong.

Little One fell silent, taken aback at this realisation. She tried to think of any moment that the pack, other than Skai, had shown signs of hatred towards her. Sure, during the hunting season, there was frustration at her need to eat more regularly. But had they treated her any differently? They rested with her, played with her, and loved her.

Does... she started, overwhelmed by this realisation. **Does this mean I have always been a wolf?**

Rae leant forward, nuzzling her side, brushing away the tears on her cheeks with her fur. Pulling back, she waited for Little One to look her in the eye before she continued.

The wild is your home, sister, and you are a wolf. You may not believe this now, but I, and your pack, will prove to you that this is true. No matter how long it takes. Rae huffed in amusement. **Mother Wolf knows that Fenris will lead the charge. He adores you very much.**

Little One released a bark of amusement. Fenris was her biggest fan right now, and she loved him for it. Even though he knew the right way to get on her nerves. *A young version of myself it seems,* she thought with a smile.

But doubt still plagued her mind. There was too little they knew about humans. Did her humanity mean she would grow as tall as the beasts they saw? Would she grow that strange fur on her body over time? Would she, as she feared she would, become a killer like them?

Little One turned to her sister, who sat watching her, patient as always. It was her calming nature that put her at ease. There was no point fearing about the future; it was time to live in the present and with her family. She couldn't repeat her past mistakes.

Rae seemed to sense her relaxing and took that as a sign. She stood and nudged her with her head. **Are you ready to retire? We have much work to do tomorrow.**

Work?

Little One almost regretted asking as Rae's body tensed, anger bubbling to the surface. Her sister had barely had time to relax since she became leader, and now was no exception.

The monsters know where we rest now. We do not know their tracking or memory skills, so whether or not they can find their way back is unknown, but we will not take that risk. Rae began walking closer to the shadowed trees where the creatures had stood, resentment tight in her shoulders.

We are to move to a new resting place. Little One went to argue and was shut down instantly. **We do not want this to be

permanent. For now, it has to be done for our safety. What they did to the rival pack, I will not allow that to—

She froze suddenly, her head pricking up into the air, her ears pointing high, twisting and flicking in different directions. Against her better judgement, Little One stepped closer, about to ask what it was Rae could hear, when she found herself suddenly airborne.

19

LITTLE ONE

She had never been weightless before. Even when play fighting or when assaulted by the wild, she was never far from the ground.

Now, for the first time, she was ripped from it. She thrashed her body wildly from whatever had her in its grasp, snapping her jaws in an attempt to latch onto something to rip at with her teeth to free herself. There was nothing in reach, and while she knew she was causing difficulty for her captor, it was clear with their tightening grip that her efforts were making it worse.

But they had made one mistake.

Before she could be stopped, she released a piercing wail into the air, listening as it echoed and bounced off the trees around them. A warm grip fell upon her mouth, silencing her. But the deed was already done.

Her eyes adjusted quickly to the movement, and within the dark, she could just make out the surrounding figures. They wore all brown, making them nearly invisible. Little One's eyesight wasn't like her family's, but she knew the dark better than these creatures, and so did her sister.

Shouts of alarm and cries of pain came to her ears from

around her, and she smiled. Her sister was a fighter, and a vicious one at that. The beasts didn't stand a chance. But Little One was still in trouble

Then suddenly, the captor dropped her.

Tumbling away, she turned, ready to fight, but froze. In front of her Kiba tore, bit, and attacked the brown-furred creature. Its face came into view as the creature twisted and turned, attempting to protect themselves. When the creature bucked Kiba off, their hind legs kicking him backwards, that Brown Fur turned tail and ran.

Kiba normally would have gone with his instincts and chased after the beast, but from the growls and snarls behind him, this wasn't the time.

Get back to the Den! he snapped, harsher than he had ever sounded, before he turned and charged towards the battle, as Little One ran away, a single terrifying thought following her:

The humans have returned.

She ran as fast as her legs could, taking her back to the open clearing and to her pack for safety. The realisation of why the humans were here buried itself in her mind. Not only had they returned, but they had returned for her.

In the clearing she found the pack on high alert; the brown-furred creatures having disappeared. The only sign that they had been there was the scuffed-up snow and mud, as well as the anxious jitters of the wolves.

But Rae wasn't among them, which made the pack nervous. None of them had seen what had happened to her.

She will be fine, Kiba barked at them. **Focus on protecting the pups and Little One at all costs!**

Then out of the thicket, she walked out, pride in her step and brown fur stuck to her teeth and maw. They released a brief collective sigh of relief at the sight of her unharmed until the tension of what they had just witnessed returned.

The smallest noise put them on edge. A snap of a twig, a

tweet of a bird, everything was a danger to them now. Then the real horror arrived.

BANG.

An echoing crack ripped across the Forest, followed by a solid thump of a falling body. There, in the centre of the clearing, lay Rune, his golden eyes wide open. Little One felt sick to her stomach at the sight. In panic, the wolves dropped to the ground, seeking to use the snow as camouflage as they sought the direction of the noise.

Another crack pierced through the air, this time the bark of a nearby tree was ripped off. BANG. Little One covered her ears, the noise echoing within them, making them ring. The pack seemed to recognise this noise and backed up towards the Den, their eyes trained on the trees ahead where they believed it had come from. Their eyes watched for any movement within the thicket, their bodies a shield for the pups above.

Little One backed up further, focusing on keeping the pups safe. She had to keep them together and get them away from whatever was out there. It was in doing this that she noticed one pup was missing.

Where's Fenris? she hissed at the others, but they were too afraid to answer.

Then, to the side of them, was a set of paw prints leading into the trees behind the Den. Little One bit her lip, turning to the pups, and then to the wolves in front of her. Without question, she knew what she had to do, another loud BANG cementing it.

She followed.

FEARING THE WORST, she was quick in her movements as she followed the paw prints. Fenris was smaller than the others. He wouldn't survive out on his own. He took after her far too much for his own good.

It was when the prints disappeared that Little One realised her mistake. *What if this was a trap?* she thought. The creatures had already proven that they played to their own rules. Anything was possible with these beasts.

Then a small bush nearby rattled, and she stood to attention, her teeth flashing. She stepped closer and stopped baring her teeth when she saw young Fenris hidden among the bushes. He had pushed himself through the sharp branches to reach the back of the bush, trying his hardest to melt into the vegetation. He wouldn't meet her eyes.

I am not afraid, he said, slowly crawling towards Little One as if to prove his point, though he didn't leave the safety of the bush. **I am just too small to fight.**

Little One crouched by the bush, locking eyes with the small wolf. She knew what he was feeling; she'd been feeling it all her life. **Well, I am afraid,** she responded, surprising the pup. **Will you stay with me so I will stop being scared?**

Fenris sniffed the air as if trying to detect any lie in her words. It was only when she shuffled backwards and away from the bush, allowing him to see her fully, that he followed suit. Clumsily, he made his way towards her.

Just as Fenris was about to step out from the bush, he froze, ears pricked. He backed up into the bush again, ducking from view. Little One understood too late the danger she had put herself in. For a moment, she reverted to her young self and considered diving into the bushes to hide alongside the pup. In the end, she was glad that she didn't.

Once again, she was weightless. Her captors had learnt from last time as a warm paw wrapped itself around her mouth. But they weren't the only ones who had learnt from their first encounter. She now expected the weightless sensation and took the movement in her stride. Using the momentum of her body, she flung her limbs widely, battering her captor at their soft underbelly. She continued to throw her weight around, trying her best to get the monsters away from Fenris. She could only pray to Mother Wolf that he would stay where he was.

But the youngling had other ideas. In his own attempt at trying to be brave, he barrelled out of the bush and towards Little One's captor, just as his father had. Snarling, barking, ready to sink his growing teeth into the monster, he bounded their way. But he was just too small. Another of the creatures appeared beside her, and before Fenris could even try, the beast levelled a swift kick at his side, knocking him away and unconscious.

Then the fiend turned to her and smiled.

Anger swelled in her stomach as her eyes locked with the murky river-coloured ones of the beast. She threw a fit, lashing out at the beast as they came closer to her. Her kicks were wild but strong. The one that held her didn't have the skill to keep up with her thrashes, their once tight grip now loosened. She caught the image once more of Fenris's small body, and she saw red.

Her teeth sank into the bare flesh in front of her, and she enjoyed the scream the monster released. Their paws dropped away from her mouth, and with her other captor dealing with her flailing legs, there was nothing keeping her silent.

She wailed loudly and in a pitch that was higher than she had ever managed. For a moment, she relished her skill and felt pride that, if only for a moment, her howl reminded her of her mother's. That was until she felt a sharp prick to her side.

Her cry was cut off by a yelp of pain. The surprise wore off quickly, and as her mouth had not been covered, she went to cry out again. But she couldn't.

Her eyes became unfocused, her mouth fell slack, and her body felt weightless, but not in the same way as she had experienced. It was as if her body was no longer hers. She went to speak again, but all she could manage was to open and close her mouth in the shape of the words. It was then that she felt a strange and unnatural need to sleep, even though she wasn't tired.

Her body recoiled at the feeling. She twisted and turned weakly, trying to get rid of the sensation. Soon the repulsion was replaced with panic. Without her voice, what could she do? And now, with Fenris unconscious, and the beasts regaining their grasp on her, she had nothing.

The two creatures spoke with one another in a foreign tongue. It was the tone in their voices, however, that frightened her most. They were excited. They looked down at her every so often as they carried her away, the excitement growing with each look. They had what they'd come for. Her.

Until Rae stopped them in their tracks.

Little One fell hard to the ground as the human Rae had bitten screamed. Turning her head in the snow, she saw through blurred vision, her sister ripping apart the brown fur of her captor and latching on tightly to anything she could grab. Little One relished in the painful yells of this beast; they deserved exactly what they were getting.

While her body was difficult to move, she attempted to roll towards her sister, hoping once she had killed the creature that they would be able to go home, and this ordeal would be over with.

But, out of the corner of her eye, she saw the other beast moving out of sight, a smocking stick in their paws. Rae had told her what these sticks had done to Shadow and from the sight of Rune's lifeless eyes not long ago, she could only assume the same had happened to him. Little One's heart started to race. Desperately, she tried to call out to her sister.

Danger to your right!

But the words didn't come out. Her mouth moved sluggishly as she tried again, but only silence followed.

Drool pooled out of her mouth, and wetness trickled down her face as she strained herself in frustration. She had been silenced, unable to move. But she refused to give up, and so, slowly, she started to roll towards her sister.

She hoped that, even at how far away she was, Rae would see her. Her prey had fallen still at her feet; all Little One needed was for her to look up at her and she could warn her.

She could do this. She had to.

A silent sob built up in her throat as she heard two clicking noises nearby. Rae's head flew up from the body at her feet, brown fur and blood speckling her mouth. Her ears twitched in the perpetrator's direction. But then her eyes settled on Little One's.

Little One screamed silently for her to run, to get out of there. To leave her. Her eyes blurred, but she blinked them quickly, refusing to lose sight of Rae. *Please,* she begged. *Go.*

She couldn't be sure, but it was as if Rae heard her then. Little One watched as her sister lowered her head, her eyes never leaving hers. It was at that moment that a single message was passed.

You will be okay.

A powerful and bloodthirsty roar screamed out around them. Little One had to close her eyes, the pain from the noise ripping through her. It was the loud thump of a body collapsing hard to the ground that forced her to open them again. Little One laid eyes on her sister, whose gaze had never left her. She watched as her chest shook heavily with panic, fear, and pain.

Her voice may have been silenced, but that didn't stop the screams that grew louder and louder in her head as her body convulsed in heaving sobs. Her body shook harder, whether from the poison or from the piercing heartbreak, she no longer cared. Whatever it was, she hoped it would kill her.

She barely had the chance to understand what she had witnessed before the humans pulled her from the ground, even the one who had been pounced on by Rae. Rage burnt in her veins, but it fell away instantly the moment she lost sight of her sister. As she was carried away, her vision blurring, she turned to stay looking at Rae. She refused to leave her, even if it was only in spirit.

Rae's eyes stayed with hers. As she was walked further and further away, her sister's chest grew slower and slower until her sky-coloured eyes disappeared from her sight and closed for the last time.

PART II

BUT GET LOST ALONG
THE WAY

20

LITTLE ONE

She couldn't see the sky when she first woke up. And that scared her. She couldn't hear the sounds of the Forest when she woke the second time. Instead, she only heard the growl of the beasts the humans rode before she fell back into unconsciousness.

The next time she came to, she stayed awake. Though she started to wish she hadn't. Her head throbbed painfully, her mouth felt dry, and her neck was sore from where she had been stabbed by the humans.

Little One attempted to stand but smacked her head into a solid object above her. Blinking, she fully came to and saw where she was. Around her, were strange short trees keeping her trapped. She wasn't small enough to fit through the gaps nor strong enough to break them.

Staring through them, Little One tried to pinpoint her location but found herself blinded by multiple strange glowing lights. As her eyes focused, she noticed that multiple small suns had been pulled from the sky and locked in the air atop an oddly short tree and held there with no possibility of escape.

Little One tried to find out what was holding it captive, but the colour was too intense to look at for too long.

Turning away from the false suns and blinking her eyes, Little One refocused her attention as best she could on where she was being taken. Just like Rae used to tell her, *If ever in trouble, use the environment to your advantage.*

Little One's heart twisted into a knot, taking her breath away at the thought of Rae left in the snow. She had to shake her head to remove the image. Now wasn't the time to grieve; she had to get back home.

Looking through the gaps in her prison again, the light of the fading sun beaming down on her as she did, she searched for any familiar signs of home, but nothing she saw made sense. There were no trees to start with, and the few that appeared to be there had been torn down and stacked together as logs for a shelter, if the people coming and going from within them were an inkling to their purpose. Add to that, the ground was covered in strange black mud that ran across the centre that looked uncomfortable to play on.

Her heart started to race in panic. *Where have they taken me?* she thought, trying to calm herself down.

Then, in the distance, she saw it.

Just beyond this strange false Forest and past the snowless hills stood the hazy image of the split mountain cavern that separated the Forest from the human world.

She had been told ever since she was a young pup that they were never to cross that barrier, no matter how desperate. Now she sat trapped beyond its protection in a world she didn't belong to.

She could barely make out the snow-covered peaks of the mountains, let alone the grove of trees that lay between it. Little One couldn't even begin to imagine how long it would take for her to return home from this place. The longer she stared at its hazy image, the more she wondered if she'd even be able to make it back home.

No time for crying, Little One thought, pushing down the lump in her throat that had started to grow. *Time for planning. Just like any hunter would do.*

Of course, no hunter had ever dealt with these conditions before. The main thing Little One found herself noticing, begrudgingly, was how everything in this not-Forest was so … loud.

As she travelled further in, more humans stepped out from their Dens to watch her. Each time they did, a loud bang would follow them as the entrance to their Dens slammed closed. Little One didn't like these Dens. It seemed odd to her that these humans kept their homes so close to one another. If a hunter ever came, they would all be wiped out easily.

Stupid humans, she thought in disgust, curling up her lips at their idiocy.

Turning away from the false Dens, she took in the rest of their land. To her surprise, there wasn't much of it. While everything was so big, it all existed in such a small area. Where are their trees? Their ponds? Their animal neighbours?

She caught sight of the smaller humans playing in groups under the false sun's light, making markings in the snow with sticks and stones, only turning away from their strange game as she passed.

Just beyond them, she could make out the Forest in the distance, but there was nothing else familiar in sight for her.

Then she caught sight of something dangling from one of the false Dens, though this one was more open than the others, a large cut in its centre making the inside visible in comparison to the rest. Hanging from a branch above the ground lay the lifeless bodies of ducks, rabbits, and even a snake.

One human stood by them, a short silver stick in their hand.

Little One watched as they took down one of the rabbits and placed it down on another wooden surface. Raising their silver stick, they brought it down on the rabbit's neck, separating it from its body – its blood spraying across the human.

Little One jerked back in fright, hitting her head on one of the poles of her cage behind her.

Is that what they will do to me? she thought in fear, her eyes darting around for any signs of a silver stick coming in her direction.

As she looked around, she came to realise that whatever had been carrying her had now stopped – the growl of the beast stuttering to a small hum in the background. Little One braced herself, ready to attack when necessary.

Now that she was trapped in place, the humans she had seen leaving their Dens began to swarm around her, speaking loudly in their foreign tongue while pointing at her. Their voices varied in pitch from so high that Little One flinched to so low that she could feel the depth of it in her bones. She noticed quickly though that the larger humans kept a comfortable distance, examining her from afar. It was the smaller ones that made her nervous.

Seeing them up close, she realised how alike these humans looked, even the smaller versions. They look just like the other beasts Little One had seen. The ones who had killed Rae.

Little One was on edge as the little humans came closer, close enough to stick their hands through the bars to poke at her. When one did, just as she had always been taught, she lashed out and clawed at their paw, hard.

The little beast pulled away crying, turning to run away to a taller human, its mother she assumed, who glared darkly at Little One.

Should have taught them better, human, she snapped.

All the little humans jumped back at that, afraid.

Little One wasn't surprised when they turned on her after

that. Just like a wolf attacked when frightened, so did humans. She wondered if that was why this land felt so familiar to her, even if it were unnaturally different at the same time.

She didn't have time to ponder before the first rock was thrown.

A growl built in her chest, growing louder as more things were thrown. Thankfully for her, the beasts had no sense of aim, most of the rocks and snow bouncing off the bars harmlessly. But they figured that out themselves too quickly.

Taking the sticks they had been using for play when she arrived, four of the younglings ran to her cage and began to stab at her with the pointed ends.

Little One snapped at them with her teeth as best she could, trying to scare them away, but soon she realised there was nothing she could do. There was nothing to fear from a caged wolf.

These beasts are truly monsters, she thought, closing her eyes tightly as one sharp jab of a stick drew blood.

A loud barking voice forced her to open them again when she heard the small vile humans shout in surprise to the new voice. In doing so, she watched as the young ones ran away from her, leaving her to breathe a sigh of relief. But when her saviour came into view beside her, she prayed that they'd come back.

Stood to the side of her cage was the brown-furred beast who murdered her sister. The monster's lips pulled back, exposing its pearly white teeth to Little One. She couldn't hold herself back after that.

Throwing herself at the cage, she tried to reach Brown Fur and scratch his eyes out. Snapping her teeth, growling, and throwing out her forelegs through the gaps, she tried to claw at the figure. But the coward stood just out of her reach. This enraged her further. She threw herself against the bars again, envisioning the moment that she would break out and sink her teeth into his neck and tear it from its body.

The beast disappeared from her sight but Little One was too far gone in her agony to even notice, continuing instead to throw herself into the bars. Her skin ached with each smack against her from the solid structure. She could feel liquid on her skin, and from the bitter taste in the air, she knew it was blood.

Let me bleed out, she thought, her rage the only thing she was able to feel now. *Just let me kill them first.* She howled for all to hear. Maybe her family would hear her too and help her take revenge. But only Brown Fur returned, and this time they weren't alone.

The door to the cage opened, and ahead of her, she could see a clear pathway point home. Without a second thought, she pounced. Flying through the air, she felt a rush at being able to feel the wind on her skin. As her limbs extended, she tried to focus only on the mountains in the distance and not the high arching Dens of the human world. She couldn't let herself be overwhelmed as she ran for her life. But in the end that didn't matter as she never even reached the ground.

They plucked her from the air with ease, and she was pulled into the tight hold of one of the beasts, just as she had been in the Forest. For a second, she thought Rae would come to save her again. But she was carried away fighting against the strong grip that held her, and as the sight of her home faded with each step, she knew she would never see her sister again.

Everything around her was white. Sharp, painful, bright, white. The harshness of this new place that Brown Fur had taken her to hurt her eyes and made her head ache.

The only saving grace was that the beings that murdered her sister were gone. But as these new figures in white coats lifted her forelegs high, spread her paws, and shone false suns in her eyes, she wished they'd come back and finish the job like they did with her family.

Soon the humans were done with her and, all together, lifted her from the cold not-ground surface, and took her to another place. Little One didn't fight this time, too overwhelmed to even consider it. But she knew she should have. A wolf should never stop fighting or allow themselves to be trapped. That's what her mother always told her. But her mother's words meant nothing now. A wolf was never to be alone either, yet she was. Alone with creatures whose eyes and features looked too similar to her own. So she surrendered and took in the small world around her.

Strange wooden logs filled this new area, most with white ice sheets on top of them. A few humans sat at these logs, watching her briefly before going back to staring at a silver boxed shaped… thing. It was the cage in front of them that then drew Little One's attention. Its grey bars were just like the cage she had been kept in before, but much larger in comparison as the bars went all the way up to the white sky of the Den. The cage stood out from most of the room, almost as if it shouldn't belong there. Just like Little One.

Locked behind the solid bars, Little One looked at the humans who watched her. Their voices excited and joyous as they spoke to one another, pointing and scratching with small sticks on these white squares in their paws as they studied her.

Seeing their joy, she turned away in disgust, trying to hold back a snarl of anger. Somewhere, far away, back home where she belonged, her pack would be in mourning. She had lost her home, her sister, and yet these monsters who had taken so much from them dared to smile and celebrate?

As a wolf, she was taught to be patient and wait for the right moment to strike. Little One had never been successful with this, her nature too curious to allow for it. Now, as she watched the monsters in front of her, she knew this was the time.

Mother always said, patience is the wolf's virtue, Little One thought, her eyes tracking every action of her captors. *It is time I learnt that.*

21

LITTLE ONE

The false sun made keeping track of time difficult. This sun was controlled by the humans, lighting up the prison whenever they pleased, and to the detriment of Little One.

Back home, Little One would curl up with her family or on the Forest grounds to rest whenever they needed it. In this world, however, whenever she tried to rest during the day, the false sun would keep her from doing so. The light was far sharper and more painful to her eyes in comparison to the real sun.

The few times she was able to shield herself from the evil light and rest, she was cruelly jabbed awake by the humans. They only allowed her to sleep when they turned off the false sun. But she needed more sleep than this to regain her strength. How could she fight back if she continued to go unrested? She wondered if the humans knew that and that's why they kept this false sun on.

At least they attempted to keep her well-fed. Unfortunately, these beasts seemed to not understand food. Let alone what to eat. Each time they bought a meal for her, they'd destroyed it beyond recognition.

Today she stared at what smelled like deer but looked nothing like one. *Where is the blood? The reddened colour? And why is it so small?* The piece was barely the size of a hind, most of it charred, and surrounded by strange smelling and tasting plants. She'd been taught to only eat what was safe, and this definitely wasn't, so she walked away from the "meal".

Little One refused the food they bought her for a few days, even though her body tried to fight her on it, growling in hunger. Thankfully, after a while, it seemed the humans caught on and brought her larger pieces of meat, though still burnt. As her stomach twisted in pain, hunger deep in her bones, she finally gave in.

These humans were tricky, however. Sometimes, the meals they provided had no meat whatsoever, instead red-and brown-coloured liquid would be presented to her which smelled of freshly bloomed spring. Instinctively, she would dip her face in drinking, only for the liquid to burn her.

The next time such liquid was presented, this time white in colour and smelling of her mother's milk, she cautiously approached to taste it, only to find that this one was much colder.

These beasts were keeping her on her toes. After each incident, she would catch them speaking to one another in hushed tones, eyes on her, as they scratched into the white squares in their paws. She didn't understand what they were saying, but she knew what this felt like.

A test.

During one of their tests, after discovering the cool liquid this time around, she had shrunk back in surprise and frustration. As she licked her paw clean, Little One noticed a long-furred human watching her. This human was different from the others in the white coats. They stood apart from them in silence, their eyes only for Little One.

There was something familiar about this human. Their fur was longer than the others, the dark fox-red fur hanging loose down their face, standing out from their body's pale colour that reminded her of snow. Their silence, unlike the others, felt calculated. Their bright blue eyes, like Rae's, were sharp, and their movements miniscule, like they were attempting to fade into the background. They were like the foxes Little One knew back home, a creature who bided their time, seeking to reap the benefits of the true hunter.

That feeling alone put Little One on edge more than anything else.

It was this uneasy feeling that kept her on guard. So, when the humans finally stopped watching her and went into action, she was ready for them.

They came into her cage quickly and in a large group, their white coats reflecting the light around them, blinding Little One enough that she didn't see them grab hold of her limbs until she felt it. Kicking out, Little One thrashed her body around, trying to dislodge herself from their hold. One unlucky White Coat, who was attempting to hold her head, faced the might of her teeth.

Little One smiled as they cried out and let go.

She couldn't fight them all six off at once though, so eventually she settled in their grip to regain her energy.

When they put me down, I will run, Little One thought to herself.

Her eyes took in the false Forest around her again, looking for an exit. But before she could find one, she was taken into a different land. As her eyes adjusted to the bright white surfaces, she realised she had been here before. This was where they'd taken her when she first arrived in this prison.

Little One was released from the human's hold and placed

on top of a solid white surface. She nearly leapt off the not-ground as her paws recoiled at the coldness. It wasn't a natural cold like snow but something stranger. Like everything else in this dreaded world.

Focus on your environment, Rae's voice snapped at her, and so she did as she was told. But it was harder than she expected.

The place itself was intense in its scent, a sort of sweet bitterness filled her snout, making her shiver. It was like she could taste the smell. On the barriers around her, white filled the room, making her eyes hurt. The only reprieve she had were the few blocks of black and cream colours that hung on the sides. They were odd though, the cream squares had other designs within them, trapped. Whereas the black had white lines running through them. Little One's head continued to ache, the overload on her senses catching her off guard. She realised too late that, in her overwhelmed state, the humans had tethered her to the platform.

Little One yanked her paw backwards to free herself, but with each tug, the tether tightened harshly against her skin. A yelp of pain escaped her. She pulled again only to receive the same pinch. Panic started to set in, but with the awareness of her enemies watching, she refused to let it overwhelm her. Instead, she continued to tug at her restraints as subtly as she could, biting her tongue to silence herself from the pain.

Being restrained terrified her, especially after what happened in the Forest. Last time she was unable to move, she had watched her sister die. What would happen this time?

Then, the fox-like human stepped into the room, and the White Coats left them alone. Unlike before, Tall Fox had changed. Their coat was as white as the room with their paws and muzzle covered by the same white so Little One could barely see them.

The two watched each other in silence. Their fox-like features narrowed in on Little One, examining her with a tilt of their head, just as Larka would do before she would leap in for the kill. As Tall Fox's sharp blue eyes locked onto Little One's, it became clear. Tall Fox was the lead female of this pack. And that made her all the more dangerous. When she took a step towards her, Little One automatically flinched.

A bubble of frustration followed as she reminded herself that she couldn't show weakness to these creatures, no matter how afraid she may feel.

When Tall Fox approached, her steps slow and deliberate, she continued to observe Little One who stayed deathly still. While she longed to lash out, a gentle touch to the side of her muzzle stopped her.

Tall Fox looked her over. Turning her head side to side, lifting her paws into her own and turning them over. The softness in her actions reminded her of Mother, the care in her movements unmistakably feminine. It almost felt like she was a mother herself, and Little One was her cub.

When Tall Fox had finished her fussing and stood, eyes locking with Little Ones, that she finally relaxed – the tenseness in her shoulders disappearing. She hadn't had a moment of peace until now, barely even processing the loss of her sister. Now, as a calm washed over her, she felt her throat tighten with emotion. It'd been so long since she'd felt at ease.

Then, Tall Fox pulled her mouth open wide and shoved something hard and sickly-sweet tasting into it. Wolf instinct taking over, Little One tried to bite Tall Fox, but as her mouth closed on the item, she found herself unable to remove her teeth from it afterwards. Her only weapon had been rendered useless. And now Tall Fox stood watching her, smiling.

She spoke her strange language before falling silent again. When she did, Little One heard the tell-tale signs of footsteps coming in behind her. It was like she was being herded, just as the pack would do when out hunting. Corner off the weakest and bring in reinforcements. She was already incapacitated, like the heel slashed deer her family would hunt, and as the figures surrounded her, she waited for them to rip out her throat.

One by one, the White Coats grabbed her front and back legs, and held her down tightly to stop her from moving. As they did, Tall Fox came in close and pulled open her mouth again, yanking out the item that she had forced into Little One's mouth. She could see the indents of her teeth on the grey material she'd been forced to taste, and now she was mad. Thankfully for her, Tall Fox hadn't moved her hand away fast enough.

A cry echoed in the room as Tall Fox yanked her trapped paw from out of Little One's gritted teeth. Satisfaction bloomed in her chest at the taste of blood in her mouth, and from the ferocity and pain in Tall Fox's eyes, it was worth it.

That feeling didn't last though. As the injured leader barked an order to her pack, she disappeared. For a moment, Little One could breathe easily and regain her composure. But when Tall Fox returned, a savage glint in her eyes, and a strange nest-shaped contraption in her paws, Little One's heart seized in panic. She knew that look. Hye had worn the same one before he tried to kill her.

Thrashing her body in a desperate attempt to escape, she tried to dislodge herself from their grip. As Tall Fox came closer, her eyes slitting, just like a fox when they smiled, she knew she didn't have a chance. A tight and biting sensation pressed against her mouth, maw, and head as the nest was attached tightly to her muzzle. She tossed her head side to side as best she could, but all that happened was a pinching sensation which made her whimper. Staring up at her torturer, anger and fear pulsed in her veins as she felt the warm trickle of blood drip down her skin. She was at their mercy.

EVERYTHING THAT MADE her a wolf was being stripped away.

The warmth of the Forest, the calm she found in the connection to her sister, and even the scent of the Den and her pack, all of it faded as water pelted into every crevice of her body. While she was not a stranger to a wash, often enjoying times in the small pools of water with her siblings, she never lost part of herself with it.

Both new and familiar faces surrounded her. After she had been moved, the ones who had held her were now pinning her and dousing her with the icy waters. The new humans added to the pain. They would step in and scrub harshly at her skin with something that felt like the rocks she was told to avoid back home. Her body felt raw and hollow. If she pushed back or growled as they worked, a harsh tug to the trap around her muzzle would occur. When it did, a sharp shooting pain against her jaw and head would force her silent.

After a while, she grew numb to the feeling. The need to fight off their hold never left, but the pain faded away. Instead, overwhelming hatred boiled within her.

They repeated the action over and over. Spray her with water, viciously scrub her, and do so again. Once, instead of a scrub, an intensely powerful scented liquid was dripped into the monster's paws. The liquid was rubbed deeply into her fur - followed by uncaring yanks and tugs at its ends. The smell overwhelmed Little One, making her feel sick to her stomach. It was as if the smell was trying to mimic the scent of the blue flowers from home, but it was far too sickly smelling that it felt like an insult.

Dowsed once again with water, the liquid was washed from her fur, much to her relief, until she realised the scent had not left. Now it was all over her. Everything from home was gone, taken over by this false nature.

Finally brought to her feet and rubbed heavily by a strange material that soaked up the water, Little One found herself carried away and back to her cage, only briefly aware of an itchy thing wrapped around her pelvis. The thought of getting away from these creatures to her prison brought her relief, a feeling she thought she would never have towards a cage.

It was only when put in the box, and her muzzle removed, that she was able to exercise the pent-up aggression and energy that had been building. *What did they do to me?* These thoughts ran through her mind as she scratched and rolled on the floor of her cage, trying to rebuild her scent.

After scratching her skin on the ground, she stood up and glared at the White Coats outside her prison. But the glare soon changed to a frown as she looked down at the fake fur wrapped around her and then back to the captors outside her cell. Looking back and forth between the White Coats and her own white coat, she found herself tugging at the soft but itchy material.

Their fur, it is just like this.

She turned back to the humans who, now watching her, bared their teeth in pride, happy with what they had done.

They saw her as kin, just as Rae had said.

She smelt like them, she was given the same fur as them, she was fed the same food as them, and they only spoke to her in their language. Rage began to build in Little One's stomach. They had stolen her from her world, and now, without even allowing her to grieve the family they had murdered, they were trying to make her … like them.

A growl grew deep in her throat at the thought.

I will never be a human.

22

LITTLE ONE

Her days after that were spent being tested. First thing when she woke up and once more before she slept. She fought back as much as she could against the testing, but as she was coming to realise, humans were far more patient than she thought. No matter what she did, how she acted, or even the physical fights she attempted to start with them, they never responded in the way she wanted.

Though they had moments when they would lose their temper, usually when she was aggressive, they never attacked back. Punishing her instead with solitary confinement. The White Coats would put her in her cage and cover the bars with a black material that blocked the humans from sight. Forcing Little One to be alone.

They must have known that wolves were social creatures. What better way to punish a wolf than to force them to be alone?

No wolf is meant to be isolated. Even lone wolves don't stay that way long. They would either find their new pack or die hungry and alone. Little One had never been alone before. Her family had always surrounded her, whether it be the whole pack, her sister, Kiba, or even the puppies.

A wolf's existence was to be with a pack. To suddenly find herself without one, without anyone, would drive any wolf to panic.

No, she snapped to herself as she paced back and forth in her cage. **You will not let them win.**

Using the cover that the humans had helpfully provided, Little One used this time to rebuild her strength. Her cage wasn't large, but from the empty rock faces to her back and left, it was just enough room to practice her skills. She would start by pouncing in place to loosen her tight back leg muscles. Then, she would use one of the rock faces to jump against to work on her reflexes for falling and dodging. There was a strange metallic log with a hole inside it near the cage's door that she'd have to watch out for as she fell.

It was on her second day of isolation training that, mid-fall, she heard a loud bang that distracted her.

Falling hard to the ground with an **oof**, she shook herself free from the ache and turned to the source of the noise.

To her right, above the soft white flat rock she slept on, just out of reach, was a light hole. She had never looked out of it before, thinking nothing of the soft noises she would often hear outside. But this time she couldn't ignore it.

Climbing up onto the flat rock, Little One grabbed onto the bars at the light hole, to pull herself up higher. As she looked out of the hole, she came face-to-face with the human's world.

The snow had melted away since the last time she had seen the outside. Now, fresh flowers bloomed in small patches outside the not-Dens of the humans. On the open pathways, many smaller humans could be seen playing with each other, while the larger ones talked in their confusing tongue to other larger beings.

She could only see this one small section of the false Forest, unable to crane her neck further to see beyond this patch of land. But it was enough to give her a sense of calm.

At least I am not completely alone, she found herself thinking as she lowered herself down from the light hole to the soft rock for sleep.

FROM THAT MOMENT ON, each time Little One was punished with the isolation block, she would take to looking out the light hole as much as she could. Only stopping when the muscles in her forelegs protested.

She enjoyed her human watching. Sometimes she even found herself creating stories for those she saw most often.

There was a taller figure who held their head high above the others that Little One would see. Other large humans would shrink around them, and even the smaller ones she saw would run away from this being. After seeing the male raise a paw to one human pup and harm them, she named him Aye, because just like Hye, a lone male wasn't to be trusted.

Another was a much older being who hunched as they walked. In comparison to Aye, this elder female was respected among the people. Many stopped to speak with them or offer support as she worked. Little One knew she was like the Nikita of the group. Nikita had been Larka's mother, and she had been respected by many packs for her fearlessness. So she named this elder Niki in her honour.

There was one being that drew Little One's attention the most. They were one of the small humans but, unlike the groups that played together, they stayed alone. From how low their shoulders sagged as they sat by one of the not-Dens, it was clear they, like Little One, didn't want to be by themself. But every time they tried to join the other small humans, they were pushed to the ground or chased away.

One day, it seemed the outcast had grown tired of trying and kept to the shadows to avoid their enemies. Little One could sympathise.

It was as she lowered herself from the light hole, her forelegs having grown tired, that she missed seeing the change.

But she did hear.

A howl of pain echoed into Little One's prison and, shocked, she pulled herself back up to the hole, ignoring her protesting muscles. Outside she saw her shadow human attacking one of the younglings who had pushed her.

She dug her teeth into the human's arm, and as her victim cried out, she let go with a smile before she was dragged away by her hair by an elder as the other humans tended to the crying pup.

Though Little One couldn't see her anymore, the smile on her face never left. She reminded her of Rae. Ready to fight when necessary and not afraid to stand up to those who hurt you or others.

This human, she thought as she finally lowered herself from the hole, wincing at her aching muscles. *This human is my favourite.*

For the next few days, the moment the test from Tall Fox and the White Coats was finished, she would spend the rest of her time looking outside for the young female.

She didn't see her often, but when she did, her heart and head would feel lighter. All the struggles of the day would fade away, and she would just watch the mundane world of the outside. It was nice to get away to that world, even if it was just in her mind. Anything was better than feeling trapped in the cruel one she lived in.

Each test in the white room left Little One feeling raw and tired. No matter how she acted, too often she found herself gagged and forced into unnatural movements. Whether it be holding strange silver sticks in her paws to eat or sitting atop the cold metal log in the cage to urinate into its hole, Little One wouldn't do it.

Every smack of a branch to her paws when she ate her way was worth it. Each angry huff Tall Fox released whenever Little One would tilt her head in confusion when she spoke to her was worth it. All of her defiance was worth it to show them she wasn't one of them.

When they took the soft material from her sleeping rock as punishment, leaving her to shiver in the cool night, Little One began to wonder what they would punish her with next.

This anxiety led her to watching the outside world more often, hoping to find the answer. She watched day in and day out as the world passed her by, and while she never understood them, she eventually found comfort in observing their routine lives to escape from her own. She liked the routine of their lives. It reminded her of home. Little One needed to see the outside world as much as she needed air to breathe. So, she enacted a plan.

On one of her testing days, she was forced in front of a black and white solid tree that let out a strange whirring noise as it glowed. She allowed them to work, waiting patiently till the moment she could act. When they finished, she began to kick up a fuss, fighting against their grips as they tried to take her back to the cage.

She knew her fighting them would be the only way to get the black shield put up to allow her to see outside undisturbed.

Thankfully, it worked every time.

With her protection in place, she was able to lift herself up again to look out into the world. An automatic smile grew on her face. One that grew wider as, after too many days, she saw the fighting girl again.

Little One couldn't help but be drawn to the girl. Just like her, she too studied the surrounding humans. If an argument broke out between two larger humans, or young pups ran past playing, she would scratch into a strange pad that she held in her paws. It reminded her of what the White Coats did, though unlike them, Little One didn't mind when she did it. It made the girl smile. She liked that.

"Artemis."

Little One recognised that voice and, in a panic, dropped down quickly from her spot at the light hole. Laying on her bed, she turned to face Tall Fox who had pulled back the black protective material and stood at the cage door.

She continued speaking in her unintelligible language to Little One, just as she always did.

Wait, did I understand her before?

Surprise took over, her attention locking on Tall Fox who had turned away from Little One to speak to the White Coats who stood behind her, gesturing to Little One in the cage. Believing she had imagined such a thing, she went to ignore them again, when—

"Artemis," and again the words that followed were unintelligible, but that single word stood out to her. There was something familiar about it somehow.

She watched as Tall Fox turned and opened the cage, the White Coats watching from behind her. As she approached Little One, a smile grew on her face. But from the glint in her eye that any prey would recognise in their predator, it was clear this smile was not one of kindness. Then her icy blue eyes latched onto Little Ones.

"...Artemis..." she said, looking directly at her the entire time.

Without thinking, Little One tilted her head at the word, still uncertain as to what it meant but hearing it all the same. She realised her mistake in showing her understanding as Tall Fox's smile grew, showing off her bright white teeth.

Standing, still smiling, she turned away from Little One and walked out of the cage, locking it behind her.

As the White Coats howled in excitement, clapping Tall Fox on the back, Little One's heart pounded heavily in her chest. The horror of what she has discovered overwhelmed her.

I am beginning to understand them.

LITTLE ONE

After that, the word "Artemis" was heard more often than before, and always towards Little One. She was unsure what it meant, or why it was being said. All she knew was that whenever it was said, they expected her to respond.

She learnt that the hard way. Whether it be a whack of a branch to her backside or smack of a paw on hers, they were unafraid to use force to get her to learn what was expected. After a while, she figured out what they deemed a good action, responding and turning to the person who calls her Artemis or eating with the strange silver sticks in her paws. And she also came to understand what was a bad action – and that was anything wolf. At least, anything wolf in their presence. She still had her cage to be herself without punishment.

Her way of processing the strangeness was by escaping to her cage window. By watching the outside world and trying to understand their ways, she hoped that maybe they would have the answer as to what Artemis was. But as she was coming to learn, nothing was ever that easy in this world.

While she could hear the voices and understand, in a very basic way, what they meant from their tone, she never heard the word "Artemis" from any of them. "Artemis", it appeared, was meant for her. She chose not to think about that; it wouldn't do any good after all. Instead, she focused on her time at the window.

The girl was back, her dark head of fur standing out from the lighter colours of the other humans, making her easy to spot.

She appeared around the same time as she had been the past few suns, watching the humans just as Little One did. Each time she saw her, she felt her chest untighten from the stress of the day, and a sense of calm washed over her at the sight of the girl.

Little One didn't realise how much she'd come to rely on seeing this little girl until she felt her heart sink on the days she wasn't there. She'd wait for her to appear, and when she didn't, she'd sink back onto her bed before going back to practice her pouncing.

On the days she wasn't there, the memories of home and the ache in her heart returned painfully. The isolation of the cage meant she was trapped with her thoughts for long periods of time, and without a distraction, her mind went back to her missing family and all she'd lost.

The heaviness in her chest brought out the worst in her. She'd fight back harder against the White Coats when they did their tests, her lips curling over her teeth, snapping out wildly in the hope of hurting them, only to be punished herself instead.

Then, when the observer returned, the sense of abandonment and loss faded away. It was still there, waiting to hurt her again, but Little One didn't feel as alone when the girl was nearby. It was a strange dependency she hadn't experienced since she was young and incapable of being left alone at the Den. The feeling reminded her of home, but in a way that didn't hurt.

When the human would leave, Little One's thoughts would drift to the happier memories of the Forest. How her mother and she would run together and play in the freshly fallen snow, when Rae had trusted her to protect her pups without a second thought, and Kiba's instant acceptance of her when they first met.

The girl gave her peace with these memories, even if she didn't realise what she was doing. Or even knew that Little One existed. She brought a calm to her isolation, even supporting her through the never-ending tests.

There was so much happening around and to her. Whether it be the expectation of responding to the word "Artemis", the constant scrubbing of her hairless body, or the way the White Coats tried to force her to speak a language that wasn't hers. It was overwhelming. It was why this human girl meant so much to her. She was the calm she needed.

She didn't know what she sounded like, what she smelled like, or even fully what she looked like beyond her fur colour. She never came close enough for her to see her face, but there was a familiarity there just from watching her watch the world, unaware of the captured wolf watching her back.

Little One knew the term "friend", companionship being an intricate element to a pack, and as each day passed with the human, she saw her as part of her pack. She considered calling out to her once, but just as she didn't understand the humans, she knew the girl wouldn't understand her. Nor would she see her from her prison. So she didn't bother trying. That's what she told herself at least.

In the back of her mind, she feared that the girl would reject her if she tried.

She couldn't risk losing the little joy she had left in this world.

Besides, she would never learn the human tongue, so there was no point in trying anyway. The White Coats, unfortunately, were not in agreement with that.

Even now, her punishments continued when she acted as

her wolf self. She didn't see the problem. Was it really so distressing to them to see her devour her meal? Every meal is to be treasured and eaten quickly before the scavengers come, her mother had taught her. Of course, in this case, the White Coats were the scavengers who took her finished meal whenever she rested.

Before, when she acted against their wishes, they had smacked her or put her in isolation. But now they had changed tactics by making her wait longer for each meal and even limiting her water. This hadn't made her nervous initially, the food always came in the end, and waiting for a meal was something she and the pack had experienced.

It had been a long time since she had gone hungry though. In her time with the humans, they had tricked her into growing dependent on the three-times-a-day meals they provided her. To go from that to smaller and irregular meals was something she wasn't prepared for.

Little One refused to be phased by this. She wouldn't give the White Coats or Tall Fox the satisfaction, not even when twice-a-day meals became once-a-day. Her body grew accustomed to hunger just like when she was at home.

Or so she thought.

It was on one day, when the sun was high in the sky above her, the snow no longer on the ground from its intensity, that Little One distracted herself once more by watching the human girl through her window. This time, the girl had taken her observation to another level, shadowing her prey in short bursts and mimicking their action.

One such victim was a large man with sun-coloured fur who walked in a manner that forced others out of his path. The girl followed behind him, throwing her forearms wide at her side and awkwardly wobbling as she walked, just like him.

Little One smiled, stretching up further onto her toes to watch, when, unexpectedly, a pain ripped through her. Her head and limbs seized painfully, her eyes glazing over, causing her to lose her sight as her muscles went limp. Soon, a weightless sensation hit her, and her body crumbled as she fell head-first to the ground.

Fear took over her as she struggled to control her movements. It was like she was back in the Forest watching her sister die. The only difference this time was she could move her limbs, though the actions were weak and clumsy. Each time she tried it just made her dizzier.

She heard the rushing of pounding feet as Tall Fox and a few White Coats sprinted into her prison, pulling her up from the floor into a sitting position. Little One couldn't see their faces, her vision blurry, but as the soft paws touched her skin and raised, panicked voices called out to others, she felt genuine care in their actions. Like a mother wolf protecting their young, they'd come to her rescue.

When her vision began to clear, she saw one of the White Coats bring in a meal and a bowl of water. It was then that she realised what had happened. Leaping desperately forward, she went for the water, ready to dunk her muzzle deep into its freshness, when she was stopped.

Two White Coats held her from behind as Tall Fox came into sight, blocking her way to the food and water. She heard angry voices coming from behind the monstrous woman, but with a single raised paw, they stopped. A soft growl grew in her throat as Tall Fox locked eyes with her, smiling.

"Artemis…"

Her heart thudded heavily, furiously, in her chest. Just then, a new White Coat entered her prison with her water in the odd-shaped item they had been trying to get her to drink from. Little One's breath caught in her throat.

This was a test.

The growl faded away, and the thirst took over. Her tongue

was dry and her throat sore from lack of water. She was too weak to fight back against them.

"...Artemis," Tall Fox said, her voice sickeningly calm. Grabbing the strange item from the White Coat behind her she turned and crouched in front of Little One, a fox-like smile appearing again. She lifted the cup to her maw and took a gulp of the water inside.

Little One automatically smacked her lips, desperate for a drink. When Tall Fox had finished, she held out the holder of water to Little One.

She was desperate. Even though she knew she was giving into her captor's wishes, from how shaky her limbs felt, she knew there was no choice but to do it. Slowly, with eyes never leaving Tall Fox's, she reached forward with her paw to grasp the item.

The action felt foreign and wrong, she could feel the coolness of the water through its shell. Tall Fox guided her, a trickster's paw tipping the casing towards her mouth, the grip she had on it clear that if Little One stepped out of line, she'd have nothing. Opening her mouth, the need to whine in relief nearly overwhelmed her as the cool liquid trickled onto her tongue and down her throat. She could barely remember the last time she had had a drink.

"Good girl, Artemis."

She finished the cup and was offered another not long after, taking to the foreign movement easily this time around.

Tall Fox and the White Coats took their leave, allowing Little One the privacy of regaining her strength. It was in the dying light of the outside world, and the switching off the false sun in this prison, that the tears came.

She was going to lose who she was.

24

LITTLE ONE?

fter that day, she did as she was told without fighting. While some things stayed the same, like her untrust of these humans, the way she ate when they were not around, and her language, everything else had to change.

Little One was not one for giving in, but the knowledge that Tall Fox understood her weaknesses and how to exploit them told her she could not give her the opportunity to take away the one thing keeping her sane: the window.

She tried her best to keep her reliance on it hidden. Waiting only until she was put behind the isolation material to look back outside, but since following their orders, she had not been put into isolation. Which meant, for the first few days of this new change, she was unable to see her friend.

At night, when the humans would leave for the night, she hoped to seize the opportunity to look out the window. Unfortunately, one would always stay behind to watch her. Though "watch" was a generous word. The Night Guard seemed to spend most of their time looking at a colourful item in their hands. Artemis only saw the inside once and noticed strange images within them that made no sense. Humans were strange.

The only time she had to herself was during the changing of the guard. For half a shadow's pass, she would lift herself to the window and look out. But she never saw her friend again. Unlike back home, the false Forest emptied at night.

Or at least, was almost empty. The dark was the time that the elder humans emerged. They were loud and aggressive at night, often starting physical fights with others. While they were something to entertain her, they weren't her friend. Eventually, the outside world became less interesting, and if she were honest, more frightening too.

So, just like before, she found new ways to pass the time. She invented games to play, just as she had with her siblings in the Forest. Though unlike home, these games were rather different. Instead of chasing butterflies and frogs, practicing their pouncing and hunting, she chased and played with cobwebs on the floors.

They'd sway violently in the air and on the ground if she moved too fast, and stay perfectly still if she did the same. She had to time her movements perfectly to catch them. But playing alone wasn't fun, and usually it led to her being yelled at when she was caught. In those moments, that rebellious side in her returned as a growl built in her chest, and while the game was there to pass the time, when she was caught and her instincts returned, it reminded her she hadn't lost herself. Not really.

She may smell, look, and feel different, but some things still stay the same.

The strength of the wolf is that of its pack, she thought to herself one day as Tall Fox presented her with her reflection.

Little One could hardly recognise herself. The scars on her face had faded away, her bark-coloured hair had been brushed straight and cut short, falling around her face just below her jaw. Even her grass-coloured eyes shone differently.

Each passing day, she was losing something. Whether it be the ability to speak in her true tongue or even remembering what home looked like, it was always something. The only thing that kept her hopes up was the night. At that time when she laid down alone and this world grew quiet, she could hear the sounds of home in the distance.

I will return, she promised them.

And for now, that small comfort was enough.

SHE HAD BEEN SLEEPING MUCH BETTER RECENTLY, which is why she found herself covering her ears in frustration and attempting to go back to sleep after a loud commotion outside her window occurred.

No wake sleepy wolf, Little One grumbled into her soft covers.

But the commotion continued, forcing her awake. Looking outside her cage bars to the White Coats' workstation area for the Night Guard, she found them far away from her, sleeping. She grinned widely.

Now is my chance!

Quickly and quietly, clamouring to her feet, she pulled herself up to the window and looked out of it. The noise was closer than usual, so she had to pull herself up higher to get a good look below her window. As she did, she found herself looking, for the first time, at the girl from afar up close.

While at this angle she could not make out her features with any detail, she would know her anywhere. The soft dark brown of her hair that fell far down her back, her odd circular eye protectors that reflected the light, and even her body fur which was a light tan colour, different to the pale of the rest of the humans here. Better still, Little One could hear her voice for the first time now. It was as clear as the sky as she shouted at the grown human before her.

Her voice wasn't what she had expected it to be, for one as

young as her; she thought her voice would be higher and squeaky like the others. Instead, it held power with its deepness, a sense of calm filling Little One as she heard the girl speak. She may have been shouting, but her sound, her language, and her image showed that she knew what she was doing.

The grown man in front of her was clearly unhappy with what she was saying, watching in exasperation as she waved her arms to the side of her, gesturing at something Little One couldn't see.

When she had finished, she stood as tall as she could, hands on hips, waiting for an answer. In a turn that surprised the girl and angered Little One, the man pushed her aside and walked away.

He hadn't pushed her hard, the girl only stumbling slightly, more in shock than anything else. But that didn't stop Little One. Instinctively, a growl grew in her throat. The want to tear the man apart for his action burnt within her, a feeling she hadn't felt in so long. One she had only had with her family.

As the man came back into sight, the growl morphed into a warning bark as he stepped just too close to the girl for her liking. Both the man and girl turned in surprise at the noise, searching for the sound. The man, once again, stepped too close to her friend as he looked around, and Little One released another growling bark.

The two of them lifted their heads in the direction of the window, and Little One snarled at the man. He stepped back and away from the girl and the window in surprise. While Little One couldn't actually tell if he'd seen her or if the noise had just surprised him, she levelled the man with a good wolf-glare all the same. Before she could figure out if the girl was okay, a large crash was heard nearby.

In a rush, Little One jumped away from the window and set about walking around the box, as if she were waiting for them to arrive. When a figure stepped into her sight, it was Tall Fox.

She stood tall, forelegs crossed across her chest, watching Artemis questioningly.

The hair on the back of her neck tingled, anxiety niggling at the back of her. *Did she see me?*

Tall Fox stepped forward and unlocked the prison door, opening it for Artemis to step out of.

This was new.

She'd never been allowed to move from her cage of her own accord. The White Coats had always come in and grabbed her, dragging her to the white room for the testing.

Was this a test? Little One wondered, refusing to move.

"Come along, Artemis," Tall Fox said, her voice gentle for once, as if she understood her nerves. Stepping back from the cage door, she crouched down. Making it clear that this was her choice.

"Trust you." She smiled kindly at her, a rare occurrence from Tall Fox, but a sight that had Artemis questioning everything.

With careful steps, she slowly exited the cell and watched as Tall Fox closed it behind her. Without thinking, she stood to the side to wait for her, watching her every movement as she placed the metal stick in the trap and turned it.

When Tall Fox turned to her and found she had not moved from her spot, waiting for her, Tall Fox smiled once more and gently placed a hand on Little One's muzzle. A warmth filled Artemis at the gesture, her heart feeling less heavy than before.

Tall Fox bent down and looked her in the eyes. "You … where … going?"

A small frown crossed Artemis's forehead briefly, her knowledge of the language still limited, but she caught onto the intention when Tall Fox tilted her head to the side of her, pointing to the white room.

Artemis brightened up and nodded, and to her surprise, Tall Fox let her lead the way. She'd never been given such freedom before, and as she smiled back and walked towards the room eagerly, for the first time, she felt pride in herself.

It was as she turned back to look at Tall Fox that her heart started to race in panic again. Behind her, Tall Fox stood looking at the window in her cell, frowning. But just as Artemis noticed her, she turned back to her with a smile and followed behind her.

For the first time, her suspicious worries over Tall Fox faded away.

LITTLE ONE?

There was something about being spoken to in a calm and controlled manner that felt different to Artemis. Every so often, she expected a return to the old Tall Fox and White Coats, a sharp word when she did something wrong and a punishment to follow. Yet, while there was disappointment, nothing like she expected happened.

In fact, she found herself enjoying her time in this prison for the first time, and more than that, she found she was interested in what they were teaching her. Her lessons focused on her listening and not speaking. The aim, she assumed, was to help her understand what the humans wanted from her so she could follow their guidance. Tall Fox was the leader of most of these sessions, her lessons ranging from reading, grand speeches, or polite one-sided conversation.

She found them all to be strange and confusing, but to have someone speaking to her in a way that engaged her, even though she couldn't respond yet, was nice. It had been a long time since she had experienced something like this.

While of course Tall Fox and the White Coats had spoken to her before, really, they had spoken mainly *at* her than *to* her. Their voices would be raised and aggressive, and every time she didn't speak back, they would get louder. Add to that, outside of the White Room, they wouldn't engage with her. Instead, they'd watch her from their desk or gesture in her direction while speaking to another White Coat.

Now, Tall Fox spent longer portions of her day talking to her. Whether it was in the White Room, in her home or even out in the White Coats' area, they spent much of their time together now until Tall Fox would leave for the night. Even though Artemis understood little of what was being said, she still enjoyed the attention.

Near the end of the day, Little One's examinations continued. The checking of her body and the prodding were still uncomfortable, but she felt less willing to snap her teeth at the White Coats for it. Instead, after listening to Tall Fox, she'd come to understand why they were doing it.

It wasn't out of cruelty or unkindness. It was just for them to see and understand her more, just like she was trying to do the same with them. They were curious creatures, like her.

Maybe this is where I get it from, she thought one day as she looked out her window after the White Coats and Tall Fox had left for the night. She stared out at the activity of the elder humans, watching and studying them, just like the humans she knew were doing with her.

Her curiosity was a human element. She smiled, remembering the frustration of her mother and Rae at her never-ending questions and explorations of the Den's territory. At least now she knew where it came from.

It was as she listened in to the conversations of the elder humans that she noticed that her lessons were coming into effect. While she didn't fully understand what their words meant, she could now understand the basics of what they were saying and mimic them in return.

I can't wait to show Tall Fox what I've learnt, she thought as she settled for sleep.

When Tall Fox returned the next morning and let Artemis out to be taken to her sessions, she was ready to show her what she had learnt. It was only when she had sat down, preparing in her mind how she was going to show her that Tall Fox surprised her into forgetting her plan.

She placed a strange, soft object in her lap. It was orange in colour, unnaturally so, and had uncomfortably dark reflective eyes that didn't move. It didn't seem to be alive and yet it felt warm on Artemis's lap. Cringing away from it – though only slightly in case she wasn't meant to – she looked between the orange-coloured figure and Tall Fox, hoping for an explanation of what this was and why it was touching her.

Laughter filled the air. Slowly, she settled, recognising the noise as one of delight rather than of malice. Her eyes stayed on the object in her lap, just in case it suddenly came to life, but her attention focused on Tall Fox as she leant forward, smiling.

"Good girl, Artemis," she said, and a smile blossomed across Artemis's face. She may not know much, but she knew that this was a good thing. Watching as Tall Fox pointed at the item and repeated, "for ... good ... Artemis."

Artemis didn't understand the sentence fully, only catching a few of the words, but what she did recognise made her feel happy and warm inside.

"Toy," Tall Fox said, pointing at the gift. "Toy ... Artemis."

Looking down at the figure in her lap, cautiously, she reached out. Pulling back intermittently, just in case, she eventually placed a hand on its soft body. Carefully she brushed her fingers over the figure, pausing when a change in feeling caught her attention. Some parts were smooth like freshly fallen snow, while others were rough like tree bark. There was no in-between. It was the head that had the strangest part. The face was made of solid parts that were cold to the touch and uncomfortable looking, yet somehow, they gave the creature life. The figure, with its whiskers like Hye's and dark eyes like a raven, smiled at her, and she couldn't help but smile back.

"...T...oi," Artemis said, the word uncomfortable on her lips.

She turned to look back at Tall Fox who clapped her hands together wildly, a giant smile on her face. It made Artemis's smile grow wider.

She had done something good, that she knew, and this strange and beautiful ... toy was now hers to keep.

For a moment, one that tugged harshly on her heart, she was reminded of her sister's pups that she had helped raise. They were once no bigger than this gift in her hands, and now, she didn't even know what had happened to them.

Her smile fell. Looking at the creature's face, the happiness she felt before vanishing instantly. On instinct, she pulled the creature close to her chest and held it there. She had seen the humans do this with the younglings when they were hurt or sad, and it seemed to help them somehow, as if it chased away the pain. In her mind, she hoped it would do the same for her, but when Tall Fox started her teaching and Little One's heart continued to ache, she knew it hadn't.

Today was one of the big talks that Tall Fox appeared to prefer. She would stand at a small distance in front of a small white sky and show strange images that she would gesture to and explain about.

This time, Little One's interest was drawn instantly as an image appeared that she recognised. Squeezing the item in her hands, she stared at the picture. The large open maw of a roaring bear lay in front of her, reminding her of the mother bear she'd come across once as a pup. She listened more intently after that, focusing in on the language, watching Tall Fox's muzzle as she spoke.

A different image appeared on screen, and it was another creature she recognised. She had to bite back an instinctual growl at the meal scavenger, reminding herself that it wasn't here in the room.

"Fox…"

Her ears pricked at the word, looking briefly at Tall Fox to try and hear it again, watching the movement of her muzzle to mimic it. She would practice that later.

The session continued this way for much of the day; Tall Fox even refused to let her be taken for her examination so they could continue the lesson. Artemis was grateful to not have to go through that today, but even more so, she was enjoying what she was learning and didn't want it to end yet.

At one point, an image of a hissing feline figure came on screen, making Artemis think of Hye. It was at this point that Tall Fox pointed to the toy in Artemis's arms and repeated the word before following it up with an explanation that Little One didn't understand.

Looking at the toy … *cat* in her hands, she smiled and stroked her finger over the whiskers on its face.

Her interest, however, was instantly pulled away from the newly discovered information when a word that felt almost familiar filled the surrounding air.

Her breath was ripped from her body the moment she looked up from her lap and locked eyes on the image. She listened, barely, to the explanation of the creature in front of her and tried to take in as much information as she could. Desperate for it all. If she had focused her mind, she would have. She needed to. Yet she just couldn't do it. Instead, her eyes stayed on the screen, locked on familiar eyes that played in her nightmares most nights.

Even after the image had gone, she couldn't refocus or pay attention to the rest of the class. Deflating at the disappointment in Tall Fox's tone when it was clear she wasn't engaging anymore, she was escorted back to her room.

With dinner prepared and left for her to eat, slowly, the

room emptied itself until she was alone, just as she needed it to be.

She wouldn't cry, she refused to. So, as she ate her meal in the room's silence, staring at the cat toy that sat before her, she tried her best to calm her heart. As she swallowed her second bite, trying to ignore the taste of dirt that came with the meal, one she knew tasted incredible usually, she focused on the cat once more.

In a burst of anger, she grabbed the toy and threw it across the small box of a room, hoping to destroy it. But it bounced harmlessly off the wall and tumbled into a hidden corner.

Her breaths came in heavy bursts, as she tried to close her eyes and rid herself of the image she had seen. She knew, deep down, that it wasn't who she thought it was, but the pain in her chest didn't stop her thinking about it.

For the first time since her arrival, she had learnt what she was in the human's eyes – or at least, what they believed she had unwillingly grown up as. Their word was like hers but said with little love or affection. An ache in her heart grew, knowing she would never hear it the way it should be said again.

The eyes of the image she had seen stuck with her. It wasn't her mother, but the beautiful white fur and warm golden eyes were close enough that she had forgotten how to breathe.

It had been three seasons since she had last been with her mother. And since being in this prison, Little One couldn't remember the last time she'd thought of her. Moving to stand, the anger in her bones thrumming with a need for movement, she knocked her meal sideways, barely flinching at the clattering sound.

How could I have forgotten her?

LITTLE ONE?

She knew she had changed. It wasn't hard to deny. From understanding the human tongue to accepting their fur cloth at her waist, it was easy to see what she was becoming. She was making it her mission not to fail them. She wanted to succeed for them, which was the biggest change so far.

Tall Fox was patient, the White Coats spent little time around her, and as a whole, she was given more freedom to roam. While she never got to leave their Den, she was no longer restrained when moved from room to room, even occasionally getting to explore the White Coats area. Though seeing as most of it was just paper with the strange words Tall Fox was teaching her and their spinning chairs, she didn't do it often.

Her new life wasn't perfect, but it was good.

They even allowed her to keep some of her wolf nature. She wasn't expected to speak their language anymore, even if there was a look of frustration or disappointment in Tall Fox's eyes whenever she looked at her confused. Artemis didn't like that look. So she kept trying to learn.

"Kip .... sowa ... doog."

Tall Fox sighed, frustrated. But at least she didn't snap or scold her. Instead, she repeated the words to her, once and then twice. Slowly and deliberately. Enunciating each word. Artemis watched and listened closely, just as her mother had taught her. She took in the sounds, watching the movement of the woman's mouth as she did.

Her mother taught her to mimic the sounds of her siblings so they would accept her and follow the movements of the natural world around them to blend and hunt. She just had to keep trying.

Tall Fox repeated the phrase one more time. There was a pause as Artemis stayed silent, and in that pause, Tall Fox went to remove the book. "Kip…"

The book stayed in place as Artemis steadied herself, pressing a paw to her muzzle to help mimic the movements. "Kip … sore a …" She pushed her lips out, working to shape her mouth to the correct place. "Kip saw … a dog."

Tall Fox clapped with elation before patting Artemis on the head with pride. That brought a smile to Artemis's face. She loved when Tall Fox was happy with her.

Yet, seeing the excitement of Tall Fox made her want to keep going. So much so that when Tall Fox was about to leave the room, their lesson finished, she stopped her with a tug at her hand.

Turning back into the White Room, she went to the learning shelf. Looking over her shoulder at Tall Fox, she waited for a nod of approval before pulling out another book. Rushing back to Tall Fox's side, she held it up to her expectantly.

Smiling, Tall Fox came back in and sat on the chair. Her blue eyes were bright with elation as she patted the seat next to her for Artemis to join her on.

As they began reading again, Artemis wondered when she became more interested in learning from Tall Fox than looking out the window. She realised with a smile of her own as she understood a new sentence in this book that it was because, finally, she had someone to be with.

She knew, in the back of her mind, that she should still be wary of Tall Fox. There was still an air about her, one that told her one wrong move would send them back to the beginning. Or worse. But the attention she received now, and the kindness in her voice, stopped her thinking about that too much.

It was after one successful session, where she was given extra food with her night-time meal, that she thought of ways to continue her own teaching. She ate her food, as close to the manner they expected her to, and once finished, she watched the White Coats, studying their actions and movements, listening to their voices and mimicking the movement of the words.

There was still a strangeness to it all whenever she spoke this foreign tongue, an unnaturalness that put her on edge. She fought all the way to ignore that feeling, going against the natural instinct to speak her own language when attempting to communicate with the humans, just so she could see the pride on their faces when she spoke theirs.

Each success ended with a gift. While she was never one to be bribed, the items, though strange, reminded her of home. Rae and the others often brought things back to the Den for the pups to play with and for Little One to enjoy. Fenris always wanted to play with her, even though she was bigger than him, and she indulged him every time. He was her favourite, after all.

Little One's smile faded. Not that Tall Fox, who was next to her reading aloud from the new story, noticed. As she read, Little One's mind ran away from her.

She wondered – and she realised she had not done so in a long while – how her family was doing. How had they coped since losing Rae? Had they found safety? Did Kiba and the others find Fenris? Were they harmed by the humans?

The fact that she didn't have answers to these questions

frightened her. She'd allowed the memories of her home and family to fade into the background, as insignificant as her own mother tongue was becoming the longer she was here.

What am I to do when I go home? Will they think me human and not allow me to return? She frowned, tuning in to the words of Tall Fox. Her comprehension of the human language had grown stronger in their most recent lessons, even if her speaking of the tongue hadn't. *Am I meant to just be human?*

A buff of her ear brought her back to the present, the shock and suddenness of the action making her jump. For a moment, an angry fire lit in the eyes of Tall Fox before it was quickly extinguished.

"Where are …. Artemis?" she said, not that Little One fully understood the meaning of the particular phrase. "… finish for … day?"

Artemis nodded her head in agreement. She had had enough for now. Her mind was running too fast and with too many questions for her to pay attention without being scolded. And she definitely didn't want to be hit in the ear again. While there was a mild surprise in her eyes, Tall Fox allowed it and let her go back to her room without complaint.

It was dark outside the window when Artemis arrived back, her meal ready on the side for her to eat, the White Coats having already left for the day. Tall Fox arrived to lock her room door as she too prepared to leave. The Night Guard would be in soon to take over anyway, giving Artemis an hour of peace beforehand. Then, with a smile and a wave, Tall Fox left.

Little One was alone in the silence. In it, she became aware of the emptiness that she hadn't been able to ignore for a while now. It took her longer than usual to realise that, unlike most nights, there wasn't even the noise outside the window to keep her company.

Forcing herself to not focus on it, she tucked into her meal. She was pleased for a moment that there was no one around, as it allowed her to eat normally; though she'd have to make it look like she had done it the human way afterwards.

They had given her extra meat rations that day, and while she was always grateful for her meals, there was a guilt now that played in the back of her mind: a sense of awareness that back home, her family would be scrounging for meals themselves, if they could find any.

It's likely they had to move on from the Den, or in the worst case, their territory itself, after the human invasion. Self-preservation always won out with her kind against an enemy that had skills and death weapons at their disposal. Having them know your location was a risk that couldn't be taken.

Would they even have food where they had to move? If they even moved at all? She realised at that moment that she wasn't even sure they were alive. They had cut her sister down without a thought. Is it possible they did the same to the whole pack?

The mundane and repetitive life she knew had numbed her to these thoughts. Mother Wolf, she had not even thought of her sister in so long that thinking of her now, a weight upon her heart held her down, and her appetite faded.

She threw the meal tray across the cell room, disgust at herself dripping from her pores. She knew she'd be punished for such poor behaviour, but for now, she could hardly care. Little One was furious at herself. How could she push aside the memories of her family so easily?

Little One probably would have caused a further ruckus just to prove a point, when a strange grating noise gained her attention.

Turning to the source, her eyes first focused on the splattered meal on the floor under the metal bars. She'd caused more of a mess than she realised. Little One sighed, she'd pay for that tomorrow. She went to turn away before she realised that her food tray … it was under the bars, not in front of it.

Standing, she walked towards the door, ignoring the squelch

of meat under her feet as she moved closer. The door wasn't in its normal place, curving slightly. Placing her hand carefully on the cool metal, she pushed, curious. With little effort, the door opened into the empty and dark room.

Little One stared out into the deserted area, her heart thumping quickly in her chest. *Could I...?*

Turning back to the cage behind her, a place that had unwittingly become a safe space for her, she considered going back to her bed and heading to sleep. Nothing would have to change that way.

Her hand stayed on the bars, the temptation to just pull it closed again in the back of her mind. The Night Guard would be here soon anyway, why risk it? It was only when the outside world came to life, the hooting of an owl, the laughter of the elder humans and the familiar-unfamiliar howl in the night that her resolve and grip on the bars tightened.

Pushing open the prison doors, Little One took her first free step out, her bare paws touching the surface of the false ground as she stepped into darkness. She wasn't sure what she would or could do as she slowly made her way to the door the White Coats and Tall Fox always used and, with shaking hands, placed a paw on it.

What she was sure of, however, as she turned the handle and pushed the door open, was that whatever happened next, she was making it home. Even if it killed her.

LITTLE ONE?

The last time she had been outside … well, she couldn't remember when that was. No matter how much she had learnt from her human teachers, she still couldn't track the time and days. The newly falling snow that fell from the sky didn't help.

In the Forest, new snowfall could give signs as to the seasons, alongside the movements of the herds. Here, that was not the case. While snow had fallen, and she had seen it do so in the times she had stared out her window, when she would look the next time, the snowy ground had turned back to the strange pathways - the icy flakes pushed to the sides in large piles, its pureness muddied by the lack of care. It was because of this that she found herself unable to track how much time had passed. Had it been a season? A singular moon cycle? She'd never know.

The ground was hard to the touch as she stepped onto it, her grown body shivering with sensitivity. She had not been this close to nature in far too long. As the cold seeped into her skin, she tightened her arms around herself to try and keep warm.

It was dark out, though the false suns that marked the human homes made the experience strange. She'd hoped to use the shadows for protection, but other than right beside the human Dens, no other shadows could be found. As the musty smells wafted close to her from the elder humans, she feared she'd be discovered quickly if she stayed in one place too long.

Add to that, she knew the Night Guard would be coming soon. She couldn't stay by the White Coats' Den forever.

She wondered briefly if she could use her human appearance to her advantage. Her captors had been keeping her well fed and clean. She could easily pass for the younglings of this place. However, she hadn't seen the young out after dark before, and her lack of human fur would bring too much attention to her. She couldn't risk being seen at all.

So, relying on her instincts, she used her size to her advantage and hid behind a pile of logs by the nearest Den. While she tried not to cringe at the cold, she watched as the elder humans swept by her hiding place none the wiser. Once they had passed, Little One leant out, glancing around the area. It was not as busy as it used to be – a fact she was grateful for. But what made this difficult instead was that other than the Dens, there were no other hiding places to duck behind.

Unlike the Forest, there was no vegetation here, no bushes or trees to duck into. The space was too open, and an open field was a death sentence, as she had been taught.

Using the shadow of the prison she had escaped, she dropped low, hoping to see below the lights any shadows she could creep to. The ground beneath her bit into her skin, but she ignored it as she looked, her eyes seeking any element of darkness she could find.

Nothing.

Holding back a frustrated growl, Little One crawled backwards and, hoping for a better outcome, headed down the opposite side of the prison, keeping to the shadows still. She walked past the door she had left from, ignoring the shiver of fear that trickled down her spine as she did.

Reaching the other end, she stared out onto a side of the false Forest she hadn't seen before. Here, there was more openness, with a field nearby. The field drew Little One's attention as, within the wooden boxed area, the field held strange white creatures with dark heads and legs. Little One's stomach dropped. They were the dead animals they had found in the Forest. The source of all their problems.

Resentment built in Little One as she watched these dumb animals eat away without a care in their world. *How is it their lives were more important than ours?* she thought bitterly.

Then she realised. If these creatures were what the rival pack had been attacking and bringing into the Forest, it meant that the Forest wasn't that far away from here.

In her haste, Little One went to run towards the hills when a loud commotion from behind her froze her in place. Dropping quickly backwards and pressing herself tightly against the wood of the nearby Den, she cloaked herself in the shadows. She couldn't see what had caused the noise, but she wouldn't risk being caught by leaning forward to investigate.

She heard the noise again, followed by a low, yet young-sounding, voice echoing around her. The voice was angry and defensive, but beneath it, there was a growing sense of fear in their tone.

Not wanting to risk being caught, Little One looked out to her escape route. The area was open but completely vacant. She could make a run for the Forest right now. The light of the moon hit the leaf covered trees behind the field and exposed the split mountain she knew so well. All she needed to do was slip into the white creatures' domain and escape to the other side. From there, all she had to do was run. Run into the wilderness, and she'd be home. She may not find her family straight away, but once she was free from the humans' sight and sound, she could call out for them, and they would find each other again.

The voice behind her grew higher in pitch, and fear rippled

off them in waves. Little One shivered and turned back for the last time to see if she could find out what was happening.

That was her first mistake.

At the end of the shadows, lit in the false suns, stood the proud and intuitive girl she had watched for who knew how long. She held herself as tall as she could, paws to her sides, with an angry expression on her face, but as she spoke, her voice wobbled in panic. Before her stood an older woman, one Artemis had not seen before, whose own voice, brittle and cruel, snapped down at the girl.

Artemis didn't realise she had been moving closer to their position until she could smell the bitter taste of the woman's false scent. It reminded her too much of the metallic taste of the muzzle she had been forced to wear some time ago.

The young girl was facing a losing battle. Her warm oak-tree eyes shimmered with tears as she spoke angrily.

"You a … mean…" She trembled. Her words made little sense to Artemis, but whatever it was she had said was not taken lightly by the elder who, enraged, raised her stick to the girl as Little One made her second mistake.

She lunged at the woman, her teeth sinking into the soft flesh of the raised arm. Her legs and arms gripped tightly to the woman who released a blood-curdling scream as she attempted to shake Little One off, which only made her cry out more as the movement made Little One tighten her jaw so she wasn't thrown off.

It was only when the woman released her stick and it fell to the ground that Little One jumped away from her, the blood she had drawn sticking to her teeth and lips, making every breath taste of this woman's pungent aroma.

The young girl stood shocked in place, and when the woman moved towards her, Little One jumped quickly in front, a growl ripping from her throat, making the elder jump back in fear.

Little One could feel the girl behind her, her body warm and her breath coming out in sharp bursts. For a moment, Artemis wondered if she had made the right decision, but when the girl stepped closer to her, allowing herself to be shielded, she knew she had.

It was as lights flashed from multiple Dens that the realisation of what she had done sunk in. Multiple elders emerged from their homes, some with smoking sticks, and others with their loud voices and toxic smoke. The woman cried out, her accusatory finger laid on Little One and Little One alone.

She snapped at the finger in retaliation, a sick sense of satisfaction as the woman cried out and fell over as she jumped away. A soft laugh from behind her made her feel proud at what she'd done.

As the humans came in closer, Artemis turned to look away and towards the hills that were just out of her reach. She wondered if she would have the chance to make a run for it.

"Artemis?"

Artemis turned away from the hills, the voice she heard familiar. Her body automatically relaxed as she searched out the source of the voice.

Amid the crowd, pushing through them, worry in her blue eyes, was Tall Fox. Artemis smiled, grateful. Tall Fox would understand.

When Tall Fox emerged from the crowds, Little One went to step towards her, only to end up taking a step back and knocking into the girl behind her in surprise.

Tall Fox's lips were pulled back in disgust as she looked down at Artemis. The worry Artemis thought she had seen was in fact bubbling rage. The blue of her eyes was cold and unforgiving. Tall Fox raised her hand and, for the first time, in a long time, she felt afraid. In her hand, she held the stick she had once used on her as punishment.

"Get her."

As fast as she could, Little One bolted to the side, charging towards the dark shadows of the wooden prison, hoping against all hope that if there was any kind of protector in the world, they would help her make it to the hills. She was young, but she was fast. Maybe not as fast as her family, but even for her kind, she could keep her own.

White Coats, and even random elders, charged after her, hoping to use their weight and height against her, but she did the same. Her slight figure allowed her to dodge their movements, ducking around and beneath them.

The space between the two wooden encampments was too small for the big humans, and there wasn't enough space to pounce, and so, zigzagging as her mother had once taught her, she made it to the other side without a scratch.

Ahead, the stretch of wilderness was laid out before her. The only thing standing in her way was a wooden blockade protecting the white creatures. She wouldn't let that stop her, not now, not when she could feel the freedom of the ground and the surrounding air.

She refused to lose that again. So she kept running.

Until she wasn't.

A screaming howl slipped past her lips as she thrashed her body this way and that, hoping to dislodge the powerful arms that held her. Her legs were free, so she kicked out wildly, aiming for any soft parts of the body to stop them. A grunt was heard, and the grip on her weakened, until another human, this time a White Coat, grabbed her legs. He took one, and another White Coat grabbed the other. Little One screamed and screamed, tossing and twisting her body any which way, hoping for some kind of weakness she could exploit.

Then the monsters holding her stopped moving, and she prayed that this meant she had succeeded. It was when Tall Fox appeared, the darkness in her eyes reaching into the depths of Little One's soul, that she felt the freedom she'd had disappear before her eyes.

"Bad girl, Artemis," she snapped. Harshly, she forced a muzzle onto Little One, its sharpness digging tightly into her mouth, making any noise or cry painful. She attempted to thrash once more, but the movement only made the muzzle dig deeper.

She had been so close, so close, and yet, as the muzzle pinched her skin, she'd lost it all again. She wanted to cry, but what was the point? She had lost. A sob built in her throat, but the muzzle dug in tightly at jaw, cutting her off. So Artemis fell silent, allowing her small, weak body to fall limp. Her captors easily moved her back into the Den's prison.

Just as the doors were about to be closed on her freedom, something she feared she'd never feel again, she caught the eyes of the girl.

Her sorrowful eyes watched her being dragged away. She was pulling against the grip of an elder, almost as if she wanted to come to Little One's aid. But she wasn't strong enough. Her shoulders dropped, defeated, but her oak-brown eyes never left Little One's until the door closed on the outside world forever.

LITTLE ONE?

Artemis knew she should have expected retaliation from Tall Fox and the White Coats. But as she stared up at where her window was, she found herself disbelieving at how soon it happened.

Three days had passed since her idiotic attempt at escape, and in that time, she had been waiting for something to happen. Other than being locked behind the isolation barrier during that time, she had been left alone. Where there had once been physical punishments, this time there was nothing.

Until they'd taken away her window, that is.

She didn't know that was their plan at the time. After three days of isolation and the routine meal drops, she'd suddenly found herself being dragged from her prison to the White Room.

There they scrubbed her raw, just as she had been when she first arrived. Though they were harsher than the first time – pulling at her tangled fur with their metal spikes until tears were pulled from her eyes or rubbing the itchy cloth against her skin so hard that they only stopped when little beads of blood were pulled to the surface.

One White Coat was dealing with her teeth, but Little One was having none of it as she bared them at the creature, a growl building.

That's when the first true punishment arrived.

A harness, similar to the muzzle she'd been forced to wear before, was pulled over her face from behind her. Panicked, Little One started to kick out and twist this way and that, but that only made the contraption scrape against her skin – drawing blood.

Surprised, and frightened of the weapon, Artemis stopped fighting against it. This harness was pulled tight against her maw and nose, forcing her mouth to stay open. When the White Coat went back to scrapping her teeth, she tried to bite at him again. But when she did, the material dug into her cheeks, rubbing it raw.

Only when they were done, they loosened the harness, allowing her mouth to close. When they stepped back, Little One finally saw the instigator of her torture.

At the doorway of the White Room stood Tall Fox, her piercing blue eyes locked on Artemis, freezing her in place.

Stomping forward, Tall Fox reached out and grabbed a loose part of the muzzle around Artemis's face. Here, she began to drag Little One away, stopping only briefly when a White Coat's high-pitched voice of protest spoke out. That quickly vanished after the glare Tall Fox sent their way.

Dragged away, Artemis struggled to keep up with the woman's long-legged pace. But thankfully, the prison wasn't too far from the White Room, and she soon found herself thrown behind the bars once again.

Stumbling and falling to her feet, Artemis turned to snarl at Tall Fox, only to find the fox-eyed fiend leaning against the bars, smiling cruelly down at her.

A strange tut sound left her lips as she shook her head at Little One.

"Poor Artemis," she said, though her eyes showed no signs of sympathy. "Neither human nor wolf." Artemis's heart clenched painfully in her chest.

"Don't worry," she continued, her eyes drifting past Artemis and to the window of her prison cell. "We make you better." Tall Fox looked back to Artemis, and her smile turned into a warning baring of her teeth.

"You just need to learn."

Without another word, she stepped back from the cell and turned away. Artemis watched as she signalled her pack to follow her, and without a second look in Artemis's direction, the group left the building, leaving her in silence.

A sense of relief filled Artemis, her tense body unclenching for the first time since being dragged back there. That relief didn't last long though as Tall Fox's words sunk in. She turned away from the bars to look where Tall Fox had and saw her worst nightmare come to life.

Her window was gone.

Where she had once seen light and heard the sounds of the outside world, there was now nothing. A single black board lay across it, keeping out everything that had given her peace. The one thing that had kept her sane and had given her a small sense of freedom had been taken from her. To add insult to injury, her sleeping cot had been moved to the opposite wall, and as she went to put it back, she realised it could no longer be moved.

Artemis stepped back and kept going until she crashed into the jail bars. Her eyes tracked across the black mark that stood out against the too-white walls and hoped for any sign or crack of light from the outside world but couldn't find one.

Walking closer, she focused her hearing, desperately seeking any noise. A false bark, the tweeting of birds, even the sounds of foul-smelling beasts who stumbled in the night would do.

Nothing.

There was nothing. No light, no sound, no sight, no smell. They had blocked everything out.

They had taken everything.

Artemis's jaw tightened as she ground her teeth together. She couldn't give the humans the satisfaction of knowing what harm they had done to her. But as her jaw moved, so did the harness, which dug tighter into Artemis's skin.

As pain overwhelmed her, she promised herself one thing.

To be strong, you must allow yourself to also be weak, her mother, Larka, had once told her.

So tonight, she will be weak. But tomorrow? Tomorrow she would show these humans exactly what a caged animal is like.

And as the emotions took over and a heartbreaking howl echoed into the night, she promised that these humans would regret the very day they stole her.

LITTLE ONE?

Artemis's plan started small. Her aim? Lead the humans on and make them believe she was following their orders. Her goal? When they gave her more freedom in response, turn on them.

She'd been examining these humans as much as they had her. Her understanding of their weaknesses was, admittedly, limited, but even knowing one was enough to get started.

As the Night Guards doubled, she took in their obsessive drinking of a black liquid that was kept near Little One's prison. Add to that their lack of coordination with the smallest of things, and she found a plan formulating instantly.

One day, after causing a scuffle with a White Coat, knocking into one of their desks, she grabbed a small handful of colourful sticks as her weapon and hid them in her bottom fur.

That night, during the break between the change of the guard, she worked to throw her weapons towards the black liquid. While most missed, and two ended up inside, it eventually ended up precariously on the edge.

Getting into her bed before the Night Guard arrived, she

waited for the tell-tale sign of a crash and found herself smiling when it happened.

Humans seemed to pride themselves on their skills, but put something slightly out of balance, and all chaos reigns.

It was during this time that she found herself taking her lessons for speaking and understanding the human tongue, which increased after her recapture, more seriously. The more she learnt, the more she could understand and use against her captors.

Outside of her teaching, Little One was largely left alone. In the silence of her prison, she found herself filling her time with training, as she had done once before, and planning new tricks against the humans. The latter was helped by the fact that the muzzle was no longer attached to her, meaning that she could make noises without pain.

It was that freedom that led to her attempts of mimicking the noises she had once heard from the outside world.

She'd never fully understood the words, but just about any noise was a comfort. So, picturing the mouths of the humans she had watched, she placed her hand to her throat or lips, and used her memory as a guide to follow the sounds she remembered.

Sometimes, when it was late in the night, and the Night Guard was delayed, she would find herself wondering the purpose of this training. She'd tell herself it was to get revenge on the humans, but when the quiet of the nights got to her, Little One began to wonder if she was lying to herself. On those days, she would find herself falling into a fitful sleep, trying to ignore the surrounding echo of her own heartbeat.

Just as she had attempted in the past, she kept her new trick to herself, concerned that the humans would take this from her too. Not that she was sure how they would do that, but there was far too much she didn't understand about them, and that made her cautious of their power.

Due to her own private lessons, she found herself ahead of the basic understanding in her lessons with the White Coats. It's why, one day, she found herself having to hide her reaction when a word she recognised came from one of the White Coats.

"They spotted wolves in the…"

Artemis's heart started to race. She knew that word and its connection to her and her family.

She tried to listen into the rest of the conversation without being too obvious and tried not to let out a growl of frustration when another of the human pack interrupted the conversation to discuss a game they had seen.

Artemis pulled her legs tight to her chest as she desperately waited for the humans to go back to what they were saying before, but they never did. Eventually they all began to pack up for the day and left without another mention of the word "wolf".

Hearing it once was enough for Artemis though, even if she didn't know why it was said. All she knew was wolves had been seen, and seeing as the mountains were her pack's territory, it could have only been them.

They are still waiting for me, she thought, a grin spreading wide across her face.

She hadn't admitted it to herself, but with her still unsure of how much time it had been, Artemis had feared her family would have moved on from her.

Kiba could have presumed her dead, like Rae, and moved the pack away for their safety. Or, the thought she most dreaded, the pack finally realised they were better off without her.

No, Artemis thought, clenching her jaw. *A pack never leaves their own behind.*

Her family was waiting for her, and she wouldn't let them do that any longer. She was coming home, even if she had to fight her way out.

❄

Day and night, she practiced her skills. From pouncing and landing to working out new ways to mimic the human tongue, her resolve to find a way out grew with each passing sun.

She added practicing her own mother tongue to her private practice. If she was going home soon, she needed to remember how to call out to her pack. Her words were as weak and as broken as a newborn pup, but she still had the ability to speak it, limited as it was.

I can, Artemis said to herself one morning as the sun rose through the windows of the White Coats' Den.

The soft reds and oranges danced across their tables and walls, reflecting off the hanging images on the far side, blinding Little One briefly. Blinking away the shine from the reflection, she heard the twisting of the lock and went to her bars, ready to watch her captors enter and examine her.

Before the door even opened, she could hear them. They were excited, their voices high, loud, and animated as the door burst open. Multiple White Coats flooded in; one in particular spoke the loudest and more animated than the others, waving their paws in the air and gesturing wildly.

They spoke too fast and overlapping for Artemis to understand, making her pull a face at how noisy they were all being so early in the day. After going from silence in the night to this, it was a little difficult to adjust to.

Just as she was about to turn away and practise her pouncing for the morning, a new and louder commotion pulled her back.

What is going— The very thought froze as she took in the new arrival.

Entering the room with cheers and jubilation was the beast from the Forest. He looked different than before, the grey fur on his head was shorter, vanishing in some areas, and he had grown some of it on his face instead, just like a wolf, but those dark brown eyes and the laughter that left him as he threw his head back, she would never forget.

That was the beast who murdered her sister.

As the White Coats ushered him in, Tall Fox arrived behind him. Her eyes came to Artemis first, and the smile that followed almost made her stop breathing.

Tall Fox turned to the murderer and gestured to the wall behind him, the one that the sunrise had just been bouncing off. The man turned towards it, and that's when Little One saw what they had all been cheering for.

Hanging down the man's back were two fur coats, neither of which belonged to him. One was a beautiful black that reminded Artemis of her father's fur, before it had started to grey with age. The other was a soft browning grey like Lobo's that, as the sun caught it, showed bits of red.

Artemis had to turn away as the banging started, trying to hold back her tears of rage and despair.

When the banging stopped, another cheer echoed around her, until the room fell silent once more, the sound of the door banging shut the only sign that this wasn't a dream.

Turning around, Artemis stumbled backwards, surprised to find Tall Fox crouched in front of the bars, watching her with a smile.

She twisted and pointed to the furs that were now disgustingly displayed for all, but especially Artemis, to see. The poor things had been hung by their tail, their limbs spread out and secured to the wall, trapping them as a sick picture for all to watch.

Tall Fox turned back to her and smiled again, as if the expression on Artemis's face was exactly what she wanted to see. Then, she leant forward, speaking slowly and deliberately, which she never did. She wanted Artemis to understand exactly what she was saying.

Her blue eyes cut deep into Artemis's heart as she told her what she had always dreaded to hear.

"You are alone. Remember that."

ARTEMIS?

rtemis grew hollow after that. She had always known there was a chance that her family had been killed. The humans had cut her sister down with barely a thought after all. Why wouldn't they do the same to the rest of the pack?

Yet, to be confronted with the reality and to have to look upon the abomination every day as the sun rose through the White Coats' windows, illuminating the horror on their walls, Artemis found herself struggling to breathe.

She'd never felt dread like this before. Each time her eyes strayed onto the fur coats that hung cruelly, her chest would grow tight, almost like it was trying to crush her from the inside out. It's like fear itself was trying to claw its way out of her chest and throat, choking her.

Only when she turned away to close her eyes and think of home, convincing herself that her family was safe and well, would the pain stop.

Until the next time the sunrise bathed the wolf furs in the colour of blood, and then she would spiral all over again.

It was only after she clawed at her chest, hyperventilating, in front of the White Coats that they finally moved the furs out of sight, much to the frustrated snarl of Tall Fox.

Even with it gone, Artemis felt no better. She began to wonder how many other furs were in this world. How many of her friends and family had been killed to decorate these humans' walls.

Artemis never slept easily again after that.

Her only comfort was knowing that, one day, she would escape again. And she would make these humans pay for what they had done. She just needed to keep working on the plan.

A FEW DAYS passed before Artemis realised the flaw in her plan.

While she knew how to be a nuisance to the humans by causing them stress and frustration, that didn't help with finding a way out. She knew last time she'd been lucky that their idiocy had worked in her favour. Now she had to rely solely on herself. The problem with that was, she had no idea what to do.

Rae had always been the planner in their dynamic. The one who would figure out the strategy of how to get the honey away from the bears without being caught, or the best way to sneak up on Kiba for a playful surprise attack, or even how to use Artemis to get to the eggs in the trees.

Without her, she was pretty much useless. All she had ever been good for was observing their target. And Artemis had observed her enemy enough to realise how unimportant that knowledge was.

Leaning against her prison bars, she looked around the night-lit room, taking in the shapes of the White Coats' desks. She knew most of their routine, having their schedules noted in detail in her mind.

Put yourself in your enemies' shoes, Rae had told her once. **It is the only way to understand how to outsmart them.**

So Artemis tried to picture what it would be like to live as they did. She would sit at their chairs, stare at the boxes on the desks for hours, poke and prod a test subject like Artemis, and then leave for the day. The Night Guards were no better; they just drank brown liquid for hours, left and then were replaced an hour later. Artemis was bored just thinking about it. She knew porcupines with busier lives than them.

A yawn racked her body, hurting her jaw, but she shook off the pain as she trotted to her bed. She wasn't exactly tired, but she needed as much rest as she could get if she wanted to escape.

Settling into bed, she rolled her eyes at the sound of the door creaking open and closed. The changing of the guard was happening.

At least I will have peace for an hour, she thought before closing her eyes.

Then the door opened again.

Artemis opened her eyes, confused. *Maybe they left something?* she wondered, rolling over to face the bars, but no one was there.

Releasing a sigh which echoed around the room, she turned away, brushing off the noise as a trick of the wind, before closing her eyes again.

Then, an echoing knock on metal woke her, loud enough that she sprung to her feet, body tense and alive with fear as she turned this way and that, searching for an intruder.

She didn't have to look far.

Standing at the bars, paws resting against it, was a small human, barely visible in the dark. A growl grew in Artemis's throat. She knew what these small beasts had done to her when she arrived.

Taking an opportunity of revenge, no matter what it would cost her, Artemis charged forward, intending to frighten them off. Instead, she found herself falling backwards in shock as she caught sight of familiar oak-coloured eyes.

Artemis crawled back quickly to her cot's side as she stared, terrified, at the figure of the young girl she had watched and saved maybe a moon cycle ago. The girl stepped back, her hands raised in front of her, as the moon's light revealed her full frame to her for the first time.

She was thinner than Artemis had expected her to be. The fur around her body hung off her so poorly, almost drowning her in its size, that Artemis wondered how she could even keep warm in it. Her brown head fur was shorter now, falling just below her jaw, shaping it in a way that drew Artemis's eyes to the warm oak-coloured brown of hers.

Then Oak spoke to her.

"It's okay..." Oak said, smiling. Her voice the soft deepness that Artemis remembered. It melted Artemis's heart, and when Oak slowly lowered herself to the ground in front of the cell, Artemis couldn't take her eyes off her. But she wouldn't move any closer.

"Okay … that's okay … you stay, I'll talk," she said with a smile.

And talk she did.

Artemis didn't understand a word she said. Her words were said so fast that it was hard to keep up. Even so, her attention never left the girl. Unconsciously, her tightened muscles relaxed as Oak's voice echoed around them.

Her voice was soft, and warm, as if she were sitting right by Artemis's side speaking to her. There was a … genuineness behind her words, as if, whatever she was saying, she said with care.

Artemis didn't realise it, but as Oak talked, she moved from her corner and onto her cot, watching her still. Oak didn't react, other than a growing smile on her face as she talked, her words fast and excited, bringing about a burst of joy in Artemis's own heavy heart.

She didn't stay long, as if she knew that the Night Guards would be coming soon. But when she placed a hand on the bars, she said one final thing before she fled into the night.

After she'd left, the Night Guard arrived and found Artemis curled up in bed, turned away. What he couldn't see was the smile on her face as she fell asleep with Oak's words playing over and over in her mind. For the first time, in a long time, her heart felt lighter than ever.

I'll be back.

ARTEMIS?

Every night from then on, Oak returned. She could only stay for short visits, taking the time between the changing of the guard to enter, and then she would vanish into the night. Neither Artemis nor Oak wanted to risk being caught.

Once, the Night Guard returned sooner than expected, and Oak had to duck under one of the desks. Artemis could only watch as Oak tucked herself tightly into the wooden wall of the desk and prayed she wouldn't be found. They finally left when the sun was beginning to rise, which meant the White Coats would arrive soon. Oak had to flee quickly without a goodbye to not be caught.

Artemis wondered if she would come back after that, but that night, she returned twice. Once when the White Coats left and before the guard arrived, and then again after the changing of the Night Guard.

While their time was limited, it never felt like it.

Oak would sit an equal distance from the cell bars and the nearest desk, just in case she had to hide again, and would tell

Artemis stories. She still understood little of what was being said, but just the fact Oak was there, talking to her, was enough.

The days were easier after these meetings.

While she still intended to use her knowledge of the human tongue to help develop her plan of escape, she now had another reason to dedicate herself to learning. The classes were hard, mainly due to the stubborn nature of her teachers, and Artemis's own struggle to keep both her mother tongue and learn a new one. But her want to communicate with the girl was enough to power her through it.

So she listened closely, quietly engaging in her classes without investing in them. Keeping her interest closely guarded so as not to tip off Tall Fox of her change in mood.

Then, as Oak came to greet her at night, she would use what she had learnt that day and listen closely to everything the girl said. Eventually, she began to understand more.

Her stories were always dramatic, if her overenthusiastic hand motions were anything to go by, and that made learning from her all the more fun. Occasionally, Artemis would hear words like "hill", "water" and "fell", but she couldn't grasp the full context. That frustrated her to no end.

One day, however, her inability to understand worked out in her favour. Oak was performing one of her stories once again, her soft deep voice enthusiastic and inviting as she told a story of a "horse" and a "boy". But something seemed off about her, even if her voice didn't show it.

Unlike before, her eyes didn't meet Artemis's as she told her story, only occasionally glancing up and then quickly looking away. Where she would normally wildly gesture with her arms and paws, this time they stayed limp in her lap as her fingers entangled with each other. The energy around her was off. Oak tried to show herself as happy with her voice, but her body just didn't show the same.

She looked sad.

Artemis, unhappy in seeing her unhappy, crawled forward slowly towards the bars in an attempt to not spook her.

Oak noticed her instantly, and Artemis froze, worried her closeness would frighten the girl. However, to her surprise, she carried on as if nothing had changed, though the widening smile on her face let Artemis know that she wasn't afraid of her. So Artemis moved the last steps and crouched at the prison bars, a piece of meat in her hands.

That day they had given her an extra ration for behaving well in her lesson. She had initially intended to eat it as Oak told her stories, but now, she just wanted her to feel better. Slowly, she extended an arm towards the bars, meat in hand, as her eyes held Oak's warm ones.

Always look your kin in the eye, Larka had always told her. **So they know not to be afraid.**

For a moment, Artemis feared she had spooked her. She'd not come this close before, and she worried that the change in routine was too much for her friend.

Artemis considered pulling her arm back when the girl reached forward with both hands and took the meat from her, a tenderness in her touch as her spare hand gently squeezed Artemis's now-empty paw.

"Thank you," she said, smiling.

Artemis smiled back, her teeth baring in the action on instinct, making Oak laugh quietly.

The two fell into a comfortable silence as Oak ate her meat, ripping into it just as Artemis would. She smiled at that. Artemis watched the girl none-too-subtly as she chewed, trying to understand her.

She didn't understand why Oak had come to her or why she continued to do so. Artemis wasn't exactly a great friend. She couldn't talk to her. Could barely understand her. All she did was sit quietly and watch Oak tell her stories. Even Artemis would have become bored of herself by now. So why hadn't she?

Oak was licking her fingers clean of the meat when Artemis refocused on her. There were so many questions she wanted to ask her, but she had no idea how to yet. But as Oak began her story again, happier than before, Artemis knew she'd find a way.

Leaning her head against the bars, closer to the girl than she had ever been, she focused on the husky voice, listening to all the different ways her tone changed. She was different from the others in that way; that much was clear. Her voice could be high and singsong-like when she was excited. It could be low and warm when something was happy. Then there were times it would be lower and almost watery when she was sad. She heard that voice a lot – whenever she heard the word "mum". Whatever she was talking about, Artemis could feel the joy in her words and the sense of adventure and longing that followed it. Her voice reminded her of home. But, as Artemis watched her smile widely, her white teeth shining in the moonlight, she realised that everything about Oak was home.

Her hairless skin stood stark against the white of the room, just as the bark of the trees of the Forest did as they stood beautifully out against the snow. She often carried with her the scent of fresh earth, as if she had been running through a nearby wood just before she came to see her. Her fur was long and dark like the night sky, and it framed her soft round face like the stars did the moon. It was her kind eyes, however, that always held her attention. They were soft and warm, like the honey from the hives she had scavenged from with Rae.

Everything about this girl set her at ease for the first time since she was stolen.

Not realising that she had drifted asleep to the calm of the girl's voice, she stayed in the clumsy position for a while until a quiet voice spoke out.

"Artemis?"

She shifted slightly, grunting at the intrusion. Seeking the storyteller's voice to rest to, she found it had fallen silent.

"Artemis?" the voice said again, familiar.

Begrudgingly, she opened her eyes, only to stare straight into the closer-than-expected eyes of Oak. Jumping slightly, she looked around the room in fear, worried that they had been caught, only to turn back to the girl again when a hand was placed atop hers on the floor.

She smiled at her and whispered, "Safe."

Releasing a breath, Artemis went to settle back into sleep, when the hand that still held hers jostled her. Letting out a frustrated grunt, she turned her eyes, annoyed, at the girl who then laughed.

"Bed sleep." She pointed to the cot to emphasise her point, or likely to help Artemis understand. "Not caught."

It dawned on Artemis the importance of what she meant. If she'd fallen asleep at the bars, the humans would find it odd and look into it. She refused to lose another thing in her life that brought her joy.

Frustrated, she clambered towards her bed but stopped, thinking. She turned back to Oak who was leaning her head against the bars, watching her. Artemis came close to her, watching with caution for any sign to stop. When she stood with just air between them, she leant forward, her nose and forehead pressing against the girl's own.

They stood still and silent for a moment, eyes closed, as Artemis brushed her nose side to side before she pulled back. She didn't smile, not yet, as she watched the girl watch her. It was only when the girl's face broke out into a watery smile that Artemis too smiled back.

She then turned and headed to her cot to lie down, just as she always did, and waited for the stories to begin. Her eyes stayed on the girl, watching as she nestled on the floor, leaning against the bars. The two watched each other in silence, at peace with one another's presence.

It was as the soft voice started back up again that Artemis

closed her eyes, the smile on her face never leaving. The stories surrounded her, lulling her into loving dreams.

As she drifted off, she heard the name she had been given once more from the girl, and for the first time, the name truly felt like hers.

ARTEMIS

Artemis and Oak's time together continued with ease, though there had been a few more close calls. Each night, Oak told a new story, and each day Artemis had a new lesson that helped her learn more for the nights - not that the humans realised this. When alone, she practiced her words, hand to her throat, and thought of what she wished to say.

"Frund." Artemis frowned. That didn't sound right.

She still sounded broken and shaky when she spoke their language, much like she did with her natural tongue now, but her confidence grew with it.

"You ar frend." She smiled after that. It wasn't perfect, but it would do.

Just as she did with the human language with Oak, every so often she attempted to work on her wolfen language. Hand to her throat, she would replay conversations she'd had with the pack and recite them as well as she could out loud. Sadly, without another to communicate with, she was struggling to make sure she was saying it right.

Only one phrase stayed with her, though not whole.

Strength of the wolf that of pack, Artemis said to herself quietly one night. Attempting to not disturb the guard. But after saying it, she felt something was wrong.

As the days passed, she began to forget more words, and as she tried to repeat the stories she knew, she found herself frustrated at her inability to do so. Not only was she losing her own language, she could barely speak the one being forced on her. It was like she was a pup again.

Artemis tried to not think about it much, worrying would do no good. Instead, she focused on Oak and her stories. The two of them had fallen into a peaceful rhythm, sitting close to the bars, watching one another as Oak animatedly spoke and Artemis bounced her head along to what she said.

When it came time for Oak to leave, Artemis would settle down for sleep and, unlike all the times before the girl had come to her, rest would come easily. Even better, no nightmares followed her in them. Instead, only images of Oak's strange stories and those warm, honey-oak eyes.

Oak always had a story to tell. Whether or not they were true didn't really matter – hearing the excitement in her voice as they were told is what made them enjoyable. Even close up, she was still expressive in her storytelling, which often ended with a few bumps and bruises.

"Ah!" she exclaimed as she banged the soft spot on her arm against the metal, the twang echoing after she did so.

Artemis smiled in amusement as Oak rubbed the sore spot and continued telling her story as if nothing had happened. This tale was different today, which is probably why she didn't want to stop. There was a wistfulness to her voice as she spoke, as if whatever she was talking about was something she was unsure how to feel about.

Artemis recognised that feeling, she often felt that when she woke up from a dream about Rae. Whether it was a dream as mundane as them playing at the Den or one as heartfelt as when

Rae told her that, no matter what, she was a wolf, Artemis's heart always felt heavy after.

She could see this with the girl as she told the story and tried her hardest to take in what was being said.

"Found a family there," she said, her fingers tapping against the bar now, a rhythmic beat following her movements. There was a soft smile on her face as she spoke. "He was ... A pack of wolves ... amazing."

Artemis jerked from her position, turning her wide eyes to Oak who'd trailed off after seeing her reaction. Placing her hands on the bars, Artemis moved her mouth, trying to form the word to repeat. She wanted to know if she had heard her correctly.

She had heard the word in passing before from her teachers, but she hadn't been taught how to say it. She needed the word to be said again and to see the girl's mouth, but how could she get her to do so? She couldn't exactly ask her to do it.

Clenching her jaw in frustration, Artemis fell backwards and onto her bottom, angry and disappointed. Out of the corner of her eyes she could see the girl watching her, waiting for what-ever she had been about to say. She just couldn't say it.

"Family?"

Artemis looked up to the girl, her eyes locking with hers. The girl smiled and repeated the word again, with a questioning tilt to her head. "Family?"

Realisation came over Artemis. She was repeating the words to help her ask what she wanted. Artemis looked at her mouth as the girl repeated the word once more, and she followed the movement with her own lips.

She frowned. It wasn't the word she wanted, but it was an important one that was clear. She shook her head; it wasn't the one she was looking for. Oak nodded her head and moved onto the next word.

This process continued with each word that had been said,

including the words that Artemis hadn't originally understood, which she now did. Initially, she feared the fallout of this repetition. She was sure Oak's patience would eventually run out, as most humans' patience did. But it never happened. She repeated the words multiple times, waiting for Artemis to sound it out or mimic the movement with her mouth, sometimes two or three times, before waiting to learn if this was the word she wanted. When it wasn't, she would nod and move to the next.

Oak hummed, trying to remember what came next, and Artemis waited patiently, no longer really caring for the answer, just enjoying the interaction between the two of them.

She turned briefly to the doors, worried that they were wasting the short time they had before the guard returned. Artemis hoped this wouldn't be how their night ended.

"Wolves?"

Sitting up straighter, forgetting her worries, Artemis watched her say the word once more, and then a third time but sounded out. Placing a hand to her mouth, she mimicked the movement and watched as Oak said it once more.

Nodding her head vigorously, both she and the girl smiled at one another, briefly forgetting the reason for this repetitive game. Then Oak threaded her arms through the bars and placed her chin on the metal. "So wolves, hmm?"

Artemis nodded.

Oak smiled, her teeth catching her lip in thought for a moment. Artemis leant forward, waiting for her to continue, but she didn't. Instead, she looked to Artemis, waiting for her. What she was waiting for, Artemis wasn't too sure. But she knew what she wanted to do.

Reaching forward, she gently laid her hand on Oak's. When those oak-coloured eyes locked with hers, slowly, she pulled the arm through the bars and placed Oak's hand to her throat. Closing her eyes, she moved her mouth to shape the words she wanted and spoke them aloud.

"Woolf famee," she said, though it sounded strange on her tongue. There was something she was sure she wasn't saying correctly, so she kept trying. Her eyes stayed closed as she stuttered her words, a small fear of seeing disappointment in Oak's eyes at her failure. "Woolf ... famlee."

She grunted in frustration and opened her eyes. She didn't care if she saw a disappointed look, the anger at herself was enough to drown her.

But that's not what she saw. Instead, Oak pulled her hand away from Artemis's throat and brought both hers and Artemis's hand to the bars. There, her other hand came up from her side and, slowly, she placed it atop Artemis's.

Frowning, Artemis stared at their hands, watching as Oak's thumb moved slowly over her skin, making Artemis feel a warmth grow in her stomach. *What is this?* she thought, tilting her head.

Turning away from the hands, she looked up at Oak whose eyes were watching their hands instead, a soft smile on her face. Artemis relaxed, the fears she'd had disappearing with each move of Oak's thumb.

"Wolves are your family?" she asked, breaking the silence suddenly, though she didn't look up from their entwined hands. "That's where you're from?" Her thumb, though it didn't move away, changed with her question, instead tapping against her hand in a strange pattern that, for a moment, distracted her.

Remembering the question, Artemis nodded and, placing her free hand on her throat, she responded.

"Yes."

Oak looked up from their hands and locked eyes with her.

"The Forest?"

Artemis smiled widely and nodded. She knew that word. That word was home. She would never forget home. Even if she forgot everything else, she would not forget where she came from and where she belonged.

Smiling back, Oak squeezed her hand gently. Artemis noticed that Oak's smile was not as strong as before. There was sadness there now much as she tried to hide it. Artemis wasn't sure what she'd done or what had happened to change Oak's smile, but it hurt seeing her sad. She turned to their joined hands and added her other one to the pile, placing it atop the girls. She wasn't sure what the intention was behind the gesture, but instinctively, she started to swing them side to side. Artemis smiled at Oak. And soon enough, Oak smiled properly back.

After that, it was time for Oak to leave. The guard would be back very soon, and they couldn't risk her staying any longer.

As their hands separated reluctantly, Oak looked Artemis in the eyes and made a vow to her. Her voice was steely and unfaltering.

"I will set you free, Artemis, I promise."

ARTEMIS

The next few days that passed with Oak were dedicated, almost exclusively, to planning. While they still made time for their usual storytelling and spending time with one another, Artemis could tell that Oak was committed to making her promise come true.

Her hand gestures were more muted when she spoke about their plans, as if she were taking the time usually put into her enthusiastic flailing into the meticulous study of strategy and scheming.

Artemis could only wish she could share the same level of dedication, but in the back of her mind, the anxiety about what Oak was organising weighed on her heavily. She'd tried to escape before and … well she knew what happened when she failed. Add in the fact that she was sure, one day, the White Coats and Tall Fox would find out about their meetings, and she'd be alone again.

Those anxieties held her back from engaging in the conversation – though she used her lack of language as an excuse. It didn't help that, because of Artemis, Oak had to go much slower when explaining. While Oak herself never lost her patience or grew frustrated, Artemis did. The feeling of uselessness intensified at her inability to help, and as time went on, she lost the ability to keep that anger to herself.

That day, Oak had stopped to repeat her phrases and explanations once, twice, three times so Artemis could understand. It was when she repeated it a fifth time that Artemis snapped, hitting the floor hard with her palms.

Oak jumped back slightly, surprised, but Artemis paid her no attention.

She barely noticed her attempts to reach through for Artemis's hand as the wolf-girl let out a silent cry, smacking her hand against her chest. She wanted to stop the tightness in her chest from spreading, even as the tears blurred her vision. All Artemis could picture was her family wondering where she was until they could no longer wait.

Artemis's uselessness would be the reason she wouldn't make it home. When she felt the hot tears trickle down her face, she stopped, curling her legs into her chest, wrapping her arms around them, and hiding her face in her lap.

What use am I? she thought bitterly.

The room stayed quiet after that, and briefly, Artemis feared that this was the last straw. Maybe she had finally frightened Oak off with her unnaturalness.

"Artemis," Oak whispered.

She held back a breath of relief at hearing her voice. Slowly, and embarrassed, she lifted her head from her folded knees.

Oak smiled softly at her, her hand reaching into the prison. Their eyes locked, and then Oak spoke again.

"I will be back," she said, slowly backing up from the cage, her eyes never leaving Artemis's until she had to turn towards the door.

Panic tugged at Artemis's heart. Oak hadn't lied to her before now, but just like any frightened animal, trust was a hard thing to believe in.

THE NEXT DAY Artemis's lessons with Tall Fox went on as usual. Unfortunately for her, she was too distracted to pay attention. A loud smack of hands in front of her face brought her back to the present with a jump.

Tall Fox bent down in front of her, blue eyes cold as ever.

"Artemis, do better," she snapped, clapping her hands at her again before she returned to the board in front of her.

Class began again, and afraid, Artemis paid attention this time. Might as well continue learning to find her own escape if Oak doesn't return.

AS THE LAST White Coat left for the night, Artemis's heart began to race.

Will she come back?

The door opened and Artemis jumped to her feet, only to see the first Night Guard entering. Artemis deflated instantly, and defeated, she climbed into bed with a sigh. Blinking back tears, she curled into herself, holding her cat toy close to her chest. She should have been used to losing her happiness by now, but it hurt all the same.

She wasn't sure when she'd fallen asleep, but from how dark it was still, it couldn't have been morning.

"Psst!" a quietly anxious voice said.

Lifting her head from her pillow in surprise, Artemis turned towards the noise and found anxious oak-coloured eyes watching her. She tried to keep her cool, but as she tumbled off her bed in an attempt to rush to the bars, it was clear she'd failed.

Oak's smile brightened the whole room.

"I'm sorry," she whispered, her eyes never leaving Artemis. "I… not mean… be gone long."

Leaning forward, Artemis pressed her head to the bars, waiting for her response. When Oak laid her forehead gently against hers, Artemis sighed happily.

Then Oak pulled back and took off a strange cover from her back. Opening it, she brought out various materials, some white paper that Artemis recognised, and even the small stick pens that White Coats and Tall Fox used to scratch into the paper.

What was different about this paper was that it wasn't all white. Instead, it was covered in an array of colours and shapes. There was a small green section closer to Artemis, but away from the other colours. In the centre was a circle, though an odd one that had sharp lines puncturing the shape and small four-legged stick figures inside. Then below that was a line of brown square shapes of different sizes and lengths. Artemis tilted her head, confused, and looked up at Oak who was watching her expectantly.

Artemis frowned in response, which made Oak smack her head with a muttered, "'Course", before she turned the paper around, the brown squares now facing in her direction. Just as she was about to tilt her head in question again, Oak pointed to the green patches at the top of the paper.

"Forest."

Artemis's ears pricked at the word, and she looked at the green patch, eyes narrowed, taking it in. She nodded, and the girl nodded back.

Oak pointed towards the circle with the lines and four-legged figures inside and said words Artemis couldn't understand. Leaning forward, Artemis looked at the image and tried to grasp Oak's meaning but couldn't. Eventually, she shook her head.

Understanding, Oak hummed slightly to herself as she seemingly tried to figure out how to explain what she meant. Getting onto her paws and legs she moved awkwardly around the floor making strange bleating noises, before pointing at the picture again.

"Animals."

Then Artemis remembered the night of her first escape attempt. Behind the prison, just before the hills, a caged area of the strange white creatures she remembered from the Forest. Oak was pointing at them in their small field.

Smiling at her understanding, she nodded at the girl and waited for her next point. Oak smiled back and moved to the picture, pointing at one of the brown squares, bigger than the others, that was just below the field, and then two lines that formed beside it.

"The lab," she said, though this time, unlike the last, her voice was tight with anger. It didn't take long for Artemis to figure out what the lab was, though she had never heard it described this way before, or even heard that term. This lab was where she was being kept. The sharpness of the word seemed fitting.

Artemis nodded, ready to move on to the next part.

They continued with this until every part of the "map", as Oak called it, had been named and marked to Artemis. She remembered, what felt so long ago now, seeing Oak with her notebook every day and wondered if her exploration of the false Forest is what gave her this knowledge of the area itself. She knew every safe space and escape route into the wilderness, almost as if she had been planning it long before she knew Artemis.

She marked on her map another line of escape. There were three now, and she explained in simple terms how it would work. In nearly every case, it involved Oak being a distraction, and Artemis wasn't sure how she felt about that. The idea of Oak getting in trouble, or ending up as she had, in this prison, frightened her. All she'd seen with this human world was cruelty, and not just towards her, but towards Oak too. That's why she'd ended up back in her prison: when another human tried to hurt her. She didn't want to risk something worse happening.

At the mention again of Oak being a distraction, Artemis voiced her complaint with a soft whine. Oak stopped mid-way through what she was saying and turned to her, frowning at the noise.

"Walk?" she asked, testing the reason for the whine.

Artemis shook her head.

"Town?"

She shook her head, and Oak sighed.

"Distract?"

Artemis huffed and nodded. Oak shook her head in response, dismissing her objection.

"Only way." She waved her hand, as if waving away this conversation. If it could even be called that. "I'll be fine."

Catching her hand through the bars, Artemis held on, forcing Oak's attention onto her, her intention clear. They weren't done with this. She still wasn't strong with the human language, and with her soon returning home, she was grateful for it in some ways. But right then, she wished she was fluent as she held the girl's hand. Hopefully, what she had to say was enough.

"Sayfee," she said, determined, holding the girl's eyes as intently as she held her hand. "You. Sayfee."

The girl held her eyes in return and didn't move away. They stayed that way for a while until the girl, shuffling forward, intertwined her other hand around Artemis, squeezing it tight, and said:

"I'll be sayfee. Promise."

Artemis studied her, searching her eyes to see if she was lying. Not that she had ever lied to her before. After a second, she nodded, ready to move ahead. Oak smiled, squeezing her hands one more time before going back to laying out the plans she had.

Soon after this, Oak had to leave. The Night Guard would be back soon, and they couldn't risk it now they were so close to getting away. Just as she went to leave, Oak placed a gentle hand on Artemis's and then another on her cheek. The two laid their heads against one another for a moment before Oak turned and left.

As Artemis watched her go, she found herself smiling when Oak looked back to wave as she slipped out the door.

Laying down on her bed after she'd gone, Artemis could feel her heart beating rapidly. She smiled as she placed a hand over her chest; she hadn't known happiness like this before.

She wasn't sure how, but she knew, someday, somehow, she would give Oak something to show her how much she meant to her. That was her promise, and she had no intention of breaking it.

ARTEMIS

They decided on a plan. There was a time, a day, and a distraction from Oak set up and ready to be enacted.

Artemis hadn't been this nervous in a long time, not since her first, and very last, hunt with the pack. It was one of the few memories she wished to forget before she was taken but since then had held onto tightly, grasping onto the image and familiarity of the home she'd lost. Now she could restore these memories and create new ones the moment she returned home.

What if home is no longer there? Then what?

She pushed away that worrying thought, that was an anxiety for another time. Right now, all that mattered was escaping, the rest would follow. Oak had confidence in their plan, and Artemis had confidence in her. She had helped her feel like her old self once more, and she would be forever grateful for that.

It was as she thought of Oak and the plan that, while the excitement and joy of the idea of finally returning home didn't disappear, there was a part of her that wondered if it would be so bad to stay.

Not where she was right now. She would never choose to stay here. How could she? But would it be possible to stay with

Oak? Would it truly be so bad to stay if the life she could lead was with her friend? She didn't think so. The time they spent together, while often quiet on her side, kept her going. Artemis couldn't imagine what she'd do without their nights together and the stories she was told.

Artemis had always been strong at denial and had become a master at burying her feelings during her time here. So, as she always did, she ignored these thoughts and feelings until they were so far in the back of mind that she no longer worried about them.

As the nights with Oak continued, the time to enact their plan for escape grew closer, and while there was a strange churning in her stomach whenever the two spoke of her going home, she pressed forward and blocked it out. Instead she focused on Oak's plan and, as much as it pained her, ignored the sadness on the girls face as she spoke.

Oak had brought the map again that night, and each time it came bearing new images and designs mixed into it. Today she had added a green material across the Forest. When Oak allowed her to touch it, she recoiled and banged her hand on the metal bars at the rough, gritty material. Oak laughed quietly at the reaction.

Artemis had reacted in different ways with each new addition, first to the soft whiteness given to the field creatures, then to the scratchy brown material of the lab. Each time, she enjoyed the laughter of the girl to her reactions, and unknowingly, did them more dramatically for her.

It was as the laughter died down that Oak's cheery smile faded, a sad sigh following its disappearance. Artemis watched her as she stared at the green material that represented the Forest, her fingers gently brushing over the space.

Oak turned to her, watery eyed, and chuckled sadly. "I wish..." she whispered, before sighing again.

Artemis had heard sighs often. Whether a sigh of frustration from Tall Fox, a happy sigh from Oak as she shared a story, or one that just meant someone was tired. This one felt different than those. It sounded longing and almost sad, as if the very action or thought of speaking what she wanted to out loud hurt.

Leaning forward, worried, Artemis caught Oak's eyes. The girl smiled briefly before quickly turning away. For a moment, Artemis was confused, until she caught the sight of a drop of water falling from her chin to the floor.

She's ... crying?

"I wish…" Oak said once more, a hand coming up to wipe at her face. Artemis listened intently, desperate to know what was wrong. "I wish I could come with you."

Stunned, Artemis lost her balance and fell on her butt. Oak didn't turn back to look at her, instead she continued to stare at the map in front of her, her fingers brushing across the green of the Forest.

Artemis couldn't understand it. Why would Oak want to give up everything she ever knew for a place she didn't?

Then she thought back to when she used to watch her from her window. Oak had always been alone. Maybe Oak hated being alone like Artemis did? This place may be where she was from, but maybe it wasn't where she felt she belonged. Almost like how Artemis had felt with her family, though in her case, other than the rare occasion with Skai, she had never been made to feel that she wasn't one of them. Maybe Oak didn't have that.

Focusing once more on the girl before her, seeing the longing in her eyes as her fingers absent-mindedly ran along the rough green, Artemis knew she must be right.

She just wanted somewhere to belong, like she did. And like that, her mind started plotting.

I would have to teach her my language. Artemis thought. *She would also be another mouth to feed, and we were pushing our luck before with our numbers. What if our hunting grounds had changed?*

Could I be dooming us by bringing her? Would the family even accept her? Was there a limit on how many human-wolves they would take? Artemis shook her head. *No, Kiba would understand, I am sure of it. Besides, it would be nice to not be the only odd one out.*

That final thought got Artemis.

Her family had always been loving, making her know and believe in the wolf she knew she was, but even with all that, she was different. Maybe having Oak come stay with her and her family, she would have someone else to be with.

They could have their own secrets, their own way of play. Maybe they could even speak the human tongue every so often to have moments for themselves, like she and Rae used to do when they split off from their siblings as pups.

Her smile grew at the thought, and she reached out her hand to her Oak. Gaining her attention, she watched as Oak blinked her eyes to refocus on the world around her, and when she smiled in Artemis's direction, she knew her answer.

Come home with me, she said in her mother tongue. She watched as, for the first time, Oak was the one who frowned in confusion at the language barrier. It was a strange feeling, but she would have to get used to experiencing it as she taught her the way of the wolf.

"You wit me, yes?" she said again, but this time in the human tongue, in the best way she could.

When the girl didn't react, Artemis feared she had said the wrong thing, that she had not explained herself well enough for the girl to understand.

It was only when Oak threw herself forward, pulling Artemis towards her into an uncomfortable embrace, that she knew Oak had understood what she'd meant. As Oak held her, her arms gently resting against Artemis back, that warmth filled the wolf-girl - her cheeks growing hot in the process.

Then Oak whispered into her ear.

"Yes."

That was all she needed to hear for her eyes to fall closed, content. She would not be going home alone.

IT WAS with this decision that the two of them, or at least Oak, worked out a way to keep the original plan with one minor difference. Oak would only be a distraction for a short period of time before freeing Artemis, and then the two would run as fast and as far as they could.

The only thing that Artemis didn't know about was how the girl would get her out of the prison. The lock couldn't be broken, and Artemis didn't know where Tall Fox kept the "key" as Oak called it. Shaking her head after being asked, Oak waved her hand, unbothered.

"I … find a way," she had said, a mischievous smile on her face that both excited and terrified Artemis.

Oak was taking an enormous risk if they failed. She was punished and ostracised enough as it was. Artemis hated to think what would happen if they were caught. And if they succeeded, even though Oak wanted to join her, she also had the most to lose in doing so. Her language, her home, her entire way of life. It may be Artemis's freedom they were gaining, but she often wondered about how this change would affect her Oak.

THWACK.

Jumping in surprise, Artemis refocused on her surroundings. Taking in the bright white walls, blinding in the false light, and dotted with images of the human form and other learning tools, she remembered she was not in the presence of a friend right now.

"Artemis! Pay attention," The White Coat snapped, the thin stick in their hand, ready to be used if need be.

She was being taught the letters of the human language once

again today, as she had been for the last few days. Her teacher determined she would get it right – the "or else" left unsaid.

The door opened behind her, and while she didn't turn, she knew instantly who it was. The unmistakable lavender scent that masked the bitterness told her as much, a smell she knew she would be unlikely to forget. As the human rounded the side of her, coming into view, Artemis looked up to face Tall Fox - hiding the resentment from her eyes.

"Trouble?"

She shook her head but stopped suddenly when Tall Fox raised her hand in warning, a clear sign that she hadn't answered the way they wanted her to. Taking a steadying breath, she opened her mouth to respond-

Then a loud crash sounded behind them, making everyone in the room but Artemis jump in surprise. Tall Fox snapped something unintelligible and stormed out, the White Coat at her heels, as they always were. With them both gone, Artemis released a breath, relieved.

Her anxieties of what would happen with Oak's plan hadn't fully passed, but she knew, whatever happened, as long as they both made it out unscathed, that was all she could ask for. She couldn't last any longer in this place, and as she heard the returning footsteps, steeling herself for more gruelling sessions, she let those final anxieties go.

She was ready to go home.

PART III

TO STRUGGLE AND LOVE

35

ARTEMIS

As the last White Coat left the lab, having double-checked the locks on the cell, like Tall Fox had made them do ever since the attempted escape, Artemis waited for the click of the door to sound before springing into action.

It's time.

All the planning and waiting was finally over. Tonight, Artemis would gain her freedom and find her family once again. No matter what happened, she wasn't returning to this prison.

Oak wouldn't come to her until the last possible moment after the first Night Guard had left. Only then would she arrive and break her out of the cell. Everything was ready. Artemis had even made sure to have her belongings in place, ready to be collected when she heard the signal.

Not that she had many things to bring. She'd collected small pieces of her meals over the last few days under her cot, just in case it took them longer than expected to make it home, and a few of the toys she had.

Fenris will love this, she thought as she looked at the cat toy Tall Fox had given her. It'd be satisfying watching it be ripped to shreds knowing who it came from.

In the back of her mind though, there was an anxiety building. This room and this place had been a source of pain for her, she should be happy and thrilled to be leaving it behind. Yet, all she could think about was how long she had been away from home and nature. What if the Forest didn't want her anymore?

She didn't know how long she had been gone. There was no telling what had happened since she'd been taken. Artemis tried not to think about it, squeezing her eyes tightly to fight off the thoughts, but the images wouldn't leave her alone. She saw her packs' broken bodies, stripped of their fur like the trophies the humans had brought in. In another, she saw them alive but now with another pack, their strength doubled but without a space for Artemis. Worse still, she pictured her family turning on her, no longer seeing her as their kin but as the monster that took Rae from them.

But there was one thought, stronger than the others, that weighed heavily on her as she looked at her small pile of belongings.

Would they remember me?

Rae's pups that she had helped raise and care for would have grown so much in the time she had been away. They'd be hunting now, and some maybe have even broken off to join another pack, if they had even survived without their mother's nourishment, of course. Or survived the humans at all.

Holding the cat toy still in hand, she stared at it in frustration, now wondering if it was even a good idea to bring it back with her at all. *It could just remind the pack I'm not one of them if I take it,* she thought, frowning.

Releasing a sigh, Artemis went to put the toy down, her decision made, when a loud bang startled her. Freezing in place, she turned to see if her new guard had arrived. That would ruin all their plans. Her first Night Guard had only recently left, the change shouldn't have happened so quickly. But no one was there.

Then the loud bang came again followed by a chorus of strange barks. Artemis turned towards the lab's door, heart pounding. A thundering of footsteps sounded outside with more barks following them. When the cries of the humans reached her ears, Artemis smiled.

The plan was in motion.

She wasn't sure when Oak would come for her, so to keep herself occupied, Artemis found herself pacing back and forth or bouncing on the balls of her feet, warming her muscles up. She wasn't sure how far they would have to travel, but it wouldn't be at a relaxed pace whatever the case. The humans wouldn't let them get away easily if Tall Fox's treatment of Artemis was anything to go by.

As time began to pass, Artemis could feel herself growing worried. Add in that her window was still covered, so she couldn't see what was happening outside. She began to bite at her claws.

Where was Oak?

She knew the plan, for the most part at least, but this waiting and not knowing whether the distraction was working was infuriating.

Walking over to her bed, she sat down, frustrated. The cat toy laid at her side, and she stared at it, resentment and longing turning around in her stomach as she did. She hated who it had come from, and yet, in the nights when Oak had come to her, she had held onto the toy as she listened. There was a comfort to the figure now, so much so that she felt conflicted at the idea of Fenris tearing it to pieces, or even leaving it behind.

Before she realised it, the toy was in her hands; her thumbs pressing deeply into its softness. She decided then and there what she would do with her cat.

CLICK.

Artemis jolted in surprise and looked up from the toy in her hands to the room outside her prison.

It was Oak.

She was dressed in black fur this time from head to toe and, as she slipped through the lab's door, she weaved quickly through the desks and to Artemis's side. Oak was smiling, as she always was, but she looked serious this time if the frown of concentration on her forehead was anything to go by.

"Soon."

That was all she said before getting to work on the lock.

Artemis had no idea what she was doing. All she could see were strange silver lines in Oak's hand that were being poked into the lock's hole. Her tongue was poking out over her lips as she concentrated.

Not wanting to get in her way, Artemis moved to her bed and collected her things. A blanket, her pieces of meat, the writing stick, and her cat toy. It was as she tucked the last of the food into the holes in her bottom fur that she heard the CREAK.

Turning, Artemis looked out the open door of her prison where Oak stood, a proud smile on her face. Artemis didn't think. She just ran and threw her arms around Oak's body, breathing her in.

Wrapped warmly and tightly in her embrace, Artemis felt the anxiety disappear as Oak sighed heavily in relief. She was a little taller than Artemis, which she should have realised before, but in her arms, she was more aware of it. She smelled of recently fallen snow and sweat, and for some reason, that made Artemis smile as she fell into the embrace more.

But they couldn't stay that way for long; time was against them. Thankfully Oak was the one who moved them into action.

Taking Artemis's hand, she moved them swiftly to the exit door. Opening it just a crack, Oak took a peek outside, searching for any sign that they weren't in the clear.

With the door open, Artemis could hear the chaos clearer

than before. It was close, making Artemis flinch at the angry shouting, but it sounded far enough away that it meant their escape route was clear. As Oak pushed the door open wider, Artemis could hear the loud bleats of anger and confusion from, she assumed, the evil white creatures from the hill. Oak's plan had included them, much to Artemis's dislike, but she had to admit, hearing the frustrated yelling from the humans trying to deal with the white nightmares made for a useful distraction.

"Let's go, Artemis," Oak said nervously, squeezing her hand gently as her eyes scanned the alley.

It was now or never. Together, they quietly slipped out the door and into the snowfall of the darkened pathway.

36

ARTEMIS

She should have realised their mistake sooner.

The plan appeared to be perfect. With the creatures causing mayhem in the main centre, most of the humans would focus their energy and sight on them, and not on the shadowed pathways. Add to that the pungent smell of the white beasts that could water eyes and with their loud bleats that covered up any noise, it should have been fool proof.

Falling into the shadows, Artemis monitored the human side, making sure no one spotted them, while Oak watched the other. Their hands stayed tightly entwined to help signal when it was time to move.

A single squeeze, stay still. A double squeeze, safe to move forward. They had also prepared a single holding squeeze for danger. Just to be safe. They'd planned for everything, but in the back of her mind, Artemis couldn't fight the thought that they'd forgotten something.

Something felt … off. As another angry bark echoed around them, Artemis kept her eyes focused on the other side of the wooden lane. Intermittently, she caught sight of a human barrelling after a section of the creatures aiming to herd them together. She couldn't put her finger on what felt wrong, so she focused on what they were doing instead. Paying attention to Oak's tugging direction.

Memories of the last time Artemis had attempted to flee came back to her, which wasn't surprising seeing as they were going in the same direction she had gone last time. It was when they reached the last part of the pathway and looked up ahead, past the broken fence of the white creature's prison, that Artemis saw her home again. The dark browns of the bare winter trees calling out to her as the bright moon above illuminated it. Finally, Artemis could believe again that she was going to make it home.

Oak covertly peeked her head out from the shadows to look down both sides of the path, making sure it was safe for them to move. There were humans around, but most appeared too distracted by the commotion on the other side to notice two young girls running about. So that's what they did.

Playing the role, the two skipped forward; or in Artemis's case, attempted to. To any unsuspecting adult human, they would come across as two younglings playing in the cooling night, enjoying the distraction their parents are facing with the animals. It'd only be if they looked closely that they'd notice there was something odd about them – the main thing being that one of them is barely dressed. Thankfully, grown humans never care for details.

As they played into the role, quickly but cautiously making their way across the path, they came closer to their goal. They'd be able to make it into the field and out without drawing suspicion. And if they did, they'd be far enough away to make it into the wild and hide before they could stop them.

They were going to make it.

Until they weren't.

It was as they crossed the fence that Artemis realised why her instincts had gone off. In the air, a familiar smell gained her attention. It was a smell that was both bitter and warm, like mud and grass, and one that reminded her too much of her family after a long tiring day of hunting. But the scent itself wasn't quite wolf, the earthy tone of the Forest wasn't there like it is with her pack.

Then a terrifying chorus of howls echoed around them. For a second, Artemis believed it was her pack, and her heart raced in excitement as she pulled Oak to a stop, turning to look for her family. As the barking grew closer, Artemis ignored Oak's incessant tugging at her arm as she looked for her pack, but when she saw them, she realised her mistake.

In the path where they had escaped through, she saw the white-furred creatures being herded through by their owners. But the humans weren't alone. Circling and leading the white beasts were three false wolves. That wouldn't have been an issue, Artemis and Oak could still escape through the pen before they made it here, but unfortunately for them, one of the fake wolves had seen them.

Which meant the humans had too.

Oak muttered angrily and grabbed Artemis's hand tighter and began pulling her towards the hill as the humans started to point at them.

When the humans shouted commands at the false wolves, both Oak and Artemis reacted on instinct.

They let go of one another's hand and bolted up the hill.

Behind them, Artemis could hear the barking of the beasts as they chased after them, obeying their human master's wishes. Artemis didn't understand why they were coming after them, but she could only assume, as they ran through the broken fence of the pen, it had something to do with what Oak had done.

She hadn't run in such a long time that her legs ached uncomfortably each time her paws hit the ground. It was like her whole body was shaking as she pushed herself to run faster, even as her breathing turned shallow. A loose stone jabbed into her bare foot, making Artemis wince. As much as it hurt, she could do nothing about it. All she could do was run.

With Oak at her side, Artemis tried to stay close to her but wouldn't slow her pace, the fear of being taken back to her prison if they were caught meant all she could think about was her own safety at that moment.

It was only when a fence, one that wasn't damaged like the first, came into view that she stopped. The fencing here was different. While the first was made of wood, this barricade was made of silver that reflected the moon's light. Putting her hand to the barricade, preparing to leap or climb over, she recoiled quickly. Staring at her hand, she watched as a bubble of blood burst to the surface from where she had touched the silver.

They were trapped.

Oak cursed again, before pulling out a small item from her clothing that glinted ominously in the light. The item was hard and a shimmering honey-colour that was coated with various patterns. It reminded Artemis of the shell of a tree nut. It was only when the shell was yanked off by the girl that she realised what it was – a weapon.

Silver like the barricade but more sinister in its glow. Artemis found herself flinching away. Whatever it was, Artemis knew it was dangerous, and that made her nervous. Shaking herself from her fear, she watched as Oak used the blade to saw through the lower line, making a safe crawl space.

Oak held onto the wire tightly, her jaw tensing in pain to keep herself from making a noise. They may have already been spotted, but they didn't want to help them by making it easier to find them.

Trickles of blood dripped onto the muddied snowy ground, its colour mixing together until they were as dark as each other. Artemis turned away, focusing instead on watching out for the false wolves. She should have done so sooner.

Ahead of them, teeth bared, maws dripping in saliva, the

beasts stood snapping their jaws. They stayed back from the two, not going into attack – whether it was from following orders or a sense of pride in the animal to not attack younglings, Artemis wasn't sure. Whatever the case, if they were here, their masters wouldn't be far behind.

She stepped sideways towards Oak, watching as the three creatures followed her movements with their eyes, growling in warning to not make any wrong moves. Now standing in front of Oak, protecting her, she waited for a sign that she and her girl could escape. It just turned out to not be the sign she wanted.

The yelling was coming closer, and the false wolves stepped back, turned, and ran off. Artemis's heart plummeted into her stomach. They were out of time. She would be back in her prison, her doors barricaded, and she would never see sunlight or feel the wind on her skin ever again.

She felt the anxiety rolling off Oak behind her, and in her mind, she knew that if she was imprisoned again, as long as they punished her and not the girl, she could accept—

THUD.

For a moment, the sky was the only thing she could see as she was knocked off her feet and onto her back before she was tugged sideways and onto her front. Then Oak's face appeared beside hers as she gestured forward.

The lower barricade was cut.

"Crawl. Now."

Artemis didn't have to be asked twice.

As fast as she could, with no hesitation, she propelled herself forward and crawled, as if she were a pup again. Keeping herself low to make sure she didn't catch herself on the sharp line above her, she shimmed out onto the other side.

The snow here was practically untouched, and while the smell of the white creatures was still potent, the coldness of the thick snow helped her to ignore it. Clamouring to her feet, she turned to check that Oak had followed her so they could finish the last of their journey running to the woods.

But she hadn't.

Instead, she stood on the other side, alone and defeated. Her smile, still there as it always was, was sad and resigned. It was then Artemis noticed the drops of blood that were trickling from Oak's hand. She was injured. Artemis went to go to her, until she heard the humans' voices coming closer, and stopped. Oak turned to glance over her shoulder before stepping forward to the fence.

Smiling, Artemis motioned her forward, sure she was about to follow, but frowned when Oak held out her hand. Artemis went to hold it, like they always did when they needed comfort, until she noticed the silver and gold weapon in her hand. Confused, Artemis turned to stare at Oak, held tilted.

Oak, voice shaking, tears dripping down her cheeks, whispered something Artemis didn't understand.

Then Oak's expression changed as she pulled back her hand and threw the weapon at her. Ducking and falling Artemis heard the thump of the weapon as it fell into the snow behind her, Artemis turned to Oak in shock.

Tears filled the corners of Oak's eyes, and it was when she closed them and took a steadying breath that Artemis realised what she was doing.

She never intended to come with me.

Suddenly, her Oak began shouting, tears falling as she screamed wildly at her, the noise hurting Artemis's ears. She caught the words here and there, and her own throat grew tight. Each word being thrown at her was cruel, even if she couldn't feel malice behind them, the viciousness took her by surprise. Frightened, she began to crawl backwards, and her hand fell atop the golden shelled weapon.

"You—you … monster!"

Turning away, Artemis could feel the tears burning in the

back of her eyes as her body shook, not from the cold, but at the harshness of the words. Confused, but desperate, Artemis picked up the weapon before turning back to Oak who held up her bleeding hands as she yelled, snot and tears trickling together as she did.

"Look what you did!" she scream-cried, her voice hoarse and broken.

Then, behind her, the elder humans appeared.

Taking a last look at her Oak, whose eyes shone with love, kindness, and despair that had been there since the day she had first seen her, she watched as she nodded at her, a smile as quick as a blink spreading on her lips as she mouthed something Artemis didn't understand. Tears filled Artemis's own eyes as she stumbled to her feet.

Without another look, even though it killed her to do so...

She turned and fled.

37

ARTEMIS

The cries and bellows of the elder humans followed her into the hills, the Forest, and the thereafter, but it was the warm eyes that haunted her as she went. It was dark and cold, winter clear upon them as she stumbled in the new snow throughout the thicket.

She hadn't been in the wild for so long, let alone in the outside world itself, that she was unprepared for the chill that ripped through her. She'd lost her blanket long ago, the hair on her arms standing upright as shiver after shiver shocked her body. The cold bit at her toes as she ran through the snow, so she waited until her feet went numb to push herself to move faster. Her injured paw stung bitterly; the cut had reopened after her most recent fall, and now fresh blood trickled down to her fingertips, leaving a trail as she walked.

There was the awareness in the back of her mind that letting an open wound bleed would attract predators. But she didn't care anymore.

Animals stirred around her as she disturbed their slumber. In most cases, the creatures ignored her, not sensing a threat, and fell back to sleep. It was the odd few creatures of the night that would stumble across her on their journeys that would turn and run in fear.

It didn't occur to her until much later, when the cold seeped into her fingers and her teeth chattered violently against one another that, being so close to the human side of the Forest that the animals here would know and fear her because … of her kind.

She supposed, beside the dirt and grime that covered her now, she looked more human than she had before her capture.

Around her waist, she wore the cloth forced on her until eventually she came to like it. She had been kept clean, absurdly so, washing away any natural scent from her homeland and pack. To the surrounding creatures, they would only see and smell human, the stench either driving them to flee or ignore her as best they could. She wondered if there would be a few who would attack her because of her heritage.

Shaking, she held the golden shell in her hands, gazing at it. So far, Artemis had been afraid to open it up and use it, wondering if the girl's blood that had been desperately shed to help her escape would cover the silver blade.

If it did, it would just be a guilty reminder that she had failed in keeping her promise, even if it seemed that was Oak's plan all along. But if it didn't, she feared forgetting or losing the memory and scent of the girl she … well she didn't really know how she felt about her.

The same had happened with her mother and Rae, though she couldn't even remember when it had happened. One day she just found herself struggling to separate the image of the two of them, each memory blending together. They had been so different from one another, but she could barely remember in what ways. Who had the golden eyes? Was it Rae she had gone honey-hunting with or Mother? How did their voices sound? She didn't know.

She couldn't bear the idea of losing another in that way.

Losing her family physically was painful enough, but to slowly lose the memories of their time together was like she was losing them all over again. What else would this life take from her?

She drew the blade.

A soft but menacing growl vibrated nearby, strong enough that Artemis could feel its intensity in her bones.

To the side of her, a cat, nearly as large as Hye had once been, emerged. Its razor-focused golden eyes laid themselves not on Artemis, but on the weapon in her hands. Her lips drew back over her teeth as she hissed.

Human.

Then she pounced.

Reacting on instinct, even if it wasn't as strong as it had once been, Artemis tumbled to the side and bared her own teeth, a growl growing in her throat as she snapped at the cat. She realised that, with her clipped claws, she had nothing to fight with. Let alone anyone to help protect her. She'd never gone up against a fellow predator without her pack at her side to keep her safe. As the cat's yellow eyes narrowed on her, Artemis, for the first time, felt afraid about being back in the Forest.

The cat smiled at her attempted display of aggression as she slowly walked closer. Artemis knew she didn't stand a chance against the cat. The creature would have no problem tearing her to pieces. In fact, she'd probably savour it if the hatred she spat out with the word was anything to go by. So Artemis improvised.

Not human, she barked, stepping backwards away from the cat to keep a safer distance between them, her eyes locking with it.

A laughing purr escaped the feline as they continued to walk towards Artemis, though instead of pouncing, she closely circled her, their eyes watching her every move. It was as if she were playing the game of predator-prey, just like Artemis had played with her siblings when they were young. This time, however, she was the very literal prey.

Not human, you say? the cat purred. Artemis followed the cat's movement, turning her own body to keep an eye on them. **You smell human...** A tail brushed her legs; she refused to react. **You look human...** Out of the corner of her eyes, Artemis could see the cat lick its salivating lips. **And I may not have tasted human but—**

With a swing of her arm, Artemis lashed out with the unsheathed weapon, before turning tail and running as fast and as far away from the cat as she could, loping into the Forest. The echo of the cat's painful yowl followed her on the wind.

She didn't know where she was going or what she was doing, but she knew that the further she got from where she had been, the better.

It was as she looked at the blade as she ran, looking at the blood-covered silver, that her own tears finally fell. Her heart pounded in her chest; fear and guilt plagued her as she felt the blood of the cat trickle onto her fingers from her human weapon. She'd just shown the cougar that they were right about her.

She kept running.

38

ARTEMIS

$\mathcal{E}$xhaustion and hunger hit her faster than she anticipated. Her resilience and strength weren't what they used to be; she'd only managed to get this far due to the fear and devastation that pulsed through her body.

Her legs collapsed underneath her, and she tumbled to the ground, face-first into the snow. She couldn't move, could barely even breathe from how heavy her chest felt. Her eyes had gone blurry, making her barely able to distinguish between the ground and sky. Closing her eyes, she tried to swallow but found her throat too dry to even try. Begrudgingly, she forced herself to her side to reach into her pocket.

To her dismay, much of what she had brought with her was no longer there. The food rations she had stored away for the both of them must have fallen out in their panicked rush. Only a few pieces were left. She took one out and put the rest back before she began to eat, slowly.

Other than the few times she'd been punished without food, she'd been fed regularly enough that, unlike when with her family, she was no longer used to small and sporadic meals. Her body groaned in protest when she finished her meagre meal, but she had to ignore it. Grabbing handfuls of the freshly fallen snow, she ate it in small bouts, hoping to gain some refreshment from the watery substance and silence her grumbling stomach. Neither was successful.

Still light-headed, she stayed lying in the snow, no longer able to feel the chill of the ground, and found herself able to relax because of it. She was about to close her eyes to rest briefly when they flew open in realisation.

Her head ached, but she ignored the warning of pain as she jumped up to her feet, searching in a wild panic. She checked her material cover, the pockets inside it, and even the snowy ground around her, digging into it until her nails turned black with mud in a desperate need to find it. But she couldn't. And at that realisation, a sob clawed at her throat.

She'd lost her cat toy.

It shouldn't have been as devastating as it was. It had only been something she had slept with. She'd gone her entire life without such a thing before it, so why did she care?

She wrapped her arms tightly around herself – not because of the cold, she could barely feel that – but to hold herself just as the girl had as a howling sob seized her body.

Her heart was heavy and her body so tired that eventually her cries drained her, sending her into a restless and fitful sleep. This was the first time since she was taken that, finally, the grief over everything she had lost – that she had buried deep inside her – was let out.

Losing her sister, her home, her language, her pack, her independence, and now Oak bubbled to the surface. It was overwhelming, and she felt like she was drowning in it, but she couldn't stop it.

She remembered the dying light in her sister's eyes as she was taken away from her. The beautiful blue that faded and disappeared into a dull hue as her chest stopped moving. Maybe if she had fought to get to Rae's side faster, she could have saved her.

She didn't know what had happened to her family, but the brutality of humans brought about such visceral images of her siblings, friends, and the younglings being slaughtered for the sheer amusement of the beasts. She still remembered the wolf skins on the walls. What if the fur she had seen had been Kiba's? Or Fenris's? In some versions of these nightmares, it was her own fur up on those walls, paraded for all the White Coats to see.

Then, as the nightmare came to its end, those oak-coloured eyes would find her. The girl would stare her down, anger and resentment in her words until, eventually, all that faded to despair. Artemis would have to watch as the tears fell from Oak's eyes, and she couldn't do anything to comfort her. All she could do was watch as she disappeared forever.

Then she would wake breathless and frightened before she remembered where she was, and the cycle would start again.

Artemis wasn't sure how long she had been falling in and out of consciousness in the snow-covered ground, but eventually she was able to stay awake long enough to realise she had to get moving. Stumbling to her feet, her legs unsteady like a newborn fawn, she walked. She didn't know where she was going, how long it would take, or what she was doing. She just knew she needed to move. Maybe in doing so she could leave these nightmares behind.

The sun had risen above her, making the Forest more visible. Animals stirred from their own slumber and curiously watched Artemis as she travelled.

She ignored them as best she could and staggered ahead, digging into her pockets to steal another stick of food. She knew she only had so much left, but her stomach ached in hunger, and she couldn't ignore it any longer.

It tasted of nothing. Every bite felt pointless, and after the piece of meat had turned to mush in her mouth and she swallowed it, she felt no different. Her legs were still unsteady, and her head swam with hunger and thirst. Tired, she stayed close to the trees, using them for balance as she walked.

When the sun reached its peak high in the sky, illuminating the whole Forest around her, Artemis sighed, the action hurting her dry throat. She still recognised nothing.

Surely, I should have seen something familiar by now, she thought in frustration as she rested against a tree trunk. She had travelled across their territory widely before. She'd trekked the whole border with Rae after their mother had passed, and she knew it stretched close enough to the mountain border of the human world that she should have recognised something by this point.

So why hadn't she?

The Forest changed with each season but never beyond recognition. No matter the time, she'd always been able to find her way home. *A wolf always knew the way,* her mother's words echoed in her mind. A burst of rage filled Artemis as she bit her tongue to stop herself from screaming.

Nothing has changed. It is just that I am not wolf enough now to remember.

Being home now, confused and disorientated, she realised how much they had taken from her without her knowledge. They'd taken her memories and love of her homeland to the point that she no longer recognised it.

Anger rolled off her in waves, scattering the few animals that had come to investigate as she ran forward. She ignored the cries of protest from her achy and tired limbs until they gave out from underneath her.

She laid in a heap, as still as the dead. Then, she screamed. Her howl was pulled this way and that, swirling around her in the wind. When she stopped, it wasn't enough, so she threw her fists into the ground once, twice, three times, more, until eventually her chest was heaving and her hands bled, but she felt a little better. Taking a deep breath, she stood up and almost fell backwards down the steep incline of a small hill. Artemis hadn't even realised she was on one until then. She was too tired to attempt to climb, so stepping down, she began to walk around it.

Pushing aside the branches of the trees that surrounded the hill, she came across a collection of collapsed treetops that had fallen down from the top of the hill she had just passed. She wondered briefly how it had stayed that way and not decayed but shrugged off the thought and continued around.

Finally, on the other side, she stepped through the trees, the empty branches catching her on her head and piercing her skin. Crying out, she moved past the trees quickly. Stopping on the other side, she put a hand to the painful area and rubbed slightly, hoping to numb the pain.

As she soothed the pain, a memory of her mother doing the same with her warm tongue came to her. Artemis smiled; she'd forgotten how often she'd been injured as a pup. Especially by the exposed branches of the Den that would usually catch her.

Sighing sadly at the memory, she rubbed at her chest, trying to dull the ache that was growing there. It'd been so long since she'd been able to picture a moment with her mother. Now, after having it, she found herself wishing she had her mother to soothe the pain in her heart.

Shaking her head free of the pain, she continued to walk forward until she froze, eyes wide.

The Den.

She turned and ran back, ignoring the tree branches that scratched her sides as she burst through them and came to the hill. Without another thought, she rushed up its side, her grip tight and the weakness in her legs gone as she charged upwards, her movements powered by pure emotion.

Emerging at the top, she laid her eyes on the fallen tree.

Beneath it, she could see the holes they had dug with an entrance near the centre of the tree that lifted higher, allowing for more space where a mother could relax and care for her pups. Just like her mother had done in this very place.

A cry slipped past her lips as she rushed forward to the Den, diving and searching every dug hole, desperate to reunite with her family.

Kiba! Fenris! It me! I home!

She received no response, and as her voice echoed in the empty land around her, only accompanied by the disturbed twitters of the birds in the trees, did she begin to realise what was wrong. It was when she went to her own resting place that the heartbreaking reality of what she was seeing came to her.

She may have been home, but her family...

They were gone.

39

ARTEMIS

She curled up in her old sleeping area and rested, having cried herself into exhaustion moments before. The few times she woke up – mouth dry, eyes sore, and body aching from dehydration – she would eat a handful of snow and drift off once more. She no longer cared what happened to her.

Her family was gone. What was the point anymore?

Outside, the weather had taken a turn for the worst. The entrance to her resting place was slowly being blocked by the rising snow, and the light of the day was disappearing the higher it grew.

Snowstorms were a rare occurrence in the Forest, she remembered. The fact one was here was a sign that winter was on the horizon. The few storms Artemis had witnessed were always intense and could last for hours, sometimes even days.

Rae, or maybe Mother, had told her when they were year-lings that, depending on how long the storms lasted, it would be a sign of what to expect with the coming winter. Long and gloomy meant they were in for a restful period as the worst had passed, but if it was short, they should prepare themselves for shorter hunting seasons and longer hibernation for others.

As she watched the snow fall, seeing it trickle into the Den, she shivered from the chill. It felt strange, being in the shelter and be as cold as she was. Normally, she wouldn't have had to worry about the cold, she'd have been surrounded by the warmth and love of her family nearby when she slept here.

Not anymore.

She wondered where her family had moved to and if they had even thought about how she would find them, or if they'd even thought of her at all. In the back of her mind, she wondered where their carcasses could have been dragged to.

Artemis had seen no skeletons on her journey, bar the bodies of the caribou and deer others had devoured. Of course, it was possible they had slowly been eaten away, as was the natural way. Maybe they had been killed further away, or died slowly from starvation, she couldn't be sure. And it was that fact that made it all the more distressing.

She would never know what happened to her family. She'd made it all the way back here, alone, leaving the only other being she had cared about behind – desperate to find the others she knew and loved to restore her broken heart, only to come up empty.

The snow trickled further in, and another shiver shook her body. Tired, she closed her eyes to sleep, hoping that this time the nightmares would leave her be.

Maybe the cold would take her in the night, and she could be with her family once more. She could see them in all their glory, run with them at speeds she could never reach before and finally feel at peace. Or maybe the humans would find her again and take her back to their world. She would go willingly this time; there was nothing more for her here.

Part of her hoped that Oak would come to find her. In her dreams, she pictured Oak running away from the human world to the Forest, and after a vast adventure of obstacles, the two met each other again unexpectedly and promised to never be apart again. From then on, they weren't alone. They lived together at the Den, travelled to the river for water and, with the blade Oak had given her, they caught their own prey.

It would be just the two of them, and she could have someone to tell her own stories to as she taught her the wolfen tongue. She would tell her tales of her and Rae, how they grew up together, and even the story of their unfortunate meeting with the porcupine, and how they were scolded for not knowing how to play nicely by their mother. There was so much she could tell her, and they would have all the time in the world – just the two of them, keeping the memory of Artemis's family alive.

Not perfect, but close enough to it.

As the storm raged on while she slept, it allowed her this one moment of peace to dream of what-ifs and tomorrows that may never come.

She rested a lot in the following days, her grief all consuming, just as it always was with wolves. Wolves grieved long and hard, their body language the sign to all creatures in the wild, and other packs, that they had lost one of their own. While Artemis did not hold the ability to show her grief in the wolfen way, her grief was no less clear. Her soft tearless wails were swept into the storm's winds and carried out into the Forest.

The Forest heard her and, as it always did, it came to provide.

Ravens appeared at the Den's entrance, resting on the branches and disturbing the fallen snow and Artemis from her slumber. They then left behind feathers and small twigs before flying away.

Next, a troublesome fox, a scavenger of meals, rested at the edge of the hillside buried in the snow. They never looked Artemis's way, nor did they react aggressively when her head appeared in the entranceway, growling to frighten them off.

The Fox stayed for some time. It was only when Artemis's cries in the night stopped did they take their leave.

Even a lone wolf came by, one as white as the snow and with eyes as dark as the night. He didn't stay long, only taking enough time to deliver a rabbit at the Den's entrance and offer her a bow before he turned and left into the blizzard.

After this, while she may have been alone, she no longer felt that way.

Her home was proving to her that they wanted her here. Enemies and allies had shown her the support she didn't know she wanted, and when their job was done, they moved along until another took their place.

As she settled to rest on her eighth night since she'd been home, eating the last of her rations, she remembered her mother's words to her about the Forest.

The Forest is not kind to those who do not know it. It is powerful, ferocious, and dangerous. Yet, if you are one with it by providing and respecting its presence, it will become your greatest ally. Prove yourself, and it will be rewarding.

Artemis smiled in her sleep.

The Forest saw her as an equal. It had shown her that, no matter how long she'd been away, she was, and always had been, a wolf.

Warmed with that thought, she found herself finally sleeping peacefully. It was as she slept that the Forest, just as her mother had promised her all those years ago, rewarded her.

A howl echoed into the night.

40

ARTEMIS

Artemis was startled awake. She wasn't sure why she'd woken up, and she felt bitter about it. It had been a long time since she had slept so well, and she wanted more of it.

Settling back into her spot, resting her head on her haphazardly made cushion of mud and snow, she closed her eyes once more ... only to throw them open in shock at the howl that echoed wildly into the Den.

The storm had grown heavier as she had slept, the wind whistling and whooshing as it whipped harshly at the entrance, almost as if it were attempting to tear it to pieces. She had never seen a storm like this before, had only heard stories of how bad they could be from her elders. They'd told her that all you could do in weather like this was seek out warmth for dear life.

She attempted to shuffle herself further back into the Den, but she wasn't as flexible as her family. They could burrow deep into the crevices without difficulty. Artemis tried, though it was far more uncomfortable than she'd like it to be.

It was as another gale of wind blasted through the entrance, blowing the fallen snow against her skin, that she heard it. Carried on the gusts of the storm, pulled so far and wide that it was barely a whisper, but its sound vibrated through the Den and into her ears. The deep tone spoke of pain and love, a never-ending hum that reminded her closely of a melody she had once heard. Artemis's eyes filled with moisture; she would recognise that sound no matter how long it had been. A wolf's howl, not a single wolf, but a pack, joining in search of one they had lost.

Was she imagining it? Surely it couldn't really be... Shaking her head, she stretched forward towards the entrance, desperate to hear it again. When seconds passed and she didn't, her heart sunk heavily in her chest.

It is too good to be true, she thought.

Until she heard it once more.

Whether or not it was her pack, she didn't care. It was familiar, and it was home.

Scrabbling forward, she pulled herself from the Den, exposing herself to the elements. She could taste the bitterness of the storm, an electricity in the air, as if nature itself were prepared to tear itself apart. Only as she ran further into the swirling nightmare, snow tearing into her sides, did she find herself surrounded by a scent of nothingness, as if the storm had wiped the world clean. The icy chill seeped into her skin, and the rising snow covered her feet and speckled her eyes, making it difficult to see. But she didn't need her sight.

She just needed to run.

Tumbling down the hill, Artemis stumbled forward, listening for any sign or direction of the howls. While the storm helped carry its sound, it threw it every way, making it impossible to figure out where it was coming from.

The chorus surrounded her, and she had to decide. She turned and ran in the direction she felt was her best chance and charged head-first into a low-hanging branch. Knocked over and into the snow, dazed, Artemis looked at the sky above, which was blocked out by the storm.

Something warm trickled down her head, blinding her in her right eye. Wiping it away with the back of her paw, she clamoured back to her feet and, brushing the blood on her hand onto her stomach, she bounded forward again.

Just as her first day back home, the cold tore through her and numbed her limbs to the point of pain. Every running step was agony. While she couldn't see what was beneath the snow, it felt as if she were charging across sharpened rocks. Each step pierced her feet, sending shooting pains up her legs and seeping into her bones.

There was nothing she could do about it though; she had to keep running. When she found her family, that numbness would fade away.

The swirling snow around her made the world around her disappear into pure whiteness. The ice stuck to her eyes, making it difficult to keep them open to see, and when closed for too long, they became stuck together. Artemis didn't have the time to panic about losing her sight. Besides, she only needed her hearing to pinpoint where her family was. She would recover eventually, so she kept her eyes closed as much as possible and carried onwards.

It wasn't safe, and it slowed her progress, making her take more cautious steps to ensure she didn't injure herself or fall into a dangerous situation. She didn't have time to fall down a hill and break bones.

As the storm swirled, it pulled the howls along its current once more, enveloping her in their song. Believing she knew which direction to go, she ran on once more, ignoring the protest in her aching limbs and starving body.

It had been too long since she'd had a proper drink or even a substantial meal, and her body was no longer capable of taking her far, no matter how much she pushed through it. Her sight may have been blocked by the snow that coated the lashes on her eyes, but as she stumbled from a sudden harsh blow of the wind, the light-headedness returned, and her ability to see was no longer just affected by the weather.

Artemis's head felt heavy, as if she had kept her head underwater for too long without taking a breath of air. The sensation was frightening, add to that the fact she could no longer feel most of her limbs from the cold, she could feel her breathing pick up in speed.

She hoped that hearing the howls once more would help her past this rising panic, but as time passed, she could no longer hear them.

Her chest tightened in anger, and her breath came out in short, sharp bursts. She pushed herself forward, ignoring the wobbling of her legs and the burning sensation in her throat as she breathed. She wouldn't give up now. She couldn't. Her family were out there, and Artemis wasn't about to give up on them.

But then her body gave up on her.

First went her legs, which buckled as she stomped forward, sending her tumbling to the ground and down an incline Artemis had unknowingly been walking the edge of. She toppled sideways down the slope, her head smacking against the hard ground just as much as her body. The fall only stopped when she crashed, hard, into a tree back-first, which knocked the breath right out of her.

Closing her eyes to alleviate the pain of the blinding snow, and maybe to pretend this wasn't happening, she laid there in agony. As Artemis closed her eyes, she fooled herself into thinking that she would just rest a moment to catch her breath before getting up again. Only when she opened her eyes again and found herself covered in a thick layer of snow, almost drowning in it, did she realise she'd fallen asleep.

Artemis tried to shake the snow off, only to find herself too frozen to even manage that. Not to mention the pain of moving. It was as if she were burning from the outside in. She didn't understand how that was possible, to be cold and yet to feel as if you were on fire. Attempting to ignore it as best she could, she curled in tightly to herself, trying to find warmth in any way she could, as one terrifying thought took root.

She was going to die.

ARTEMIS

rtemis kept drifting in and out of consciousness, and each time she opened her eyes, the world around her looked different. Sometimes bright, too bright that Artemis would have to close her eyes again. Others were so dark that she wasn't even sure she'd opened them.

Once, she opened her eyes to find her line of sight blocked by a blurred shadow that sniffed and nudged her face before disappearing into the storm as quickly as it had arrived.

She found herself wondering if it was the cougar she'd attacked. Maybe the cat would put her out of her misery and eat her. Then she remembered they often eat their kill while they're still alive and she took that hope back.

When she opened her eyes again, the blurred shadow had returned, but not as close, and not alone. Three others stood with them, skittering forwards, backwards, and even out of sight. Like dancing.

Artemis remembered one of the picture books Tall Fox had shown her once, when she was being "kind". In it was a false wolf named Benny who danced and played in the meadows with his friend Bunny. She liked that story because Benny's loving nature reminded her of Kiba.

With that story on her mind, Artemis watched the figures as they flew across her eye line, coming closer before skittering away. As they moved, she replayed the story of Benny and Bunny in her head once, twice, three times until she remembered one of the stories Oak had told her.

As the figures crept closer, she revisited Oak's story, barely noticing as the shadowed beings surrounded her. While she was not telling the story aloud, her understanding of her mother tongue too broken to use, it was as if the figures themselves could hear it.

This was her favourite story from Oak. One about a pack of wolves in a distant land, untouched and separate from the human world, except for a single explorer. The pack had never felt fear of humans, and though they were guarded, the pack felt no threat from the man – not that he ever could have been one.

Oak had said that this man respected the wolves, and he studied them extensively so the world could one day understand them just as he did. His mission was to show that humans should help protect them and that the wolves were not a threat to them. Even if it wasn't a simple task. Knowing there were good humans for wolves out there had always put Artemis at ease. It's why she liked replayed it in her mind.

By the time she could open her eyes again, Artemis couldn't see the shadows anymore. But she could feel them.

There was a warmth that encircled her once more, and for a moment, she felt panicked – a fear of the ice burning within her from the cold came to mind. But that wasn't the case this time. Instead, this warmth was softer, kinder, and one that didn't overwhelm her.

She was enveloped by it, every inch of her body and skin was wrapped up in warmth, and while the idea of being surrounded should have been terrifying, Artemis only felt comfort. As if, whatever was covering her, was helping her.

It could have been her mind playing tricks on her, a delusion just like the howls of her pack, but it was one that, even if it was, it would at least give her a last moment of peace.

Settling to rest once more – her eyes heavy, her head sore, but the ache fading – the weight against her turned heavier, as if, whatever it was, was intending to rest alongside her. She would not be alone, and that's all that mattered right then. Closing her eyes, she settled into the weight against her, and slept.

ARTEMIS DIDN'T REALISE she was being moved until she woke up to the sensation of being dragged. Her instinct to fight back came rushing up. As strong as she could, which wasn't much, she tossed and turned, trying to release herself from their clutches.

The figure that had been pulling her let go instantly.

She dropped to the snow beneath her which, thankfully, cushioned the drop. Her body ached from where she had been tugged; it seemed the figure had let go so she wouldn't hurt herself. Artemis could feel the bite marks on her shoulders and the warmth of saliva around the bite. The hold on her was similar to that of the way a mother wolf would soften her maw to carry her young in her jaw.

Why were they moving me? she thought, just able to open her eyes and look around. The shadows and the storm made it diffi-cult to tell where she was.

It wasn't until she noticed the lack of snowfall around them that she looked up, taking in the sight of an overbearing shadow. A tree, she assumed.

The figures had carried her as best they could out from the

direct line of the storm to a more covered shelter. Her body, while still numb and freezing, felt more alive than it had before.

While she still could barely see, the ice attached to the hairs around her eyes had caused enough damage that it hurt to open her eyes more than a squint. She turned to the figure behind her that had been pulling her.

Thank you, she said, hoping her wolfen tongue was strong enough to be understood. And from the soft, warm nuzzle to her head, it was.

Under the protection of the shadow tree, and the warmth of the surrounding bodies, she fell asleep once more.

THE NEXT TIME SHE WOKE, she felt some of her warmth missing. It was a strange feeling depending on another once more for her safety, just as she had once been with her pack. Family relying on one another was part of the dynamic. A dynamic she hadn't had in a long time.

Then the missing warmth returned in the form of the blurred figure, though it didn't return to its original place at her cold side. Instead, it laid something beside her head, before laying down, nudging its gift closer until it pressed into her face.

She could recognise that smell anywhere; the warming ooze of blood that dripped onto her lips stirred a hunger within her that hadn't been sated in so long. With a sudden burst of energy and need, she dove forward and tore into the meal given to her, taking her time to savour every bite.

Artemis recognised the taste of rabbit as she devoured the meal. She hadn't had it in a long time, but the memory of her first catch wasn't hard to forget.

Kiba had taken her from the Den, without telling Rae, to help her in feeling like a contributing member of the pack. He had always understood her at that deeper level, more than any of the others, and even more than Rae and her mother some-times. He had shown her the way to track and to use agile manoeuvres that would be essential in trapping small prey. She hadn't been successful at it – failed at it like she did most things. Yet, Kiba had never made her feel that way. He took his time in teaching, never getting frustrated or scolding her for her fail-ures. Oak reminded her of Kiba in that way, always taking her time and waiting for Artemis to make the decision that worked for her.

As she ate the rabbit, those memories of Kiba and Oak stuck with her, filling her with warmth. It was as she ate, the dribble of blood trailing down her face, the fur of the beast tickling at her face, her teeth sensitive as she tore at the meat, that she heard it.

A soft whine of hunger which sounded so familiar that she stopped instantly.

She laid down the meal into the snow as one figure, a crea-ture of blackish-grey colouring, jumped forward ready to tuck into what she had left. Then another snapped. This one was a figure of grey and brown with bright amber eyes. It snapped its jaws at the smaller creature, warning in its action.

With this act of aggression, Artemis wondered if she should be nervous. These creatures could hurt or turn on her if she went against their wishes, but she didn't feel afraid. In fact, she was sure there was something familiar about them. It was when the grey-brown figure licked at her face in a comforting manner, its warm tongue catching her ice-covered eyes, that Artemis came to realise why they felt so familiar.

The creature slowly pulled back from her face as if he could sense her thoughts and was waiting for her to say what she hoped was true. As her no-longer ice-coated eyes began to adjust, she could see those loving amber eyes watching her.

Artemis stayed silent as she blinked heavily, taking in those eyes – ones that reminded her that she was truly home. Reaching out, her fingers tangled in the fur, like she had done so long ago. Unshed tears filled her eyes as she leant forward, pressing her head to the creatures before her. When they reciprocated the action, nuzzling her cheeks, her neck, her head, sighing in doing so, she finally spoke.

Kiba...

A soft tongue pressed against her skin again, washing away a fallen tear, before she leant forward to wrap her arms tightly around him. It was a human action, but one that Kiba allowed as a heavy breath escaped him, a wistful and emotional tension in his own voice as he responded.

Welcome home, Little One.

42

ARTEMIS

As the storm faded in the passing days, Artemis's strength began to recover as she basked in the love of the four wolves from her pack that stayed and cared for her as she healed.

Day after day, she found herself able to move further along on their journey to the pack's new home, always staying close by Kiba's side. He filled her in on all that she had missed since she'd been gone, which, as she was told, had been an entire season. She'd been taken just before the cold period and returned in another.

Kiba told her about the aftermath of the humans trespassing and how, after losing Rae and her, the pack had almost fallen apart. He had to step up, alone, to keep them together. But, without his soul, it was hard for him to be the symbol of strength the pack and their pups needed.

The family never considered a new leader, even after we had mourned, Kiba had told her as they walked, his body strong enough to support the leaning weight of Artemis beside him. **We continued as we were, waiting.**

Wait? she asked, confused. Her words broken but understandable enough.

Kiba's ear flicked in her direction at her words as he huffed a laugh.

For you, of course, Little One.

Artemis stumbled in surprise, her grip tightening on Kiba's fur. Not that he complained at the action.

Our family could not heal without being able to find out what happened to you. We knew not whether to mourn or search, so we did both. It was the least we could do... His voice turned sorrowful. **...for Rae.**

A sadness took over the both of them as they walked on, the other wolves forming a protective stance around them. Not wanting to fall into the despair that was close to taking over, Artemis turned to look at the other wolves, unsure of who they were. Whether it was a foggy memory or they were new wolves to the pack, she wasn't sure. If it was the latter, then their protective nature confused her. Why would they protect a wolf they didn't know? And go out of their way to do so?

The wolf to the side of her, the one who had tried to eat the last of the rabbit, the blackish grey, was the one that intrigued her the most. He seemed to stick closer to her than the others, both as they walked and as they slept.

Frustrated at her faded memory, she missed the moment the wolf caught her staring.

I know you do not remember me, he said. There was no judgement in his voice, though she could sense a silent sadness behind it.

Artemis caught his eyes, a vibrant amber just like Kiba's, and while guilt washed over her at the realisation that she had known this wolf, a sense of relief that they were not angry at her relaxed the tension in her shoulders.

Exhaustion slowly filled her, and with the wolves able to sense when this was happening, they settled under a nearby canopy of trees to rest for a few shadow passes before continuing.

As she lay down to rest, Kiba assured her it wasn't long now until they reached their new home. Then he and one other headed out to scrounge up another meal for her, leaving Artemis with the blackish grey and another grey under the tree.

I can sense you are still unhappy with yourself, the blackish grey said to her as he curled in at her side, keeping her warm. **Do not be. I was only a pup when they took you. A lot has changed since then.**

Just a pup? she thought, surprised. There had only been so many pups when she had been taken, but only one had the blackish-grey fur of his grandfather.

Placing a hand, carefully, on his back, Artemis spoke her thoughts aloud.

Fenris?

He turned his head towards her, leaning his body more heavily against her paw. **I have missed you, elder.** His head dropped to the ground, curling around her shoulder and nuzzling her cheek lovingly. **Thank you for coming home.**

With a smile on her face, and the warmth of her family around her, Artemis fell asleep filled with love. Her family may not be as complete as it once was with Rae gone, but to know that those she loved wanted her home was all she ever wanted.

And now she had it.

It took another day and a half until they reached the new Den. They emerged over a hillside, and up ahead, with the backdrop of the mountainside, their home resided. It was not as well positioned as their old one, nor as comfortable, Fenris said, but it was home all the same, and it offered them the safety they needed to control their territory.

The rushing water is what first drew her attention, and with a speed she hadn't had since her escape, she sprinted to the water's edge and drank. Since she had been found by her pack, this was the one thing she hadn't been able to receive from them, and as she gulped heavily, she realised how desperately she had needed it.

As she drank, an electricity of excitement and trepidation filled the air. While her senses were not as keen as a wolf's, she could feel the pack watching her, waiting for her next move.

Once she had had her fill, she turned to the wolves and felt suddenly parched once again.

Seeing them all, both those she knew, and those she didn't, whether it was from ageing or faded memories, she wouldn't know for a while, but finally. Finally. Her family was here. They had been waiting for her. Had been searching for her. Had wanted her.

Slowly, as if she were a new member, she lowered her head and body to the ground and crawled forward. Her message was simple: I am not a threat. I am one of you. I am back and never leaving again.

Artemis wasn't able to continue her plan of submission when, suddenly, a pile of bodies pounced on her, warm tongues lashing against her skin. The actions took her back to her days of caring for the young pups, the young pups that were neither young nor pups anymore, as they danced and played with her.

Laughing loudly and without fear, she partook in the game. Tackling one wolf, tugging at another's ear with her teeth, and submitting when she was overpowered. It was as if she had never left, and maybe that's how it should be.

Her family didn't ask what had happened when she was taken, though Kiba, as he always had, offered her an ear if she ever needed to speak. She had smiled in thanks but passed up on it, wanting just as much as the others to forget that that time away had even happened. The memories were too raw to think about.

Instead, she focused on the here and now, looking to her future with the pack. Unfortunately, forgetting the humans was not as easy as she had hoped.

Due to their stain on the Forest, the pack discussed together that, sadly, it was possible that they may have to move around every new season to keep from being found.

Guilt filled Artemis at this, realising that it was possible that the humans could come looking for her in the Forest once again, but the wolves quickly shot down those thoughts of hers. The human beasts were the only ones to blame, and as Fenris said:

The strength of the wolf is that of its pack. And you are a member of the pack. Always.

They planned patrols in the following days. As Artemis learnt, since their move to the new Den, they had sent out groups in search of her and to patrol their territory at the same time. The pack was sent out in fours, some to plot the borders of the territory, others to guard and search for signs of the humans.

Artemis wasn't happy about it, fearing that straying too close to the human side of the Forest would put them at risk.

It will be fine, Little One, Kiba had said as the first patrol since her return was sent out. She watched as Fenris and Yue, a new yearling member, left the inner territory. She knew the dread in her stomach would stay until they returned home. **They are stronger than you think and have become used to such tactics.**

They not have to, she snapped, though with how broken her words were, it did not have the effect she intended. The scar the humans left on her came in many forms now. Whether it was the patrols they needed or her being back to basics with her language, they had taken something from all of them. **Dangerous.**

Artemis remembered the sight of the wolf skins on display and tried to wash away the image from her mind.

Find your calm, Little One. Do not worry.

Taking a breath, she centred herself. She believed in Kiba and his leadership, so she trusted his judgement. For now, she would focus on the day ahead.

She and Kiba were to work on her hunting once more, both to offer support towards the pack's hunts but also in case she ever found herself lost again. The latter confused Artemis, however. What was the point? She would never be without her family again.

I cannot bear to think what would have happened if we hadn't found you, Little One. Please, allow me this one comfort.

Artemis understood and followed him out to begin her teachings. It was as they walked that she opened up about the one thing that she had feared speaking aloud upon her return.

Little One... she said, waiting for Kiba's attention. As his caring amber eyes fell on hers, his attention solely on her, she felt brave enough to continue. **Not my name now.**

Only for a second, his eyes dropped from hers, and she could sense the disappointment within him at her words. Kiba was always far too kind, and as quickly as a blink, his eyes were on hers once more, and his voice was as soft and loving as always. **I see,** he said, **then what do you wish to go by?**

Thinking of the name that had been forced onto her, she wondered if maybe she should tell him to ignore her, that she would go by Little One once more. It was, after all, the name her mother had given her when she had brought her in to raise as her own.

It was then that she heard Oak's voice saying her name. The way it had sounded coming from her lips, as if it were the most important word, as if Artemis were the most important being she could speak to. Oak, saying her name, made her feel like she mattered. Each time she had said her name, she felt a little less lost in the world she had been trapped in. It was for that reason she decided.

Artemis, she replied to Kiba, a smile on her face. **My name Artemis.**

While there had been sadness before in her best friend's eyes, now, having watched her come to this conclusion, he looked lighter. Happier. As if, all this time, he had been waiting for her to believe and find herself so he could find peace. A soft sigh escaped him as he leant forward and rested his head against her chest.

I am glad to have you home, Artemis.

THAT NIGHT, after a successful return from the patrol and an initial start to her hunting training and relearning in wolf, Artemis found herself unable to sleep.

She was surrounded by family, with a stomach well fed, and a thirst that had been sated. There should have been no reason for her to struggle sleeping. She was exactly where she wanted and should be.

Yet, the memory of the girl she had left behind plagued her. The memory of her name upon her lips had stayed with her throughout the day, and now, as she tried to sleep, it came back in full force. The intensity of her eyes, the sound of her laugh, and the look on her face as she cried watching Artemis leave. She knew Oak had saved her life, in far more ways than one, and though she had attempted to block her memories of that place as best she could, there was one thing that she never wanted to forget.

Oak.

Watching to make sure her family did not stir, she pulled the golden-shelled knife from her hidden patch in her bottom fur and stared at it, her fingers brushing over the intricate designs. As carefully as she could, she unsheathed the silver blade. In the moonlight that shone through the entrance, she could see the blade fully for the first time. It unnerved her seeing the weapon even now. It looked and felt unnatural in her hands. She wouldn't risk it, but from what she'd seen, even the smallest touch of the silver to her skin would draw blood. It was as she looked the blade over that she noticed a strange carving in the side. The letters, while not clear, she recognised from her classes.

JGY.

Artemis wasn't sure what it meant, but she was sure that, somehow, it was connected to Oak. Her nail drew over the engraved letters, and a warmth grew in her chest as she thought of the last smile she had seen.

The blade sheathed and clung to her chest. Artemis stared out of the Den's entrance, taking in the Forest before her.

As she felt sleep finally taking over, eyes drooping and the noise of the Forest soothing her into slumber, she thought with a smile,

I hope I see her again.

JAMIE

Winter had come and gone when her father returned from his trip. She hadn't seen him in over a year, and while normally she would have been excited by his return, ready to hear his new adventurous stories, this time she didn't care.

She'd been staying with a distant auntie this time around in the middle of nowhere, and it had been made clear that no one here was happy that she was there. The fact her father had grown up and run away from here said enough about what he thought of the place. Apparently though, he didn't have an issue dumping his daughter there to be miserable and alone. Again.

Being alone wasn't anything new to her. Her father was away more often than he was with her, so she was used to being abandoned in new places when it suited him. Each town or city was just as boring as the last. The only thing that kept her going were the stories her dad would tell when he came back to get her.

Like her dad, she wanted to explore the world. Each time he planned a new trip, she begged to go with him, but she was always left behind. This last expedition of his was the final straw for her. She used to want to be just like him, but now, she wanted nothing to do with him.

In the log house where she had been left, with an aunt who seemed happy to ignore her very existence, she waited for him to return with his stories. She was ready to reject him and give him a taste of his own medicine.

As she waited in the living room, she had to admit that at least this place was homier than the others she'd been dropped at. There was a fireplace she was allowed to use when she wanted to read, the house was large enough to be explored, with new secrets around every corner to uncover, and there was an expansive library filled with fiction and scientific journals that her aunt allowed her access to. The place was nice, but it wasn't home. She didn't have one of those.

The fire was going as she waited. She was sitting close enough to feel the warmth on her skin but far enough away to not be hit by the occasional spitting embers. It was as she watched another spark of flame that she heard the click at the door.

He was here.

Taking a breath, she turned to face the door she knew he would enter from. She was ready for what she had to do. It was as the creaking door opened and he stepped through, his smile wide and loving as his eyes landed on her, that her resolve was destroyed.

Jumping from the ground, she rushed forward and threw her arms around him as his own arms encircled her. She may hate him for leaving her, but he always came back.

He crouched slightly without letting go, coming down to her level as he always did, a sign of respect he had called it. As he pulled back, his hands at her shoulders, holding her, she took him in.

His beard had grown bushier, which explained why it had scratched at her cheek, not that she minded, and his skin was more tanned than its natural pale. It was the eyes that stayed the same, a piercing blue that contrasted the brown she had gotten from her mum.

As she looked at him, he smiled that wide and charming smile – a smile that Mum had told her was what convinced her to marry him – before he placed a hand on her cheek.

"I have a story for you, Jamie," he said, just as he always did when he returned.

Their reunions were always like this. There were no hellos, I missed you, how was your trip, how was your new, soon-to-be-old, home while I was away. Instead, everything they wished to say was shared through a story. It had been their way of communicating since she was young, a tradition started by her mum, and was one they carried on after they had lost her, as if it kept her close.

She smiled but didn't answer, which seemed to surprise him. Turning away and shrugging not unkindly from his grasp, she moved to the armchair by the fireplace. She could hear him follow her, intrigue in each step, followed by a slight pause as she took the chair and turned to face him.

Without having to ask, he smiled and sat down on the floor before her, just as she would when he would sit to tell his stories. Usually, hot chocolate would have been made, or a soothing tea, but that would have to wait till later.

"I have a story to tell," she said, her voice strong and her tone one of drama and importance, just like her father's voice when he began his own storytelling. "It is a story of friendship, villainy, and a girl who was not quite a girl."

His eyebrows raised, and just as she always had, he leant forward, resting his chin on his hands as he watched her. Waiting.

She smiled. Her dad always had a story, but this time, it was her turn to tell one.

As she told the tale of her year, sparing no detail, even the ones she thought could get her into trouble later, she fiddled with a toy in her hands. Every so often, her eyes would drop to the matted thing, its mud-stained body ruining what it was meant to be, but she refused to even consider throwing it away.

Tears filled her eyes as she came to the end, her eyes never leaving the disfigured form of the toy cat in her hands. The cat toy, more than ever in that moment, meant more than any gift her dad had ever given her from his travels, or even the stories he would bring home to her.

While it may not have been given to her, it was something she could hold and have to remember her adventures with the girl who never even learnt her name.

What can a mere ten-year-old do in the face of trouble?
Get her dad, the world-explorer and naturalist, to help, of course.

The story will continue with the short story, *Before I Go*, that follows the aftermath of Jamie's actions in *Home to the Wild* and the lengths she will go to protect the girl she saved.

Head over to www.francescamcmahon.com to find out when their journey continues.

How far would you go to save the ones you love?

Jamie has lived with the memory of Artemis, the girl she helped save, for over a decade. Now in her final year at university, she discovers that the forest her childhood friend grew up in is under threat of deforestation. And only Jamie seems to care.

With her father, best friend, and frenemy at her side, she strikes out to the Swen Forest, determined to protect it. But things don't go according to plan.

With danger around every corner, Jamie and Artemis must reconnect if they have any chance of saving the forest. But what happens if, along the way, something is stirred between them?

Follow their story in this second instalment of the Into the Wild series, *Way of the Wild*.

Head over to www.francescamcmahon.com to find out when their journey continues.

What happens to a wolf who's hungry and alone?
They become desperate.

Can't wait for the next part of the story? You can check out *Echoes of the Past,* the prequel short story set before the events of Home to the Wild, out now on all eBook platforms.

ACKNOWLEDGMENTS

A huge thank you to my incredible beta readers, Andrea S. U., Brontë Pleasants, Caitlin Santos, Elliott Quirke, Erica Ito, Katie Mack, Libby Driscoll, Lijia Wang, Michael Griswold, Nicole, Robert Gaymer, and Tia Hammad.
To my brilliant editor Carly Catt, you are a legend, and this book is stronger because of you. Of course, no story is without its own visual beauty. Thank you to Arthur Bowling III for the incredible cover art.
Special acknowledgements to my mum who put up with me talking about this project all the time and to the friends who allowed me to badger them for feedback.

ABOUT THE AUTHOR

Francesca McMahon was born in Oxford, England, to a Scottish father and an Essex mother. They gained a B.A. in Creative Writing at Edge Hill University and was shortlisted for the university's Dame Janet Suzman Playwriting Award in snow2019. Since graduating, Francesca has worked consistently in publishing while working on her writing of fantasy, horror and romance fiction, as well as various tabletop RPGs and screenplays. As a queer person, their work is dedicated to the LGBTQIA+ community, and she hopes that they will all find a home in her imaginary worlds.

You can learn more over at www.francescamcmahon.com or follow Francesca on social media, via Twitter, Instagram, and TikTok (@adoseoffran).

www.ingramcontent.com/pod-product-compliance
Lightning Source LLC
Chambersburg PA
CBHW061605190726
48288CB00007B/2177